A TASTE OF PARADISE

Jillian was too caught up in the smell and feel of this man. She was wallowing in a heady experience, something totally new for a woman who seldom deviated from her plan. It felt surreal to be sequestered in a fantasy world, with no scheduled meetings or hectic deadlines.

Ben's arm circled her neck. She rolled onto her side, twining her arms around him. He blew a soft breath against the hollow of her throat. When he kissed her again, the safe little world that she'd been cocooned in shattered. Emotions too new to examine surfaced. Caution was thrown to the wind, and Jillian went with the flow.

Dear Reader,

Arabesque is excited to publish the Ports-of-Call summer series for 2005, featuring four romances set in exotic locales, including Venice, Italy; the Fiji Islands; Trinidad; and Accra, Ghana, in West Africa.

In Sandra Kitt's *The Next Best Thing*, April Stockwood tags along with her friend Stephanie on a business trip to Italy, but finds herself stranded in Venice when her passport and wallet are stolen by a pickpocket. When handsome Hayden Callaway, a foreign-service agent and old high school acquaintance from Philadelphia, comes to her rescue, April finds her holiday fling involves more than just sightseeing.

Set in Fiji, *A Taste of Paradise* is the backdrop for Marcia King-Gamble's steamy island romance. When hotel acquisitions director Jillian Gray is sent to the South Pacific to buy a run-down old property, with plans to turn it into a luxury resort, she doesn't count on sexy African-American transplant Benjamin Fuller getting in her way. But he has other ideas about the old hotel and Jillian.

When actress Kenya Reese visits Trinidad in Simona Taylor's *Then I Found You*, she thought it would be under different circumstances. But with the threat of blackmail and extortion, the rising star is forced to hire security advisor Damon St. Rose, a handsome and imposing figure. Despite their disagreements, the two find suspense and romance a potent mix amid the excitement of Carnival.

In a sequel to *Once in a Lifetime* and *After the Loving*, Gwynne Forster's *Love Me or Leave Me* follows Drake Harrington, the youngest of three successful brothers who own an architectural, engineering, and construction firm. When the Harrington brothers take a trip to Ghana to view a potential project, Drake invites local TV anchor Pamela Langford to come along. Although both enjoy the cultural and historical sites in and around Accra, the trip to West Africa also pushes their love to the limits.

With best-selling and award-winning authors Sandra Kitt, Marcia King-Gamble, Simona Taylor, and Gwynne Forster contributing to this series, we know you'll enjoy the passion and romance captured in each exotic destination.

We welcome your comments and feedback, and invite you to send us an e-mail at www.bet.com/books/betbooks.

Enjoy,

Evette Porter
Editor, Arabesque

A Taste of Paradise

MARCIA KING-GAMBLE

ARABESQUE
BET BOOKS

BET Publications, LLC
http://www.bet.com
http://www.arabesquebooks.com

ARABESQUE BOOKS are published by

BET Publications, LLC
c/o BET BOOKS
One BET Plaza
1900 W Place NE
Washington, DC 20018-1211

Copyright © 2005 by Marcia King-Gamble

All rights reserved. No part of this book may be reproduced, stored in a retrieval system, or transmitted in any form or by any means without the prior written consent of the Publisher.

If you purchased this book without a cover, you should be aware that this book is stolen property. It was reported as "unsold and destroyed" to the Publisher and neither the Author nor the Publisher has received any payment for this "stripped book."

All Kensington Titles, Imprints, and Distributed lines are available at special quantity discounts for bulk purchases for sales promotions, premiums, fund-raising, and educational or institutional use. Special book excerpts or customized printings can also be created to fit specific needs. For details, write or phone the office of the Kensington special sales manager: Kensington Publishing Corp., 850 Third Avenue, New York, NY 10022, attn: Special Sales Department, Phone: 1-800-221-2647.

BET Books is a trademark of Black Entertainment Television, Inc. ARABESQUE, the ARABESQUE logo, and the BET BOOKS logo are trademarks and registered trademarks.

First Printing: July 2005

10 9 8 7 6 5 4 3 2 1

Printed in the United States of America

This book is dedicated to James Jesserer, "the English Major." Your chip-toothed smile was my inspiration. Thanks for the helpful critiquing and for making me smile.

Chapter 1

"What do you mean the hotel is full?"

Jillian Gray got into the face of the olive-skinned clerk behind the reception desk, daring him to answer her.

Unperturbed, he flashed even white teeth and said, "I'm sorry, Madam, but you've arrived early and there simply isn't room."

Jillian huffed in a breath and stared at the Jimmy Choo shoes on her feet. A big mistake that was, flecks of a pinkish liquid were splattered all over the expensive beige pumps. She took a step forward and one shoe stuck to the woven mat. Miraculously she managed to lift the foot up.

No one had bothered to clean up the liquid on the tile floor, a sure sign of a hotel in rapid decline. Glancing about her, she took in the oversized Tikki hut with its faded upholstery and rickety rattan chairs. Gigantic vases held orchids that must be several days old. It was no wonder the Bula Resort in Taveuni, Fiji, had lost two of its stars.

"There's fruit juice on the floor," Jillian pointed out. "You really should do something about it."

The hotel clerk grimaced at the mess. "Housekeeping has already been notified. I'll call them again if you like."

Not if she liked. It should have been second nature to clean up the spill, if not for aesthetics at least for liability's sake.

"While you're at it," Jillian snapped, "get your manager down here. He'll find me a room."

The clerk blinked in shock, looking at her as if she were an annoying bug he'd like to squash.

"My manager cannot manufacture a bure if we don't have one," he said.

"Bure?"

"Cottage."

"We'll see about that."

Jillian knew she was being high-handed. But no way was she about to be dismissed and sent off to find lodging elsewhere. She'd arrived at the Bula Resort one day earlier than expected, counting on the element of surprise to be on her side. Her purpose in doing so was to see how the hotel really performed. So far it had failed miserably. There was no heartfelt welcome and certainly no warm "hello," as the name "Bula" signified.

Jillian was director of property acquisitions for the Elite Resorts chain. It was her job to find ailing hotels with promise and see if a lucrative deal could be made. She would perform due diligence, then take her findings back to Michael Rosen, her boss, who then presented them to the owner, Peter Fontaine, with a recommendation to bid or pass.

Based on what Jillian had witnessed—no visible bellhop at the door, a lobby that desperately needed refurbishing, so-so service, and non-existent air conditioning—the Bula was ripe for the picking.

The front desk clerk was shaking his head and making "tssking" sounds, infuriating Jillian even more.

"My shoes are ruined," she said, bending over to remove the pricey pumps and plant them on the counter. "Now what are you going to do about them?"

The clerk shrugged and swept the pumps aside. He sighed loudly and rolled his eyes. Clearly he was not empowered or didn't care about resolving the situation.

Jillian was not normally impatient or arrogant. But jet lag had kicked in, making her cranky and intolerant. She longed for a shower and something to eat, not necessarily in that order. Now all of her exhaustion was being directed at an indifferent hotel clerk whose monthly wages were what she made in a day.

Jillian's fingers smoothed her tightly cropped hair. She fingered the pearl in one earlobe and prayed for patience. Because she traveled frequently, she opted for a low-maintenance look. She'd just had a nail biting flight on a puddle jumper, crawled off the plane in sweats, ducked into the airport bathroom, and changed into the austere business suit.

Peter Fontaine, Jillian's employer, the aging scion of Elite Resorts, still ran his business as if it were the 1960s. Employees were forced to adhere to a strict dress code. Despite the humidity, Peter expected his executives to dress as they would for a stuffy boardroom.

It still amazed Jillian that a man so mired in tradition had hired a thirty-two-year-old African-American woman to be his director of property acquisitions, a role that came with incredible stress and many responsibilities.

"Do you have comment cards? A resolution process? A *manager*?" Jillian asked the still gaping clerk.

She fingered the pearls around her neck and tried her best to ignore the cotton shell now soaked with perspiration. Giving up, she tugged off the tailored pinstriped jacket and dangled it off one finger.

The employee was still frozen and the line of impatient vacationers waiting to check in began to complain.

"Are you the only one on?" a crotchety female voice said from behind Jillian.

"How long are we supposed to wait for service?"

"Get your manager," Jillian insisted. "I need a room and I'm not moving from here until one is found. These people need service."

Something about her tone must have prompted the man from inertia, or maybe it was the sight of a tall woman in stockinged feet that signaled she just might be crazy. Whatever it was, he picked up the old-fashioned phone, dialed and jabbered away in rapid Fijian.

The conversation done with, he pecked at his keyboard, his demeanor quickly changing when he read something on the screen. All of a sudden his hospitality kicked in and a slow smile broke.

"Oh, Ms. Gray," he said in dulcet tones. "I am so sorry. You should have identified yourself. Of course we will find you a room. Go to the bar, they may still be serving lunch. Our manager, Marlon Hinds, will join you shortly."

Not even an offer of a complimentary drink, just a wave of the hand in the direction of what Jillian assumed was an outdoor restaurant.

Jillian gestured toward the sweating bellman leaning against a brass trolley with her stacked Ralph Lauren luggage. "My bags? What is he to do with them?"

"I'll hold your things until we find you a room."

She managed a curt nod. There was nothing further to be gained by standing there. The people behind her, judging by their snorts and sighs, were close to erupting. Reclaiming her ruined shoes, Jillian vowed to take up the matter with Marlon Hinds, the property's manager. No way would she incur one dollar of expenses for something that wasn't her fault.

Squeezing the once spotless Jimmy Choos back

onto her swelling feet, Jillian minced off in the direction of the outdoor restaurant bar.

Outside, the hot sun beat down on her face. Jillian followed a pebbled path lined by flowering shrubs, eyeing with distaste the untended gardens. Massive fan palms and tubs of bougainvillea were haphazardly positioned throughout. Even the pink and white hibiscuses swaying in the humid breeze couldn't keep the grounds from looking shabby.

The Bula might have been something in its heyday, but not now. Now it looked like a middle-aged woman who'd run out of steam.

Fumbling through an oversized Kate Spade bag, Jillian found and withdrew her Palm Pilot, bound and determined to take notes.

"Don't tell me you're working?" a male voice said from behind her.

Turning, she smiled at an overweight couple. Both were dressed in loud tropical gear.

"I am."

"No one conducts business during the warmest time of the day," the man said, sidling by her, tugging his companion along.

"You're right, shame on me."

Jillian shoved the electronic gadget back into her bag. Three weeks at the Bula Resort would give her plenty of time to record her observations.

She continued down the path, her eyes bugging out as she caught her first glimpse of a white sand beach and a bluer-than-blue ocean. She'd give anything to peel off her clothes and jump into all that cool water. But that would have to wait.

Looking around, she could see the property's four pools and water gushing from a platform of rocks. The pool area needed new chaise lounges, cabanas were needed on the beach, and updated water sports equipment wouldn't hurt either. More importantly, the employees needed customer service training. With a little sprucing and some innovative thinking, the Bula Resort could be a world-class resort again.

Jillian came to a Tikki hut that was a larger version of the lobby. A good-sized crowd sat finishing lunch. The bar held a combination of locals and tourists drinking and acting as if they didn't have a care in the world.

Ignoring the curious glances thrown her way, she slipped onto a barstool. The day's specials were written in chalk on a blackboard behind the bar and Jillian mentally made her selection.

"Something to drink?" a rotund bartender asked, a smile creasing his face.

This was more like it, at last she was getting a warm welcome and experiencing the famous Fijian hospitality she'd read so much about. What a big difference from the terse greeting and uncaring attitude of the clerk at the front desk.

"Kava," Jillian responded, opting for the popular local drink. She'd been told it used to be prepared by virgins who chewed the root into a soft pulpy mass.

Another smile told her she'd won a new friend. "Good choice," the bartender said. "Now what about lunch?"

"Lunch sounds like a great idea."

He beckoned to a beautiful Indian woman wearing a hibiscus behind one ear.

"Madam wants lunch," he said, tossing another smile her way.

The man's hair was woolly and his features an interesting mix of Melanesian and Tongan. Anywhere else he would easily have been mistaken for African-American.

Jillian chose a local dish, figuring it might be worth sampling the chef's specialty to see if he was worth keeping. Property inspections were usually tough.

Once the staff knew who you were, and knew that their jobs were in danger, they pulled out all the stops.

"I'll have the kakoda," she said to the waitress.

"Fish steamed in coconut cream," the woman translated, jotting down her order.

She left to wait on another table, and as was the custom, Jillian lifted her glass and downed the kava in one quick swallow.

"You drink like a native," the bartender said, another wide smile creasing his face.

"It's delicious."

Her answer drew agreeable nods from those openly listening. The man next to her raised his bottle of Fiji Bitters in salute. "You'll fit right in. Soon you will be one of us."

Jillian doubted that. She'd be much too busy to become a native.

An animated game of volleyball was being played on the beach. It looked like locals had erected a tattered net on the sand. Whoops and hollers floated her way as one side or another scored a point.

Even watching the teams play made her sweat. Jillian longed to strip off the severe business suit, discard the uncomfortable pantyhose and shed her expensive pumps for sandals. What she wouldn't give to soak her feet in the cool ocean. Peter Fontaine and his sycophants would never find out. Yes, she decided, the hose had to go. She would not endure the confining nylons for another minute.

Jillian grabbed her purse off the bar. She'd seen the sign for restrooms somewhere. It was doubtful lunch would arrive before she got back.

Wending her way through crowded tables, she eventually found the ladies room. The offending pantyhose was quickly discarded and stuffed into her bag. She splashed water on her heated face and tried to envision herself in shorts and a halter top.

When she emerged again, a man in a crumpled linen suit was walking around. Jillian guessed this might be the missing manager, Marlon Hinds. She gave a tentative wave to which he responded with a nod.

She'd certainly expected a more effusive welcome. Marlon Hinds had to know who she was. As she was about to introduce herself, a huge uproar came from the beach as several players chased an escaping volleyball. It bounded toward her and Jillian leapt up onto her toes, preparing to catch the wayward ball. It ricocheted off one wall and diners ducked. Jillian chased after it until the heel of her pump caught in the hemp mat. She pitched forward and broke her fall with her palms.

"Oww!"

"Are you okay?" the man she thought might be the manager asked, crouching down beside her.

"I'm fine, just had the wind knocked out of me." Jillian still had one arm around the ball.

The man eased her into a standing position and Jillian tried putting weight on the now aching foot. "Ooow!"

"No, you're not. Sit." She was shoved into an empty chair. Her rescuer beckoned to someone she couldn't see. "Bring me ice."

Still holding onto the ball, Jillian closed her eyes and fought the pain.

Another voice, an American voice, dreamily familiar, and with a compelling cadence to it, said, "I'd get rid of the other ridiculous shoe if I were you."

Jillian's eyes flew open. A bearded, shirtless man, droplets of sweat glistening on his copper back, knelt at her feet. One large hand held her leather sole. He pulled off the remaining pump and tossed it across the room. Then his rough palm cupped her sole, examining the throbbing ankle.

"Yup, Marlon, she just might have a fracture," he confirmed. "I'd have her see Doctor Charles."

The man spoke as if she didn't exist or wasn't worth addressing. Despite the pain, Jillian decided that she could not and would not simply sit there as if she were an inanimate object.

"Let go of my foot. Who are you?"

The new arrival sat back on his heels, regarding her with a chagrined golden gaze. The beard and bandanna he wore added to his pirate look. Only his slightly crooked nose and chipped front tooth kept him from being pretty. She had the feeling those eyes had raked over her before. But that was impossible. He was comfortable on the beach and clearly uncomfortable with her.

"Does it matter?" he asked, slowly releasing her foot and unfolding his body from his subservient position. "The ball, please." He gestured to the volleyball Jillian still clutched.

She gaped at his wide expanse of chest; a hint of gray hair dusted his solar plexus. He had to be in his early forties, she guessed, though his muscular body didn't indicate that. Mesmerized, she dropped the ball and watched it roll across the woven mat covering the restaurant's floor.

With one long stride, the stranger scooped up the rolling ball.

"I'll be back," he said, sauntering off.

"Who was that?" Jillian asked, staring after him. "And who are you?"

A crisp beige business card was produced and deposited on her lap. "Marlon Hinds," the strapping Caucasian man confirmed. "And you are Ms. Gray?"

"Jillian Gray, the acquisitions director for Elite Resorts. If you'll give me a minute I'll find my card."

The manager quickly masked his surprise and said

smoothly, "That can wait. Right now we need to take care of that foot."

As if by magic the bohemian from the beach reappeared carrying a small towel-wrapped bundle. He squatted down and pressed the cloth against Jillian's rapidly swelling ankle.

The sudden coldness of it made her flinch, but pain aside, she would persevere. She did not like it that a stranger had possession of her foot. She liked it even less that he was prodding her ankle in a most unsettling way.

Another waitress, the one who'd taken her order, sauntered over. "The lady's food is getting cold," she said to the still nameless man.

"Food will have to wait. Prepare Ms. Gray a tray to go and find Dr. Charles and let him know we need him here."

"I don't need a doctor," Jillian protested, leaping up again and trying to stand on the ankle. The excruciating pain sent her reeling back into her seat.

"Now that was a dumb move," the stranger said.

Dumb or not, what she needed was a room, a place to lie down and take a nap, a place she could soak the aching foot. Even so, Jillian's mind kept working overtime. She knew the man. He even sounded familiar. She was certain she'd seen him before. They'd spoken. Not once, often.

Marlon Hinds was speaking into a walkie-talkie that he'd produced from somewhere. "I need a golf cart," he said to the person on the other end. "A VIP got hurt. We'll need to transport her to her room."

They'd found her a room. That was a good thing.

Jillian was suddenly conscious of the people around her, of hushed whispers and curious glances thrown her way. The ankle throbbed and had blown up to twice its size. Just what she needed when she had work to do.

"We weren't expecting you until tomorrow, Ms. Gray," Marlon said, making her focus.

Like she didn't know.

"I completed my business in New Zealand and took an earlier flight."

There was a commotion at the door as the golf cart pulled up. Marlon motioned to Jillian.

The stranger from the beach leapt from the vehicle. He came to her side and picked her up like a package. She was left with little choice but to twine her arms around his neck.

"Put me down. I can walk," she hissed.

He ignored her as if she hadn't spoken. Turning toward Marlon he asked, "Where shall I take her?"

"The bridal suite. It's vacant until next week. I'll grab the tray and bring her food."

Despite her agony, Jillian saw the humor in the situation. Even with a full house, the Bula management was pulling out all the stops. They were housing a lone woman in a suite designed for honeymooners.

She was carried through the gathering crowd and plopped down into the golf cart. The volleyball game on the beach had ceased and several players stood shading their eyes.

"Give me a minute," the mystery man said, loping off.

He returned and hopped into the driver's seat. After whizzing them up a series of paths they stopped in front of another medium-sized hut that Jillian heard the driver refer to as a bure. This one had privacy walls surrounding it.

Both men got out of the cart. After a brief exchange they linked their fingers together and made her a makeshift chair. Jillian ignored the crippling pain and hobbled toward them. Without another word, she sat.

Entering a courtyard she noted a sprawling lanai

holding potted plants and comfortable deck chairs. A bamboo-lined path led to a gigantic oak front door. Off to the side, shrouded by more bamboo, was a covered hot tub.

"I haven't been checked in yet," Jillian said, still looking around. Aching foot or not, she was captivated by the ambiance, her borrowed slice of paradise.

"Taken care of," Marlon said, waving a skeleton key in front of her face. "Now let's just hope Dr. Charles tears himself away from his golf game and shows up. If he's not here within the hour, we'll bring a doctor in from town."

"I don't need a doctor," Jillian assured him. "Get me Epsom salts and a basin, and I'll soak my foot."

She wanted to be alone. The aching ankle aside, she was ravenous and needed a shower.

Sensing her need for solitude, Marlon turned to his friend. "Ben, get Ms. Gray's food. I'll give her time to eat, then I'll come back."

They entered the bridal suite, a spacious room with a very South Pacific theme. Jillian was delighted to see a living room and L-shaped kitchen. She was quickly seated in an oversized chair and the injured foot propped on an ottoman.

Ben went off to fetch the tray, which he brought back and set down on her lap. Marlon brought over a cordless phone and placed it on the table next to her. "Call me when you're done," he said.

Jillian's eyelids drooped and popped open again when she overheard Ben say, "Only a woman would chase after a volleyball in killer high heels."

She glared at him.

"I've done my duty," he said. "I'm out of here."

The door slammed behind him, leaving Jillian awestruck.

Chapter 2

It was Ben's turn to serve.

Holding the ball in one hand, he prepared to send it flying over the net, aiming for the weakest person on the team. As he closed his fist and prepared to give the ball a good whack, his thoughts returned to the annoying woman in those silly high heels. She reminded him of someone.

She wasn't a native, that was for sure. The local women didn't wear dowdy little suits nor did they strive to be androgynous. Ladies in Taveuni, the "Garden Island," as it was called, wore their femininity like a badge. Not this one, she looked like one uptight miss.

Miss? The truth was he didn't know whether she was married and simply didn't care. Their encounter had been blessedly brief. He'd done what any human being with a heart would do; he'd delivered her to her cottage safely.

"Come on, Ben," an impatient female voice called. "You held us up. Now serve the damn ball."

Ben's answer was to give the ball a close-fisted thump. It sailed toward the net and his teammates groaned. Breaths whooshed out when it made it over with inches to spare. The players on the opposing team dove, banging into each other. After several fumbles, the ball rolled out of bounds.

"Way to go, Ben!" another teammate shouted.

Ben pumped his arms. If it continued this way, the game would end soon. He had a meeting with Marlon and Franz Herrman, the owner of the Bula, in less than an hour, and he needed to shower and change.

Ben was bound and determined to come to a verbal agreement today. He was counting on his relationship with Marlon to make that happen. Like Ben, the hotel's manager was an American transplant who'd become more native than the natives themselves.

Marlon clearly understood what it meant to the Fijians to have work. If Ben were lucky enough to acquire the Bula, he meant to guarantee the locals jobs. He'd already lined up the financing for the most part. Now all he had to do was to come up with some way to run that Elite woman off.

It had surprised Ben that Elite, a white bread company, had sent an African-American woman to Fiji to do their negotiations. But he wasn't going to let shared pigmentation stand in the way. Corporate America would not get their hands on the Bula if he could help it. He had plans for the place.

The game ended fifteen minutes later than he liked, but at least his team won by a sizeable margin. Ben draped a towel around his neck and prepared to leave. Cyndy, one of his teammates, announced to anyone in hearing range, "Let's grab a beer. I'm buying."

Ricky Lohman, a muscular Rotuman, grabbed a fistful of Ben's wet T-shirt and said, "Man we're out of here."

Ben added in a louder voice, "Neither of us drink and I'm running to a meeting. Catch you all next week."

Out of earshot, Ricky let out a belly-busting guffaw; his Polynesian features registered true amazement as he wound a muscular arm around Ben's neck. "We already went to one earlier today."

"This is business, not that kind of meeting."

"Bula business, I take it."

Ben grunted.

Ricky already knew that Ben had given his heart and soul to corporate America. But life had changed drastically after September 11, when his priorities shifted. He'd lost his entire family in a horrible airplane disaster.

"Catch you later," Ricky said.

Ben was bound and determined not to take a maudlin trip down memory lane. His old life was something he didn't want to remember. Back then he had a family and a whole other purpose.

Ben made it back to his bure in record time. He shaved and took a quick shower before climbing into chinos and a polo shirt. Fifteen minutes later he was banging on Marlon's office door.

"Hey," Marlon said, letting him in. "I thought for sure you'd forgotten our appointment."

"Sorry. I got here as quickly as I could. The game went on forever. There was no one to take my place.

A grunt came from a smoky corner. Ben looked over and spotted Franz Herrman, the German owner of the Bula, ensconced in a leather swivel chair. A cigar dangled from his lips. He didn't get up. But that was typical.

"I've got exactly ten minutes," Franz said, tapping the face of his watch.

Ben took the seat that Marlon pointed to. "I'd like to make a bid on the Bula," he said without preamble.

"Yes, and so does Elite. I'm sure you've heard their representative is currently occupying the bridal suite."

A picture of the Elite representative popped into Ben's mind. She was an attractive woman despite the severe haircut and prim little suit. Her face, though not classically pretty, had been interesting. Her height and regal bearing gave the impression of class. Even the ridiculous Jimmy Choos sent the message— a nonconformist, definitely an individual with an independent spirit, and tough as nails, Ben would guess. He'd recognized the shoes instantly. The designer was his wife Karen's favorite.

Forget about the Elite woman. Concentrate.

"You'd be willing to turn over the Bula to a conglomerate?" Ben asked Franz.

"Money talks," the owner quickly replied. "It's time to cut my losses and move on."

"What if I were to match any offer Elite makes?"

Franz seemed taken aback, but quickly masked his surprise. "Where would you get that kind of money?"

"I am quite well connected."

The Bula's silver-haired owner stood up, towering above Ben who was well over six feet. "After I meet with Jillian Gray and hear what she has to say, we'll talk again."

He was out the door before Ben could say another word.

"How do you think that went?" Marlon said the moment the door slammed shut behind Franz.

"At least he's open to further conversation. Fill me in about this Jillian Gray."

"She's got a hairline fracture, if that's what you're asking."

It wasn't what Ben had been asking. He'd hoped to get the scoop on his prim and proper competition. Still, her minor disability could buy him time. And time was what he needed.

"That's too bad. Did the doctor say how long she would be out of commission?"

Marlon raised one eyebrow slightly. "She's to stay off the foot for a couple of days and use a cane. Why the sudden interest?"

A TASTE OF PARADISE

"Just need to know what I'm up against."

Marlon glanced at his watch. "I promised I would check on Ms. Gray. Want to come with me?"

An opportunity had presented itself, one that Ben wasn't about to walk away from. "Sure, why not?"

He followed Marlon out the door, refusing to admit that he was actually intrigued by the thought of seeing his nemesis again.

Jillian stared up at the beamed ceiling of her bure. She was angry with herself—angry for getting hurt. She should never have given in to vanity and worn those damn high heels. Now this little mishap would set her back several days. An unnecessary inconvenience since she had work to do.

A knock at the door saved her from self-pity.

"Come in!" she shouted, pushing away the table holding her leftovers. She'd somehow managed to shower and struggle into shorts and a crumpled linen blouse. Then she'd grabbed a pad and began compiling a "to do" list. Sleep had been impossible and she'd never been good at sitting idle anyway.

Marlon Hinds entered, followed by a tall man Jillian barely looked at.

"How are you doing?" Marlon asked, rolling the table with the remains of her lunch toward the door before picking up the phone and speaking into it briskly.

"Get up to the bridal suite on the double," he ordered.

The man who accompanied him hovered at the entrance.

"Who are you?" Jillian asked somewhat rudely.

"Ben Fuller. Don't you remember we met earlier, Jill?"

"Jillian."

His name even sounded familiar, and there was that cadence to his voice. Jillian stared at him, recognition slowly dawning. He was the person who'd picked her up unceremoniously and brought her here. Now clothed and minus the bandanna he was almost unrecognizable. He looked more like a successful businessman at leisure, and an attractive and familiar one at that.

"Do we know each other?" she asked, squinting her eyes at him.

Ben's tawny gaze roamed over her. For a moment Jillian wasn't sure how to interpret the spark in his eyes before they became shuttered. His expression overall grew distant and remote.

She'd heard his name before, of that she was certain. A long time ago. The name had once commanded respect. It had made people sit up and listen. But this man was no executive. There was a roughness to him and he looked like he'd lived quite the life.

"Do we?" he asked, with just a tinge of haughtiness to his tone, a steeliness that told her it was better to leave well enough alone.

"Where are you from?" Jillian inquired.

"Chicago."

"So am I. But you live here now?"

"Yes, I have for the last two years."

Clearly he wasn't about to elaborate and she got the distinct feeling that she had just crossed some invisible line.

Marlon ended his phone conversation and returned to her side. "I assume that in my absence you two have become acquainted."

Ben nodded. "Yes, Jill and I have been chatting. How is your ankle?" He asked in a gentler tone.

Jill again? The nerve of him. She hated the abbreviated name.

"Throbbing and uncomfortable, fortunately not broken, at least that's what the doctor says."

"Can I get you anything? Tea maybe or aspirin?" Marlon interjected.

"Thanks but the doctor's given me painkillers. What I'd like from you is a list of rates and your occupancy and vacancy reports."

Marlon seemed momentarily taken aback but quickly rallied. "Are you sure you're up to that task?"

"I'm sure."

"I'll have them sent to you then. Now if there's nothing else you need, I've got several urgent matters requiring my attention." Marlon gestured to the phone. "Call me if you need me. Coming, Ben?"

"A pleasure getting acquainted with you, Jill," Ben Fuller said. "Take care of that ankle."

A brief salute followed as he headed out. He surprised her by turning back. "Do you have dinner plans?"

"Dinner plans?"

"Yes. You do eat, don't you?"

Again, Jillian was totally captivated by the cadence in his voice. She found it mesmerizing, but not the man. Now how to interpret this dinner invitation? She pointed to the ankle.

"This little mishap prevents me from doing much. My plans tonight are with room service."

Ben's white smile, a flash of ivory against the pecan of his skin, did something to her insides. She explained it away as being overtired, jittery and on the edge. Now he seemed warmer and more approachable. She imagined that if he piled on the charm, there wasn't a woman around that wouldn't crumble.

"That's settled then. You'll have dinner with me. I'll be by with the golf cart to pick you up at eight o'clock. That should give you plenty of time to rest."

Sure of himself and likes to be in control, Jillian thought.

But spending an evening cooped up in a bridal suite wasn't exactly appealing either. But what were his real reasons for inviting her to dinner? He didn't seem to like her. Not that she'd given him any reason to.

Still Jillian found herself saying, "I'll agree on the condition that you call me Jillian. We'll be eating on site I take it?"

"Yes, *Jillian*, at the bungalow I rent. See you at eight then."

It took everything Jillian had to keep her jaw hinged. *Dinner at* his *place?* He really was nervy. Before she could say another word, Ben was out the front door, Marlon behind him.

Left with nothing but time and an aching ankle, Jillian reflected on the exchange. Suspicious by nature, she wondered what had prompted Ben's visit and the subsequent dinner invitation. Maybe she was making too much of it. Ben Fuller probably worked for the Bula and was doing what he had to do.

Contemplating all of it made her more exhausted. She set the alarm on her watch and closed her eyes. Rest might take her mind off the aching ankle and put her in a better frame of mind.

What seemed like minutes later, Jillian was jolted awake by a buzzing sound. Struggling to sit upright, it took her a while to locate her watch. She put weight on the ankle and a sharp pain sent her sinking back into her seat again. Finally, biting down on her lower lip, she hobbled into the bedroom to get dressed for dinner.

Forty-five minutes later, Jillian was ready. She'd managed to slip on a sundress with tiny spaghetti straps and force her feet into thongs. After adding a dab of make-up, she watched a silent TV replay the evening news.

At eight on the dot there was a knock at the door. With the aid of her cane, Jillian painstakingly went off to answer it. Ben stood before her—or at least someone that looked like him. His tawny eyes roamed over her, open admiration in their depths.

"You look nice."

"Thank you."

What was different about him tonight? Jillian found she couldn't tear her gaze away. Ah, yes, he'd shaved off the beard and his curly black hair had been slicked back and secured by a thong.

A white, billowing linen shirt added to the pirate effect and brought out the copper in his skin. Slightly wrinkled black linen slacks covered the muscular legs she'd seen earlier. Jillian did her best not to stare. Ben Fuller looked like he should be on the high seas commanding a schooner. The name "Captain Ben" popped into her head, producing a grin.

"Looks like you're ready to go," Ben said, offering her the crook of his arm.

"Yes, I'm ready. You did say eight."

Jillian took the elbow he extended, curling her fingers around a muscled arm and tried to ignore the delectable smell of citrus wafting her way. She reacted by pulling away. Centering her weight on the orthopedic cane, she gingerly made her way down a lantern lit path and toward the golf cart.

"You live on the property?" Jillian asked when she was seated.

"Yes, I was able to rent a time share. It's a bungalow much like yours."

"How long have you lived there?"

"The last three months or so."

Ben started up the vehicle.

Jillian wanted to ask him why he'd chosen to make his home on Taveuni but refrained. She sensed from his body language that further inquiries might be rebuffed. The silence continued as he steered the golf cart up a series of paths and away from the main thoroughfare. Finally he pulled up in front of a sprawling bungalow that was set back from the road. On the wraparound verandah, a woman shaded her eyes.

"Mr. Ben," she called out, "Is that you?"

"Yes, Anna, I've brought our guest. Anna is my housekeeper," he said under his breath.

"Welcome."

The little woman, who looked more like a gnome, waddled toward them. Jillian could not see her face but the cheery greeting immediately put her at ease.

"It's nice to see Mr. Ben with a woman, and a beautiful one at that," his housekeeper confided. "He seldom brings anyone home."

"Anna," Ben Fuller warned sternly.

The woman clapped a hand over her mouth. "Sorry, Mr. Ben, but you know that is true. Come, my dinner is growing cold. I made *chevrettes*—fish and taro, it will keep your teeth healthy."

Jillian couldn't help smiling. Aided by Ben, she slowly climbed the three front steps and stepped onto the spacious verandah. Tiny white lights rimmed the railings and banisters. On the verandah was a rattan table set for two.

Jillian hoped she wasn't gawking. This seemed such an intimate setting for a business dinner. Again she wondered what had prompted him to invite her to dinner.

"I figured we might be more comfortable sitting outside," Ben hastened to explain, holding out a chair. "Anna, please bring us some coconut water."

"Right away, sir." The housekeeper waddled off, then turned back to say, "Make yourself comfortable and I will be back soon."

Ben sank into the seat across from Jillian. She had the distinct impression she was experiencing déjà vu. She'd met Ben Fuller before and in fact knew him well. A vague memory of a younger man, an autocratic one, began to take form. Now she remembered him clearly. She'd worked for Ben ages ago. Back then he'd been demanding, opinionated and brashly aggressive—a major pain in the butt. She'd been his intern, one of several.

Benjamin Fuller had been the boss from hell.

Chapter 3

"I know who you are," Jillian said, the words popping out of her mouth before she could stop them.

Ben's head listed to one side. One imperious brow rose. "What's that supposed to mean?"

"You were my first boss. I worked for Jamison and Fuller. God, it has to be at least fourteen years ago."

Ben stared at her as if she had two heads, as if she'd completely lost it. "I don't remember you. I was a fledgling in the real estate business. My company speculated on properties, buying them cheap then selling them for a sizeable profit."

"Yes, I know. I was one of the gophers you hired while I was still in college." Jillian ran a hand across her cropped head of hair. "I had wild hair and wore ugly granny glasses. I tried to blend in to the woodwork. Some might have even labeled me a nerd."

"Hardly a nerd now," Ben muttered, his eyes roaming over her, taking in the sundress and her exposed shoulders.

She'd gained Ben's full attention. He sat up straight, his eyes returning to her face, clearly trying to place her.

The company Ben had owned, Jamison and Fuller,

had prided itself on acquiring commercial properties. The two partners—James Jamison and Benjamin Fuller, Ben didn't exist back then—scoped out areas being gentrified, buying up decrepit old buildings. They fixed them up and flipped them, making an incredible profit in the process. The monies were then invested in other rundown properties.

Back then, the two cocky African-American Ivy Leaguers had gained a formidable reputation for having incredible business acumen. This was no easy feat in a tough real estate market, dominated primarily by white men.

The staff, for the most part, was made up of interns recruited from black colleges, brought on board to learn the real estate business. This young, inexperienced team served in every capacity, ranging from resident gophers to construction workers. Although the pay was abysmal, the waiting list to come onboard kept growing and growing. Students wanted to work for two young upstarts that looked like them. It gave them hope that they could achieve what Benjamin and James had.

And truly, it was a win/win situation for all. Jamison and Fuller kept their overhead down by not extending health insurance or benefits, and eager students lined up for their chance at the pie.

"Why don't I remember you?" Ben growled, squinting at her, his mind apparently working overtime. "I unloaded that business ages ago. And I prided myself on knowing my staff."

Jillian steepled her fingers and looked him squarely in the face. "As you said, it was a long time ago. I worked for you for six months and then got hired by a competitor paying a decent salary. You, on the other hand, went on to build a business and a reputation right up there with Trump."

"The Donald? I should have his money," Ben muttered, rolling his eyes. "Can we change the subject?"

"The coconut water is served," Anna announced, reappearing at the opportune moment. "It's chilled like you like it. Want me to pour?"

"Please." Ben's attention was now totally focused on his housekeeper. "You may also bring out the food, if it's ready."

She set the pitcher down on the table, then disappeared through the door from whence she had come.

"Well, what do you think?" Ben asked as Jillian took the first sip of the beverage. There was still no offer of wine, she noticed. It seemed very strange.

"Delicious," Jillian said, swirling the drink around her tongue. She'd had coconut water before, but nothing that tasted quite like this.

"I've become addicted to that water," Ben admitted. "The trees in my backyard make it that much more convenient."

Jillian changed the subject and pointedly said, "I love your house, what little I've seen of it."

Ben glanced at her ankle. "I'll give you the tour if you can manage."

"I'd like that." She struggled to her feet, centering her weight on the cane.

Ben took her elbow and guided her inside. His touch triggered a reaction—one that she would examine later. On their way in, they passed Anna, balancing dishes in both hands. She beamed at them before edging by.

"We'll be back soon," Ben quickly reassured her. "I wouldn't want that delicious meal to get cold."

Inside was pristine. The living room had highly polished wood floors and comfortable rattan sofas. Colorful batik pillows were stacked around a teak coffee table. An urn, overflowing with birds of paradise and razor grass, provided more color. Entering the galley kitchen,

Jillian noted it was amazingly clean, no evidence of a meal being prepared. A small dining area off to the side held a mahogany table and a glass breakfront.

Jillian followed Ben into two airy bathrooms. Rectangular skylights gave a glimpse of a starry night and the beginnings of an orange moon. Next, she was whisked through an austere guest room holding a bed and two nightstands. Ben then led her into what must be his room.

Although the bedroom was masculine, hints of Ben's personality could clearly be seen. Jillian eyed the stacks of books and magazines piled on built-in shelves. A solitary golf club was propped in one corner. French doors led out to a secluded verandah, and cream-colored walls held framed murals of island scenes.

Ben's bed, a gigantic thing, was shrouded in mosquito netting. On it were plump pillows and even more books.

"You read?" Jillian asked, breaking what was starting to be an uncomfortable silence.

"Every chance I get. You sound surprised."

She was. Ben Fuller had never struck her as the intellectual sort. There was more to him than she'd initially thought.

Quickly, Ben steered her out the way they had come.

On the table were steaming dishes. Anna, the housekeeper, stood to the side waiting for instructions. Ben held out Jillian's chair and she slid into it. Instead of taking the seat opposite, he sat to her right. His close proximity unsettled her, as did the scent of citrus. She was experiencing sensory overload, Jillian decided.

A perfumed breeze blew across the verandah, ruffling gauze curtains at an open window and billowing the sleeves of Ben's shirt. *Focus, Jillian. Stop staring at the hollow of his throat.* But even that caution didn't seem to work. She continued to stare, her eyes taking in the cleft in his chin—a cleft she hadn't noticed before because of his beard. Why was she having such an erotic reaction to a man she once feared?

"Uh, um." Ben cleared his throat.

Jillian now turned her attention to the food Anna ladled onto their plates: fish and taro, red bell peppers, fluffy wild rice, assorted vegetables and breadfruit. The pungent aromas made Jillian's stomach growl.

"Did you say something?"

"No, I didn't."

How embarrassing. She kept her eyes focused on her plate but managed a sideways glance. Ben picked up a skewer and bit into the succulent shellfish. When he looked up and winked at her, her stomach did a little dance.

"Don't stand on ceremony. Dig in," he commanded.

Jillian quickly forked food into her mouth. She gave another sideways glance at her host. Ben's full lips were the kind a woman wanted to nibble—that is, when she was into nibbling men's lips.

As if guessing her thoughts, Ben's golden eyes twinkled. He looked at her questioningly, "Something wrong?"

"Nothing wrong. I was just thinking how delicious everything is. Sitting here under a Fiji moon with stars I would never see in Chicago has a magical effect. If you told me I'd be doing this six months ago, I would have thought you were mad."

Ben muttered so low Jillian had to strain her ears to hear him. "And if anyone had told me that I would be living in Taveuni, I would have had them committed."

This time it was Jillian's turn to raise a brow. "You don't enjoy living here? Then why did you move?"

Ben used a cream-colored napkin to wipe his full lips, lips that she was having a difficult time tearing her gaze from. "I needed a life change. Taveuni presented an opportunity. I took a vacation, fell in

A TASTE OF PARADISE

love, and stayed. Now this has become my island and these are my people."

Words popped out before Jillian could stop them. "You fell in love? I thought you were married. I remember seeing a picture of a wife and a family."

Ben's entire demeanor changed then. His shoulders stiffened and he refused to meet her gaze. One moment stretched into another. Annoyed, Jillian repeated her words.

Finally Ben mumbled, "I meant to say I fell in love with the island." After a few beats went by, he added, "How does another drink sound?"

Clearly that was the end of that. She would get no more out of him.

Jillian sure could have used a strong drink. But there was still no offer of wine. Given the elaborate meal that had been cooked, she would have expected at least a Chardonnay. Maybe Marlon had told Ben she'd been prescribed painkillers.

She mulled over what Ben had just said, wondering what kind of life changes had so affected him? The man Jillian remembered had had the world on a string. He was on his way up. And nothing could put a crimp in his style.

Jillian slid her still half-full glass Ben's way. "How did you get hired by the resort?" she asked.

"I don't work for the Bula."

"But you were with Marlon earlier. You used the golf cart."

Ben shot her an amused look. "You presumed since Marlon and I are friends, I must be an employee. I live on the property and I'm considered trustworthy."

There was a story here and one she planned on unearthing. The old Ben Fuller had been polished and immaculately turned out. He'd worn tailored suits and monogrammed white shirts. His hair had been closely cropped and he would never have been seen dead in the bandanna he'd worn earlier on the beach.

In the recesses of her mind, Jillian remembered a scandal, something quickly hushed up. The story would come to her eventually if she gave it some thought.

"You're with Elite," Ben said, subtly shifting the conversation away from himself. "How come they chose you of all people to look over the property?"

Jillian eyeballed him, sensing the question behind his actual words. "I'm the most qualified person Elite has," she offered. What Ben really meant to say was, "How come Elite sent an African-American woman to negotiate a deal so monumental?" She'd expected far better from him.

"No doubt you are, but why is Elite interested in a rundown property that needs sprucing up? The service is abysmal, lackadaisical at best, certainly not up to American standards."

Jillian chuckled at his droll delivery and decided to play with him. "Ah, but the Bula has a distinctive charm to it. It's the kind of property that attracts a more adventurous patron, guests who want to immerse themselves in the culture. That kind tends to be more tolerant. If Elite makes an offer, we'll change things. The Bula will be returned to the world-class resort it once was."

"Sounds like you've already made up your mind that you'll be making an offer."

"Maybe. Usually I don't make up my mind that easily. There's quite a bit to be considered. Books will have to be looked at, revenues and expenses examined."

"You easily made up your mind about me," Ben said, eyeing her over his glass. "What is it about me that makes you uncomfortable?"

His direct approach took her aback, but Jillian rallied. "You're hardly part of the equation."

"I could be if you'd let me."

What was behind his comments? Was Ben Fuller hitting on her? Every caution button lit up. The thought occurred: What if Ben was scouting out the property and needed information to see what he was up against?

Well, Ben was in for a rude awakening. She'd learned from the best—James Jamison and Benjamin Fuller. This acquisition was her turning point; if she were successful, she would move into a whole other league. It would ensure her a vice presidency.

No, Ben's interest in her could not possibly be romantic. The man was just used to getting what he wanted. He would use his blatant sexuality and good looks to ferret out information—find out what she knew. Jillian needed to be on her guard.

Ben had been the ultimate strategist, not one to walk away from a lucrative deal. Jillian would "Google" him as soon as she got back to her bungalow. While fourteen years might seem a lifetime to some, a leopard usually didn't change its spots.

Jillian moved her vegetables around her plate. Choosing her words carefully from now on might not be a bad idea.

"So what exactly is it that you do now? How do you make a living?" she asked.

"I manage to keep busy."

"That's rather cryptic."

Ben chuckled a mirthless sound. He reached across the table and took her hand. "I feel like I'm getting the third degree. If you'd consider having dinner with me again, I might be more forthcoming. What do you say?"

Ben was definitely coming on strong, and her traitorous body was responding to his touch. Electricity surged through her veins and even the tips of her fingers tingled. Why the sudden interest in her? She wasn't the type powerful men went for. They liked trophies, Barbie dolls that kept them youthful and looked good on their arm.

Jillian remembered Ben's wife. From what she recalled of the photograph she'd seen in a rare visit to his office, she'd been petite and doe-eyed. The fragile type, who gazed up adoringly at her man, as if intrigued by everything he had to say. Two kids had flanked the couple, dressed in uniforms from an expensive prep school.

That memory made Jillian withdraw her hand. She'd not come to Taveuni to find a relationship and wasn't the least bit interested in a quick hop in the sack.

"You're married. What would Mrs. Fuller say to this?" she said tersely.

That produced a coughing fit. Jillian slid Ben's glass of coconut water closer. He gulped it and managed to regain control.

"There is no Mrs. Fuller," he said somewhat sharply when the coughing fit ceased. His eyes were now shuttered and his expression guarded.

Bingo. That's what had brought him to Fiji—a bitter divorce. That was the scandal.

"I'm sorry," Jillian sputtered, kicking herself for being insensitive.

"Not as sorry as I am," Ben whispered, looking completely morose. "Anna, please bring us out dessert."

The housekeeper silently materialized, quickly picked up their dishes, and scooted back inside. She returned holding a bowl. "Coconut custard," she announced, ladling the creamy substance into two coconut shells. "Would you like coffee?"

Jillian declined. Caffeine was not a good idea. She was already too wired. What she needed was a good night's sleep and time to strategize. Aching ankle or not, tomorrow she would make some calls and find out all there was to know about Ben Fuller.

Ben silently made short work of the delicious dessert. His flirtatious mood seemed to have ended as quickly as it had begun. Jillian wondered what had gone so terribly wrong with his marriage that he could no longer discuss his wife or family. She set her spoon down.

"Would you like more?" Ben asked, eyeing her empty coconut shell.

"No, thank you, I'm stuffed. Everything was delicious. Your housekeeper outdid herself." She yawned.

"Tired?"

Jillian nodded.

"If I can't get you anything else maybe we should call it a night."

Ben was equally as anxious to get her out of his house as she was to leave. Jillian wondered if it was because she'd been totally non-committal about agreeing to have another dinner with him.

Tomorrow would be a busy one, and, yes, she was tired. Jillian swallowed another yawn and reflected on her plans. She'd review the Bula's occupancy rate and see what the profit margin was, if indeed there was a profit to be had. She'd set up meetings with department heads. These preliminary interviews could be conducted over the phone.

The advertising company would be the first call on her list. They were located in Hawaii, and she would bet her last dime no one had checked up or held them accountable for their lack of effort in a really long time. Their focus would be on bigger game, more upscale resorts with money to burn.

Ben jiggled the keys to the golf cart at her. "Ready?"

"Yes, I am."

He placed a hand on her elbow and Jillian allowed him to help her up.

"It's been a lovely dinner," she said graciously. "I must extend my compliments to the chef."

"Anna," Ben called, "Ms. Gray is leaving."

The housekeeper quickly emerged. Her previously cheerful countenance registered her disappointment.

"You're leaving so soon?" she asked, glancing at the table and the still steaming coffee urn.

"Ms. Gray has been traveling all day," Ben explained. "She's exhausted."

"You will come back soon."

This was said with such sincerity that Jillian could not resist touching the woman's shoulder. "I might consider it, if I'm ever invited."

"You will be invited," Anna said, as if she knew something Jillian didn't.

Despite the earlier invitation, one glance at Ben's face confirmed that might not be so.

He waved a pecan-colored hand toward the exit. Lightening quickly, again his mood had changed.

Why was Ben in Taveuni? What had brought him here? It had to be the Bula. If that were the case he'd soon find out what he was up against. Jillian had worked too hard to let Ben have his way. She was determined to make vice president and acquiring the Bula at a decent price would make that a certainty.

Chapter 4

The same miserable dream consumed Ben—a dream that had been replayed one too many times, a dream he would never forget. He watched helplessly as the plane did a series of loops before plunging to the ground. The acrid smell of smoke burned his nostrils and the hysterical screams of agony filled his ears. The images were so vivid that Ben sat up in bed, expecting to find the charred bodies beside him. When would the horrific nightmares end?

He plumped up the pillows, determined to find a more comfortable position, and counted innumerable sheep. Sleep still would not come. The evening's events replayed in his mind. He'd vowed not to like Jillian Gray, but the truth was, he'd enjoyed her company immensely. Both were aggressive about what they wanted and determined to get their way.

Jillian's announcement that she'd been an employee of his had come as a surprise. For the life of him, he couldn't remember her, though that was to be expected, he supposed. Jamison and Fuller had hired hundreds of interns in the fourteen years they'd existed. And Ben had been too busy building a business to get to know his staff or form personal attachments.

Giving up on sleep, Ben wandered into the kitchen, opened the refrigerator and retrieved the pitcher of coconut water. What he really wanted was a nice stiff drink. Funny but that urge had never left him, pretty scary after being sober these past two years.

From attending Alcoholics Anonymous meetings, he had learned that urge would stay with him for a lifetime. He would have to deal with it a day at a time and celebrate every single day of staying sober.

Still, like the old cigarette ad said, "You've come a long way, baby." At least he no longer started out his day belting down a drink, nor did he end it with enough liquor in his system to ignite a small fire. For too long, drinking himself into oblivion had been the only way he could get to sleep and deal with those horrific nightmares.

Alcohol had provided a diversionary haze during the difficult period after September 11, 2001 when he'd lost the things he loved most and his world ended.

The memory of that time, getting that call, would forever be emblazoned in his mind. That event had changed his life and made the country realize it wasn't invincible. God knew it had changed Ben's life irrevocably. He still hadn't totally recovered.

"Mr. Fuller, sir! Come see what's going on!"

Ben turned to see Anna behind him. She slept in a smaller bure out back. She was disheveled and he'd never quite seen her like this, in pajamas and robe, and her usually neat hair spiked out like a halo.

"What's the matter, Anna?" Ben asked, worried that something terrible had happened.

"One of the hotel buildings is on fire. Please come outside and take a look."

Carrying his glass with him, Ben followed the tiny

woman out to the verandah. Sure enough, flames licked the sky and people were running in every direction. Panicked shouts filled the air. Words he couldn't quite make out.

"Call the fire department," Ben ordered. But even as he issued that command, sirens screamed in the distance. "No, don't bother. Try reaching Marlon Hinds instead. His number is programmed in my phone."

Ben was climbing into shorts and a T-shirt before he knew it. When he returned, Anna, looking like the world had stopped, still clutched the phone.

"No one's answering," she jabbered. "What do I do?"

"Nothing right now. I'm heading over to take a look."

"I'm coming with you."

Ben didn't look back as he covered the short distance and entered what appeared to be Hades. There was soot and smoke everywhere and sparks showered down on the gathering crowd. Many were in various stages of undress, awed by the unexpected pyrotechnics. Firefighters aimed their hoses high, trying their best to manage the blaze.

"How did this start?" Ben asked a waiter he recognized.

The man shrugged. "Who knows, maybe someone fell asleep with a lit cigarette."

Where was Marlon or his designee? No one seemed to be in charge. Ben remembered Jillian Gray and her incapacitated state; she must be panicked, wondering what was going on.

"Do you think they can save the building?" Anna asked, tugging on his arm.

"I hope so. I'm going to walk around and see if I can find Marlon. I wonder if anyone's thought to call Franz Herrman?"

He left the housekeeper and elbowed his way through the crowd. The flames had subsided a bit but ashes still rained down, covering every available surface. Female guests sobbed loudly, as did some of the employees, the ones who'd spent the night on the premises. A man bellowed orders using a bullhorn, urging guests to go to the lobby, where refreshments were served.

Again, Ben thought about Jillian. *She must be beside herself.* He'd make a quick stop at the main building, get an update, and then head over to the bridal suite.

The lobby was swarming with people as he elbowed his way to the front. Marlon held court, trying to calm down a group that had grown hysterical.

"The fire's under control," the manager announced. "And no, we have no idea how it got started. Your safety and well-being are our primary concern. Go enjoy the buffet. Help yourself to coffee and drinks. All refreshments are compliments of the Bula."

This was no time to take Marlon off to the side. Ben continued on his way. A few employees had been roped into standing guard on the grounds. They held flashlights, lighting the way. Ben took a shortcut through the undergrowth and headed for the bridal suite.

When he arrived, the gate to the courtyard was closed, so he pushed it open. All of the bungalow's lights were on and the building was lit up like a Christmas tree. On the lanai was a woman who must be Jillian.

"Who's there?" her wobbling voice called.

"Ben Fuller," he announced.

"Oh, Ben, thank God it's you. What's on fire? The sirens and smell of smoke woke me up."

Ben climbed onto the lanai before answering. For the first time he noticed Jillian's state of undress. She was wearing skimpy boxer shorts and a matching camisole. She had a hand on the railing of the lanai, supporting her weight. The cane she'd used to make the short journey hung from a balustrade.

"Get off your feet and I'll tell you what I know," Ben

said, gesturing to a deck chair and holding her by the elbow with his free hand. An electric bolt seared him when his flesh connected with hers. What in the world did that mean?

He broke contact as soon as Jillian was seated. She drew up her long legs—legs that were so perfectly proportioned, she could have been a hosiery model.

"Marlon was worried about you. He asked me to stop by," Ben lied, trying not to stare. "In your condition, it's not as if you can get around easily."

Jillian's expression signified her surprise. "That was nice of him. I did try calling the front desk. But there was either a busy signal, or the phone rang and rang."

"One of the bures caught on fire," Ben hastened to explain. "The firefighters are working to get the blaze under control. Perhaps someone fell asleep with a lit cigarette. No one knows for sure."

"Hmmmm," Jillian said, "any possibility of arson?"

That thought hadn't even entered Ben's mind. "I can't imagine why anyone would purposely set fire to the Bula."

"I can. The property is in financial difficulty. Insurance money could be the answer."

Ben wasn't sure how to take that. Did Jillian think he might be conspiring with Franz and his friends?

"Neither the owner nor the management would stoop that low," Ben said coldly. "They have always conducted business aboveboard."

"I'm just thinking out loud," came her equally churlish reply.

Ben couldn't imagine Franz Herrman or any of his investment partners desperate enough to resort to the despicable, but you never knew. Franz would never soil his own hands. But what Jillian said couldn't be totally discounted.

Remembering the lateness of the hour, Ben stood. He'd done what he'd come to do: calm Jillian Gray down. Now time to return to the main building, take Marlon aside, and find out what he knew.

"Try to get some sleep," Ben said, preparing to leave. "I'll call if I discover anything worth knowing. Need help getting back inside?"

Jillian's smile took the sting off her words. "No, thank you. I am perfectly capable of making it on my own. I hobbled out and I'll hobble back." She pointed to her cane, making her point.

"If you're sure then. You would not be imposing asking for help."

"I know that." Another wide and amazingly warm smile followed.

Ben left Jillian inching her way back inside. Begrudgingly, he admired her independence and her smarts. She'd be a worthy opponent. Certainly not your run-of-the-mill woman.

By the time he reached the lobby, the crowd had dissipated and only a handful of employees and guests remained. Ben scanned the surrounding areas looking for Marlon. The manager was nowhere in sight. He made his way to the back offices, and hearing the rumble of conversation coming from behind a closed door, knocked.

When no immediate response came, Ben tried again.

"What?" snapped a deep voice he recognized as Marlon's.

"It's Ben."

The door opened a few seconds later and Marlon motioned for him to come in. Franz and a handful of employees were seated at a round table in the midst of what seemed like a heated discussion. No one even acknowledged Ben's presence.

"I'd give Jillian Gray a call if I were you," Ben whispered. "What might be even better is a visit in person."

A muttered expletive followed as Marlon thudded

his open palm against his forehead. "I've been so involved with this crisis I forgot the woman was on the premises."

"I already covered for you and made your excuses. You might want to phone her, then send a room service tray over with your apologies."

"I'll go one better." Marlon crooked a finger at an employee. The woman scooted out of her chair. "Do we have courtesy vouchers for the spa at the Guest Relations Desk?"

"Yes, we do," the attractive East Indian woman answered.

"Please call room service and have a tray of tea and sandwiches made up for the bridal suite. I want orchids on that tray, and I want a courtesy voucher for a facial, massage and manicure. I'll handwrite an apology. You, our guest relations manager, will deliver it rather than shove it off on the room attendant.

"Consider it done," the manager said, heading off.

"Can you talk?" Ben asked after she'd left. "Any idea how this fire got started?'

Marlon shrugged, jutting his jaw in the direction of the people at the table. "Hopefully the fire chief will have something for us soon."

"Okay, I'll leave you to it. Call me when you know something for sure."

"How about we meet for breakfast on the outdoor patio, say around eight," Marlon said, ushering him out.

"I'll be there. Hopefully by then you'll have an update."

Marlon snorted. "I'd better have something, or heads will roll. Of that, you can be sure."

Chapter 5

Three days later, the swelling on her ankle having subsided considerably, Jillian managed to get around without a cane. Her incapacitation had served a purpose, forcing her to stay put and catch up on the tedious paperwork that came with the job.

She'd had ample time to analyze the Bula's comprehensive room occupancy report and to figure out if they were even making a small profit.

As she suspected, the hotel was gradually losing business. There had been no conscious effort made to retain repeat guests beyond heavily discounting rooms. After speaking with the agency account executive handling the resort's advertising, Jillian became even more concerned. He clearly did not have a plan or the desire to send business the Bula's way.

What Jillian didn't get was why a resort like the Bula, with such infinite possibilities and private funding, would be allowed to fall into disrepair. All the hotel really needed was some cosmetic improvements and some innovative thinking. Sure the public areas needed sprucing up, but the bures were comfortably appointed and had a certain charm to them.

Wooden ceilings and a spacious layout brought the

outdoors in. Jillian often felt as if she were sleeping in the middle of a lush tropical garden. So far, her stay had been very relaxing. And yes, the drapes and upholstery needed updating, but technically there was little other than that that was wrong with the accommodations.

Jillian had quizzed the account executive relentlessly as to his advertising plans for the year. She hadn't liked his responses one bit. Clearly the Bula was not his number one priority, since all of her questions had been answered evasively. She'd gotten the distinct impression he'd made up his mind there was no way to save a sinking ship so why bother.

She would bet that unless a guest—translation, one of the repeat variety—specifically requested the Bula, he would direct them to a more upscale property. Frustrated with the man's less than enthusiastic responses, Jillian had given him a directive. Send her his plan to drive business and increase revenues, and do it right away. She'd already decided if Elite acquired the Bula, the advertising company would have to go.

What she needed was a breather, time for her. Since the ankle was feeling much better, she'd decided today would be perfect to take Marlon Hinds up on his gracious offer and receive her complimentary spa treatments. She would enjoy that massage and facial. She'd have her nails done, and with her ankle feeling so much better, even have a pedicure.

Jillian had just hung up the phone after making the appointment when the phone rang.

"Hello."

"Good morning, Jillian," Marlon's clipped greeting resounded in her ear. "Will you be attending Moonlight Madness? If you'd like, I'll send a golf cart around to get you."

"When is it?" Jillian asked, not remembering an invitation.

"Tonight."

"Tonight?"

What she'd probably done was stick the invitation under the sheaves of paperwork she'd been going through. Still, viewing the entertainment and leisure activities of any property came with the territory. Jillian doubted whether the event would be spectacular but it was something to do, and she was beginning to get tired of being holed up in her room.

"The festivities begin at eight. Weather permitting, the party will take place on the beach," Marlon said, breaking into her thoughts.

"What's the dress code?"

"Leisure attire. Comfort is the name of the game. Is your ankle up to it?"

"It's much improved and the swelling's down. Thank you for asking."

"See you tonight, then," he said. "Please call if you'd like to have a golf cart sent around."

Jillian hung up thinking that her time at the spa wouldn't really be wasted. She'd justify the pampering as hands-on experience, and, of course, she would be taking notes.

She threw on a pair of shorts and a tank top, stuck her feet into flip-flops, and prepared to take off. Opening a desk drawer, she removed a map of the resort and traced a finger over the route she would take.

Even as she did so, a vision of Ben Fuller popped into her head. She hadn't seen or heard from him since the fire. And he hadn't followed through on his promise to update her. She'd questioned Marlon during one of his phone calls but he hadn't been forthcoming either. He'd simply said, "The matter is under investigation. I'll be sure to fill you in when I know."

Something was up. Deep down in her bones, she

still believed it was arson. She suspected the fire had been set deliberately to force Elite to back off. She'd "Googled" Ben Fuller but there had been very little public information about him after 2001. But Jillian strongly suspected that he was still buying and selling run-down properties, or why else would he be here?

Stepping gingerly, she made her way down a pebble-strewn path, crossed a small bridge and followed the route outlined on her map. Closer to the spa, she came across the bungalow that had been on fire and stopped to stare.

Although the area was roped off, the stench of smoldering wood still lingered. The cottage's thatched roof had been destroyed and a prominent *No Trespassing* sign erected.

Jillian stared at the mess, wondering which poor guest had been displaced. She meant to ask Marlon that question later, along with some others. Her sandaled foot kicked a metallic object and it skittered across the path. Absentmindedly, she bent down to retrieve the object and, realizing it was a pen, stuck it in her pocket. She continued on her way.

Five minutes later, Jillian swung through glass double doors and entered an airy oasis. A cross section of guests and locals were seated in the waiting room, some impatiently flipping through pages of glossy magazines.

Crossing spotless tile floors, she headed toward a batik-covered couch. As Jillian was about to sit, a smiling receptionist called to her.

"Hello, Ms. Gray, we're ready for you."

Word must have gotten around that she would be gracing the place with her presence.

Swallowing a grin, Jillian followed the pretty Asian woman into a backroom where clients of all shapes and sizes struggled into and out of clothing. She was handed a sarong and ordered to undress.

"You've got a full hour blocked for your massage," the receptionist said, ushering her into another room.

Periwinkle walls held framed photographs of island women and pink orchids dangled from the ceiling. On closer inspection, Jillian realized the plants weren't real. But they added to the ambiance and the feeling of tropical decadence, as did the comfortable beige divan urging you to lie down, close your eyes, and dream.

Piped-in soothing music played from the speakers in the ceiling, and candles flickered in recessed alcoves. Mesmerized by the music and the wonderful vanilla scent the candles emitted, Jillian began to disrobe. An object clanged across the tile floor. Jillian bent down and picked up the pen she'd found earlier. Absentmindedly, she tossed it into her Kate Spade bag and wrapped the sarong around her.

A discreet knock came from the door, followed by a male voice calling, "Madam, are you ready?"

She was as ready as she would ever be.

A burly native entered. His size intimidated her, and his bulging muscles indicated he was no stranger to weights.

"Come with me," he said, opening a door that led into an adjoining room.

Jillian followed the man into a tiny room that held only a massage table on wheels.

Sliding white cotton sheets down, he told her to lose the sarong and make herself comfortable.

"I'll be back," he said, disappearing again.

Jillian stripped off the sarong and slid under the covers. Another delightful smell permeated the room—one she recognized as aromatherapy rose petals. Heaven.

Three hours later, she emerged a new woman. The soothing massage performed with aromatic oils helped ease any stress she might have been harboring. The deep cleansing facial convinced her she'd been neglecting herself for far too long. She'd even allowed the manicurist to paint her fingernails and toes an attractive shade of coral. Now she was in full resort mode and determined to go with the flow. Forget Peter Fontaine, her boss, and his restrictive dress code.

Jillian tipped the attendants and headed for the exit. She was surprised to find the waiting room still teeming with people.

A rumbling voice came from behind her, making her jump. "Jillian, is that you?" the masculine tone inquired.

Turning around, she faced Ben Fuller.

"What are you doing here?" she asked, unnerved by his appearance. He was the last person she'd expected to see in a salon.

Ben stood, towering above her. "I need a haircut and this is convenient. You look nice," he said, assessing her carefully. "I mean nice and relaxed."

"Thanks," she muttered.

Jillian was conscious of his appreciative gaze and his predatory ogling of her legs. No mistaking it, Ben liked what he saw. She hated the fact that she actually felt jittery around him. There was something about the man that turned her to mush.

"How's the ankle?" Ben asked.

"Much better, thank you."

"Will you be attending Moonlight Madness tonight?"

"I'm thinking about it," she said, trying not to stare at Ben's wide expanse of chest. The fitted short-sleeved T-shirt he wore left little to the imagination. It gave an unfettered view of a sculptured upper body and two sinewy arms.

"Weren't you supposed to call me?" Jillian said sharply, her goal to remind him who she was.

Ben cocked his head to the side, "Was I now?"

"Yes. You promised to tell me what you'd found out about the fire."

"Nothing to tell. Marlon should be the one providing you with an update."

Jillian doubted that he knew nothing about the fire. The old Benjamin Fuller accumulated information for information's sake. He would want to know everything there was to know about the fire. He was keeping something from her and was deliberately being evasive.

"Mr. Fuller, Peng's ready for you," the receptionist called before Jillian could press him further.

Ben, who seemed eager to escape, beat a hasty retreat. "See you later, maybe."

She was barely able to nod before he loped off.

Jillian's eyes focused on his broad back as he followed behind the attendant. She warned herself to be careful. A man like Ben Fuller used his looks to get what he wanted. He wasn't a distraction she could afford. She was too behind in her work. All of her energies needed to be concentrated on the Bula and not on some man.

Ben hadn't expected to find Jillian in the salon. He hadn't planned on being here himself, at some froufrou spa that primarily catered to women. But he needed a haircut and this was the closest place. Time was at a premium today.

Two of his key financial backers had flown in from Australia. One was his old friend, James Jamison. Ben had managed to get an audience with the other, a private investor who accompanied him. He hadn't seen James in years and thought it might not be smart having him think he'd been living under a rock.

An androgynous stylist waved Ben into a seat. The man's streaked blonde hair contrasted sharply with his Asian features. A half-dozen earrings dangled from one lobe.

"What are we having done today?" the stylist asked, draping a cape around Ben's neck.

"Taking it all off."

"Are you sure?"

"As sure as I'll ever be."

It had been almost two years since Ben's last haircut. Now he wore his naturally curly hair, a legacy from a Native American grandfather, down to his shoulders. His outward appearance was usually something he didn't care about. Except today it was important that he make an impression.

Ben sat stoically as the stylist went to work. Occasionally he glanced at the tile floor watching as wisps of hair accumulated. He wasn't particularly attached to the unruly mane but it had provided security and represented for him a whole new identity. In Taveuni, the wilder side of him had emerged—a side that during his married years he'd kept under wraps.

No, he would not go there. No morbid thoughts for him. Hair would easily grow back. He just had to convince the money people that this was a worthwhile project, and they would make a profit.

The Fiji people were his family now and many needed jobs. If he was able to acquire the Bula and all that wonderful acreage, he could put hundreds of natives to work. He'd build a plant in the midst of the coconut grove and bottle all that delicious water. He would use the copra to make butter, soaps and oils. The husks could easily be turned into souvenirs. In good conscience, how could he allow the Americanization of this resort?

Another twenty minutes went by, and a growing pile of hair accumulated. Finally, Ben was handed a mirror and urged to look at the results. He gazed at his reflection while the stylist, who called himself

"Peng," kept up a steady stream of compliments. Summoning his colleagues over to take a look, he rambled on saying, "Mr. Fuller looks like a magazine model."

Ben refused to react to the stranger in the mirror. It had been years since he'd been both clean-shaven and shorn. And truthfully he looked at least ten years younger than his forty-four years. He'd need an edge for the upcoming meeting. Hopefully this would be it.

Ben had cashed in his stock after dissolving his partnership. A few sound investments had made that money multiply. He was willing to put up a large portion of it because he knew deep in his bones that a coconut plant would be a huge success. But even more funds would be needed to assure him the upper hand. Those monies needed to come from Ilya and Tony.

Ben already had commitments from four local people that were part of the island leadership. He was also counting on Elite to make an embarrassingly low bid. The corporation was known to buy things cheap. They were also known for cleaning house and firing employees. Ben had a deep love for the island, and the locals needed to win.

He was counting on Franz Herrman, who'd married a local woman. He had ties to Taveuni, whether he lived there year round or not. The man would want to see the Bula restored to its former elegant self. Elite, on the other hand, would modernize and run the hotel like an American chain. And they wouldn't know what to do with his precious coconuts.

Foreigners would be brought in to manage the resort—people with hospitality training, but not a clue as to what warmth and South Pacific graciousness meant.

Ben would be damned if he would let that happen. The strategic Ben Fuller was back.

Chapter 6

"Right this way, madam," the man who'd been her bellhop said, making a sweeping gesture toward a torch-lined path.

Jillian had passed on Marlon's offer of a golf cart, reasoning that she needed the exercise. Now faced with the incline ahead, she wasn't sure that had been a good idea.

The echo of drums and an innate curiosity made her take a deep breath and continue on her way. Judging by the raised voices, Moonlight Madness had drawn a good-sized crowd.

Slowly and carefully, she continued the climb, acknowledging the friendly greetings of employees whose sole job was to point the way.

"*Bula.* Hello," they greeted.

"*Bula,*" Jillian responded.

When she arrived at the top of the cliff, one of several native women approached and encircled her neck in a lei.

"*Vinaka,*" Jillian remembered to say. "Thank you." It was one of the first words she'd memorized in her guidebook.

A heavyset Fijian woman broke away from the

group and escorted her down several wooden steps and onto a deck. The raised platform overlooked the waters of the Somosomo Straits where tables with colorful cloths were set up and guests busily sampled the fare. Waiters holding trays of exotic drinks circulated amongst them.

Jillian accepted a hollowed-out pineapple with a hibiscus garnish and stood for a while sipping her drink, taking it all in. She spotted Marlon chatting up a couple and keeping an eye on the gala. When he looked over in her direction, she waved to him.

Excusing himself, Marlon made his way over, stopping to greet the few guests intent on waylaying him.

"I'm glad you could make it," he said when he was finally able to disentangle himself. "So what do you think so far?"

"It's a beautiful setting," Jillian answered carefully, "and everyone seems to be enjoying themselves."

He took her elbow, propelling her into the crowd. "Let me introduce you to some of the locals. People you might enjoy meeting."

Marlon guided her in the direction of a middle-aged white couple.

"Sam and Lydia, this is Jillian Gray," he said. "Jillian's here to check out the hotel and make us an attractive offer."

They made the requisite small talk. And the couple invited Jillian to come to their restaurant any night she was free.

Jillian was then led over to a group of younger people. "Fern is our head concierge," Marlon said, introducing them. "The gentleman in blue is Desmond Bailey." He gestured toward a tall African-American who smiled broadly at her. "Desmond owns a scuba diving business and his partner, the man who hasn't stopped gawking, is Keith Chan. You should see them if you can make time to take a little excursion."

Keith greeted Jillian by raising his glass and patting the vacant seat next to him. "Please join us."

Jillian didn't sit right away. She waited for Marlon to complete his introductions.

"Across from Keith," Marlon said right on cue, "is Twyla Garcia. Twyla owns one of the swankiest boutiques in town. And last, meet William Leone, our resident banker."

In unison, all repeated Keith's invitation. They wanted her to join them. In fact, Keith was already on his feet, holding the empty chair out, urging her to sit. Jillian inched up the ankle length tank dress she'd thrown on because it was comfortable and took a seat. She was still relaxed from her massage and determined to go with the flow.

In a festive spirit, she'd added hoop earrings and a touch of make-up—actually more make-up than she was used to—convincing herself that the extra effort had nothing to do with wanting to impress Ben Fuller in the off chance he did show up.

A handful of people gyrated to the band on the beach, while lines began to form at the buffet. Jillian listened to the animated conversation that had little to do with business and centered more on the people in attendance. In a very short time she knew who the locals were and who were hotel guests.

"What say we grab something to eat?" Desmond Bailey suggested to no one in particular. "Looks like there's quite a feast." He took Jillian's hand, walking with her toward the laden banquet tables.

There a server handed her a shell plate and utensils. Jillian helped herself to roasted chicken fillet stuffed with lime, basil and pine nuts. She scooped noodles onto her plate, adding a lime, honey and garlic sauce. Noticing a prominent sign for grilled walu fish with coriander, she decided to try it. Cinnamon rice, mint and chutney completed her choices, then with Desmond's urging, she added roti and mixed salad greens to her already heaping plate.

It was more than she was used to eating, but Jillian was determined to sample the fare. Retracing her steps, she caught a glimpse of a magnificent sunset—one so beautiful it literally took her breath away. A kaleidoscope of soft pinks, magentas, crimsons, and golds contrasted beautifully with an emerald sea, almost merging into it.

"This is utterly awesome," she heard herself say.

"It is, isn't it?" Twyla Garcia uttered, sighing. "The first time I witnessed a Fiji sunset, I was convinced that this was what paradise must look like."

"Where are you from?" Jillian asked the woman who, by virtue of her last name, she assumed to be Latin.

"California. L.A. I've been living here these past few years. Followed a man I met on vacation. He's long gone but I stayed."

Jillian didn't know what to make of that so she turned her attention to her meal. She'd demolished most of what was on her plate when William Leone, the banker, exclaimed, "Ben Fuller certainly cleaned up for the occasion."

Every head swiveled. With an escalated heartbeat she refused to acknowledge, Jillian looked over at the spot where everyone was staring.

Twyla's loud outtake of breath gave Jillian reason to glance over before focusing again on Ben. Truly he was striking. Sheer white gauze pants and a matching short sleeve shirt set off the copper in his skin. Denzel, move over.

What was different about him? Jillian eyed him surreptitiously over her pineapple, realizing it was the haircut. She'd made the assumption earlier he'd meant to get a trim, but surprisingly he'd gotten all his hair cropped off. He looked more like the Ben

Fuller she remembered, younger, polished and definitely in charge.

Ben was flanked by a man and a woman. All, with the exception of Ben, held drinks. They were chatting animatedly and appeared not to have a care in the world. Even Ben seemed relaxed and approachable.

"I'm going to go over and say hello," William said, leaving them.

"Sure, he is," Fern, the concierge, muttered once William was out of earshot. "More likely he's looking to cement some deal."

"That's our William," Twyla responded, her gaze still riveted on Ben. "Ben Fuller is hot. But he keeps to himself. God knows there isn't a woman around who hasn't tried bedding him. We're all beginning to wonder if maybe he plays for the other team."

Desmond guffawed. "Not our Ben. He's straight as an arrow and still in mourning."

"Mourning what?" Jillian couldn't help asking.

The group at her table looked at her as if she were an alien.

"Ben lost his wife and kids on September 11, in one of those American Airlines crashes," Keith explained, draping an arm around the back of her chair. "From what I've heard, he hasn't been himself since."

Jillian almost choked on her chicken. So that's what Ben had meant about no longer having a wife, and she'd thought the worst of him. Now the pieces all fit together. It was that tragic loss that had driven him to Taveuni and made him stay.

She set down her knife and fork and looked around for a waiter. Ben and his party, accompanied by William, were heading their way.

Now she needed a stiff drink. She was suddenly conscious of her appearance. Was the lime-green jersey dress she'd chosen too loud? Did it contrast sharply with the coral on her fingernails and toes?

Did the hoop earrings make her look like a hoochie mama and not a successful business woman? Should she have added more make-up?

Spotting a waiter, she flagged him down, this time opting for rum and coconut water. Her new friends meanwhile ordered another round.

William brought over the threesome and began making introductions. Jillian wasn't sure whether Ben had spotted her so she used the time to carefully examine him. His newly shorn hair made his cheekbones look as if they were carved from Taveuni wood. His golden eyes held a sparkle that hadn't been there previously. Did the woman he was with have something to do with the cleaned up Ben Fuller?

When it was Jillian's turn to be introduced, Ben didn't even fake surprise at seeing her. "Oh, Jillian and I have met," he said smoothly. "In fact, we had dinner recently."

"You've been holding out on us," Twyla whispered under her breath.

Jillian ignored her, her eyes still on Ben's face. He nudged one of the accompanying men forward. "James, do you remember Jill? She was one of our interns."

The dreaded "Jill" again. She chose not to correct him though she'd hated the nickname. It reminded her of nursery school, when she'd been taunted mercilessly and the kids had sung the nursery rhyme "Jack and Jill went up the hill to fetch a pail of water . . ." over and over again.

James was James Jamison, an older James, but her ex-boss, nonetheless. He'd gained weight and there was more salt than pepper in his hair. He wore rimless glasses, a recent addition, she'd guess.

James took his time looking her over. "Can't say that I do. When did you work for Jamison and Fuller?"

"In the nineties."

"Impossible," he said, grinning down at her. "I would have remembered an intern as stunning as you."

Jillian, despite her vow to remain cool, blushed. "Thank you," she managed.

The woman accompanying them was introduced as Ilya, an Australian. By virtue of the fact she was glued to Ben's side, Jillian guessed that they were more than acquaintances.

Meanwhile, two employees had been persuaded to find another table and more chairs. Ben's party would definitely be joining them. Jillian wasn't sure how she felt about that. Maybe she'd do a lot of listening and learn a thing or two.

The tables were slid together and extra chairs added. Ben eased into the empty seat next to her.

"Your spa date paid off," he whispered. "You look wonderful."

Jillian wasn't sure how to take the backhanded compliment. "Thank you," she said, refusing to admit he was responsible for her jumpiness.

On the beach, fire dancers put on an exuberant performance. Two men swallowed fire, then exhaled the flames, while an awed audience clapped.

"Amazing!" Jillian said, her eyes glued to the dancers.

"Takes a lot of practice. But these guys have been doing this forever. Shall we take a walk and see them up close and personal?"

"I'd like that."

Jillian could sense the others' speculation. Ilya looked none too pleased. But this was her opportunity to ask about the fire.

She accepted the hand Ben offered, twining her fingers through his.

Twyla's face registered astonishment but she quickly covered up when Ben said to the table in general, "Anyone else want to come?"

No one answered right off and Jillian exhaled the

breath she didn't know she was holding. Wending their way through a growing crowd, she was able to find a position affording a good view of the men who were now dancing on smoldering coals.

A velvet sky looked like a handful of diamonds had been tossed across it and an orangey-red moon bathed the spectators in a golden hue. Picture perfect was all Jillian could think of, every sense heightened. She smelled the frangipani, heard the rhythmic drums, and savored the coconut and rum as it easily slid down. She was painfully conscious of the man beside her.

"If you've had enough, shall we walk on the beach?" Ben asked.

Jillian hesitated, wondering where this was leading. "What about your friends?"

"They're adults and can quite easily manage."

Together they walked in silence, watching the waves bang against the coral rock. Ben slid an arm around her shoulders and her immediate response was to tense up.

"Relax," he said. "Enjoy the evening."

Okay, she'd see what he was after.

"How long will you be here?" Ben asked after an interminable silence followed.

"Probably another week or so. I am a little behind in what I'd set out to accomplish. All on account of my ankle."

"You seem to be managing reasonably well."

"So far so good."

Jillian shifted the conversation abruptly. "I'm sorry about your wife and children," she said.

"So you heard." His mood changed to one more somber.

"It's gotta be painful losing loved ones."

"Harder than you imagine. But time is a wonderful healer."

"And you've had time?"

A TASTE OF PARADISE

"Time to at least think and adjust. Look at the moon," he said, pointing upward.

Jillian looked in the direction he pointed. It was truly magnificent, larger than she'd ever seen.

"Maybe we should start back," he said, coming to an abrupt halt.

"Maybe we should."

Ben's arm around her waist tightened and he made a quick U-turn. The sudden change of pace made Jillian stumble. Had it not been for Ben's steadying arm around her, she would have fallen.

"Easy," he said, holding her even closer. "I wouldn't want you to hurt that ankle again."

A bewitching scent of citrus tickled her nose and she felt herself responding. She stood for a moment trying to regain her equilibrium.

Ben moved so quickly she didn't even see it coming. His arms tightened around her and he brushed his lips against hers.

"Wh-aa-t? Wha-a-t are you . . ."

Her protestations were cut off as he stepped away.

"I apologize. I shouldn't have done that."

But it had been a heady experience, brief as it was. She regretted not giving in to the moonlit night and her promise to go with the flow. *Sensory overload. Time to get things back on a normal footing.*

"Shall we start back?" she asked.

Ben nodded and they continued on their way, wrapped up in private thoughts.

The party was in full swing when they returned to the deck. Marlon had been looking for them and he waved as they approached.

"You're hogging our guest of honor," he said, making a wry face. "I'd hoped to at least get a dance, providing Jillian is up to it."

Ben turned Jillian over to Marlon and headed back in the direction of their table.

"Having fun?" Marlon asked, twirling her onto the makeshift dance floor.

Jillian was still dizzy from Ben's brief kiss.

"Yes, I am," she managed. "Moonlight Madness is turning out to be quite the event."

An event she had not anticipated.

"Desmond Bailey is interested in you," Marlon said, taking the conversation in a totally different direction. "He wanted me to find out if you were available."

Jillian was so surprised she missed a step. She quickly recovered. "Did you tell him that my time is limited? I'm only here for a few days and most of that time will be taken up by business."

"One should always take time out for a little fun."

"I already did," Jillian responded, keeping an eye on the tables that needed clearing. Marlon or a designee should be overseeing his people and whipping them into shape.

"Have you found out what started the fire?" Jillian asked, figuring this was as good a time as any to broach that delicate subject.

Marlon's gait stiffened. "Funny you should bring that up. The fire chief contacted me earlier. The inspector thinks a candle may have tipped over and the rug caught on fire."

"There was someone occupying the bure I take it."

"Yes, a gentleman and his friend."

"Have they been questioned?"

"Yes, they both were. Of course they denied lighting the candle. In fact, they weren't even there."

The tune ended and Marlon led her off the floor. But Jillian wasn't quite done with him. "What is the insurance company saying?" she inquired.

Marlon seemed uncomfortable by her question. "The truth is," he said after a while, "the policy's been allowed to lapse."

"What do you mean?"

"Our accountant delayed paying the bill."

"But how could that happen?"

Marlon guided her toward the table, where now only Ben, James and Ilya sat.

"When a property is experiencing financial troubles, you delay paying your bills."

"That was a stupid judgment call. An insurance payment should be top priority."

"Be that as it may, it is simply the way it is." He spread both palms wide. "Franz is already unhappy and heads are going to roll. Mine is definitely up for the taking."

In spite of herself, Jillian felt sorry for the man. He was charged with the hard task of running what used to be a world-class resort with limited funds. She'd found it interesting that Franz Herrman hadn't made the time to meet with her. Not a good sign.

James and Ben got to their feet as she joined them.

"Desmond and the rest apologize for leaving," Ben announced, holding out the chair she'd earlier vacated. "Seems they had another engagement. He left you his card. He wants you to call him and arrange a scuba lesson. You must have made quite an impression."

Jillian didn't know how to take his droll delivery as he folded the card into her hand. Marlon chose that time to move on, claiming he'd neglected several guests.

Jillian passed on another alcoholic drink and accepted a bottle of water just like Ben was drinking. She'd decided, given what transpired on the beach, it was best to keep a clear head.

"What brings you to Taveuni, James?" she asked, noting his amused look.

"Business in Brisbane. Ben and I are involved in a project, and I was nearby. I thought, Why not have our discussion in person?"

Made sense to her. Jillian wondered if their project

had anything to do with acquiring the Bula. During their earlier encounter at the salon, Ben had never once mentioned his old partner would be visiting.

"How long will you be here?" she asked, echoing Ben's earlier question.

"As long as it takes to get what we need to have accomplished."

He might as well have told her it was none of her business.

She turned her attention back to Ben. "Did you know the Bula has no insurance?"

"That's impossible."

He seemed visibly shocked.

"Marlon just told me the policy lapsed."

Both men exchanged looks over her head.

"How could that be?" Ben asked, shaking his head. "You can't run an operation as complex as this one without coverage. That would be like an accident waiting to happen."

"Well, they did."

"Their financial situation must be bad," James offered.

Jillian didn't say a word. She'd seen the books. Let these two do their own due diligence, especially if the Bula was what they were after.

She'd worked too long and too hard to let these two move in on what she wanted.

Her gaze locked with Ben's. The memory of his touch produced another blush.

Get your act together, she cautioned herself. *A kiss is just a kiss. It meant nothing—and certainly nothing to Ben.*

Chapter 7

What in the world had possessed him to do such a stupid thing like kiss Jillian Gray? Ben couldn't even blame it on alcohol. He'd stayed away from the stuff and made sure that he stuck to the coconut water he loved so much. He'd simply given in to an urge.

Moonlight Madness was responsible, or maybe it was because his day had gone so well. His meeting had been a huge success. James, his old partner, still had powerful contacts and those contacts had come through. That's why Ilya and Tony were here.

It had been a stroke of genius contacting James in New Zealand and convincing him to come to Taveuni and see the Bula. His old partner had always had a good eye. He'd seen the resort's potential immediately. Now the two people accompanying him had the wherewithal to make Ben's dream come through. Ilya was an investor with the right connections. And Tony, who'd opted to pass on the festivities, had more money than he knew what to do with. Both were well respected, plus Tony had done business with Franz Herrman before. He knew all the hot buttons to push.

How Ben wished he were a fly on the wall of Jillian's bure. She was a tough one to read. Now that there'd been a fire, would she recommend Elite acquire the property? She'd seemed shocked to discover the insurance had been allowed to lapse. Now, in addition to mere cosmetics, Elite would have the additional expense of replacing an entire structure.

Ben questioned whether Jillian's company was even familiar with its target market. What would it take in terms of dollars and cents to advertise such a property? Would the potential yield even be worth it to them? Ben, on the other hand, already had a plan. He knew the area and knew it well. The coconut manufacturing plant would help subsidize the hotel when occupancy rates were low.

The phone rang as he was considering calling it a night. Impatiently, Ben picked up the old-fashioned receiver. "Hello."

"I'm sick as a dog. Might even need a doctor," his old partner said.

"Why? What's wrong?"

"All of a sudden I'm nauseous. Not only nauseous, but dizzy and light-headed as well. And so is Ilya. I just gave her a call."

"Sorry to hear that. I can get Doctor Charles for you. He lives on the premises and he's paid to make house calls," Ben said.

"I already tried phoning but no one's picking up."

"Let me see what I can do. I'll contact Marlon or a staff member; then I'll be right over."

Ben hung up puzzled. James and Ilya had seemed fine when he'd walked them to their respective doors. Ben had invited James to stay with him but he'd declined, joking that he needed his privacy in case he got lucky with some woman.

Rather than phone, Ben decided a quick stop at the lobby might be in order. Maybe the attendants were asleep on the job or inundated. As he approached, he heard loud voices. Ben entered the lobby Tikki hut swarming with people, some only half dressed. Many hugged their stomachs and were bent over in obvious stages of distress.

The reception desk was unmanned. One bewildered employee warded off the crowd barreling toward the guest relations desk. She was almost run over.

Ben pushed his way to the front.

"Where's your manager?" he demanded.

That started the crowd chanting.

"Where's the manager! We want the manager!"

The woman at the guest relations desk, looking clearly terrified, took a step back. Realizing there was no leadership present, Ben took over.

"What's going on?" he demanded.

A rotund man in a wildly colored shirt spoke up, acting as ambassador.

"These people are all sick. Food poisoning, we suspect."

"Has anyone contacted Dr. Charles?" Ben quizzed.

"We demanded a doctor, but he's nowhere to be found and no one was answering the phones. That's why we came here."

Placing two fingers in his mouth, Ben let out a shrill whistle.

"Okay, everyone sit! I am not an employee but I will find someone who is."

A few people were actually retching in nearby flower pots. The putrid smell almost made Ben gag. Some hurried toward the public facilities, barely making it.

"Pull yourself together," Ben whispered to the harried employee, who looked like she would rather be anyplace but there. "Take charge and tend to these people."

He shoved through the crowd and headed for the back offices. No one was visible and every door was locked. Using a side entrance he escaped to try and find Marlon and the rest of his group.

Cutting through the coconut groves, he found the manager's bure shrouded in darkness. Not a surprise really, Marlon maintained an apartment off-site as well. Still, there should have been a manager on duty. Ben thought for a moment and then decided paying a visit to Dr. Charles wouldn't hurt.

The doctor's tiny porch was bathed in a golden light, as was the front room. The silhouette of a man's head could be seen through the window, reading a paper. This was pretty typical of the doctor to remain oblivious to the goings on around him. His sole focus lately seemed to be on his golf game.

Ben banged on the door, refusing to let up until he got an answer.

"Who's there? What's the racket all about?" an ancient voice croaked.

Charles was as old as snow, and sometimes hard of hearing. He was an English gentleman who'd made his home on Taveuni for as long as anyone could remember. When his wife passed away, he'd sold his house. The Bula had offered him a position as resident physician, figuring that he was up to the task of handling a few cuts and bruises.

"It's Ben Fuller. Open up."

"Ben who?"

"Fuller."

It took a while before the door was thrown open. The doctor, clad in a cotton bathrobe and holding his newspaper, squinted at him.

"Better get dressed. There's a lobby full of people that are deathly ill," Ben said.

"It's late and I'm about to go to bed." He yawned.

Ben glared at the man. "Look, late or not, people are ill. My guess would be food poisoning but I'm not a doctor—you are. Two of my friends came down with the same affliction. I'm off to pay a visit to them."

As he was about to lope off, Ben turned back. He wanted to make sure the man fully comprehended the urgency. "You might want to hurry," he added. "Eventually these guests are bound to find out where you live and I wouldn't want to be in your shoes."

Realizing almost half an hour had elapsed since his conversation with James, he hurried back the way he had come. When he arrived at James's cottage, banging on the door produced no results. He tried Ilya's, which was right next door, but she too had left. Maybe they had gone to the lobby.

Ben retraced his steps, heading for the large Tikki hut again. As he rounded a bend, he almost ran into Marlon, who had a walkie-talkie in hand and was bellowing loudly.

Ignoring the fact that his friend was in the midst of conversation, Ben started in, "Where the hell were you? Your staff's pretty much useless. You damn near have a riot in the lobby. Several guests are sick and no one seems to care."

Marlon's hand shot up, backing him off like a traffic cop. He spoke into the transmitter. "So you think it may be that walu fish?"

A crackling voice answered. "Yes, and Dr. Charles can't be found. Uh . . . wait a moment, here he comes."

"I'll be right there," Marlon snapped, disconnecting. His attention returned to Ben. "Now what is it you were saying?"

Ben had a horrible thought, one he immediately put into words.

"Better send someone to look in on Jillian Gray. It would be a disaster if she came down with this intestinal thing."

The pathway was dimly lit but Ben could swear that Marlon had turned a peculiar shade of yellow-green.

"Oh, hell! Again, I forgot. This may be the final straw. Can you do me a favor and check on the woman? Pray to God she didn't eat that fish."

Ben squinted at the face of his watch. "It's after midnight, a phone call might not be welcomed at this hour."

"Who's talking about a phone call? Walk over and see if she's okay."

Ben considered it for a moment. Jillian wasn't exactly on his list of people he wanted to see right now. He'd acted out of character already and wanted some time to think about what he'd done and why.

"Fine," he begrudgingly agreed. "But only if you'll check on Ilya and James for me. Extend my apologies and let them know I'll be with them as soon as I can. Neither is in their cottages and both are sick."

With some misgiving, Ben continued up another path. He was still not sure this was a good idea. Jillian had made it clear earlier that his advances were unwelcome. She might think he was harassing her.

He'd lost his mind, giving in to an urge and kissing her. Since Karen's death he'd not been physically attracted to a woman. And certainly not the type of woman like Jillian Gray who did not have one ounce of emotion in her body and had a calculator for a brain.

Jillian was thinking of going to bed when a knock at the front door got her attention. Hastily, she saved the report she was in the midst of and shut down her laptop.

"Who's there?" she called, unable to imagine who would be visiting at that hour.

"Marlon asked me to check on you," Ben's gravelly voice responded.

Jillian hesitated for a moment wondering if that was really true? Ben's behavior earlier was inconsistent with the man she knew. But what if for some reason or another he had decided she was an easy target? What if he thought by turning on the charm she would willingly share what she knew?

Gathering her robe around her, she cautiously opened the door and peered out. The muted light from the lanai revealed Ben's worried expression.

"Is something wrong?" Jillian asked.

He raised an eyebrow. "You're not ill?"

"Should I be?" Jillian took a tentative step outside. She closed the door firmly behind her. "You're here at a rather late hour. Why?"

For a second too long, Ben's eyes roamed over her. Oh, lord, the robe was probably transparent in the light. Too late to do anything about that now.

"Marlon is tied up. He asked me to check on you," he said, finding his voice. "Several of the guests are ill and food poisoning is suspected. Did you have the fish?"

Jillian thought about it for a moment. She'd taken a bite but had been so full she'd left the majority on her plate.

"I tasted it," she admitted.

"No wooziness, no feelings of nausea?"

"Not so far. Exactly how many people are sick?"

Ben grimaced. "I didn't count but there were probably about fifty people in the lobby, and lord knows how many are in their cottages unable to move."

"This isn't good," Jillian said, shaking her head. "In the space of a few days, there's been a fire and now several guests are ill. Makes you wonder, doesn't it?"

Ben took a step toward her. "Just what are you getting at?"

Jillian folded her arms across her chest. "Seems almost intentional. I'd be curious to find out if mishaps occurred before I arrived."

"How would someone benefit from a fire or food poisoning, for that matter?

He made it sound as if she were a stupid woman.

"Oh, come on, you're a smart man," Jillian snapped back. "To get me to back off. The only reason this place was packed was because room rates were so low and staying here was a no-brainer. Now guests are probably going to check out and demand money back once they recover. If I recommend Elite not make an offer, this provides the perfect opening for another speculator to move in and snap up the place."

"You have a vivid imagination," Ben said curtly. "Since you're obviously all right, and as cynical as ever, I'll let you get back to whatever you were doing."

Turning abruptly he made his way down the steps.

"Ben, wait!" Jillian yelled.

Her words halted him. "Yes?" he answered over his shoulder, his disdain for her quite clear.

"Where are you going now?"

"Back to the lobby. I'm going to find my friends. Both are sick to their stomachs."

"Give me a minute to change," she said. "I'm coming with you."

Despite her feelings that Ben was somehow the enemy, there was a lot about him she liked; his compassion, for one. He clearly cared about the property and people. Besides, there was no way she could fall asleep now.

Chapter 8

"Jillian, Mr. Fontaine would like to speak with you. Are you able to hold?" a nasal secretary inquired.

"Certainly."

If Peter Fontaine himself was calling and bypassing Michael, her boss, it meant only one thing. Trouble.

Jillian shuddered, thinking if Peter could see her now, in her canary yellow capris and fitted tank top, he would have a stroke. She held on to the receiver, becoming tenser as the minutes ticked by.

Finally Peter came on the phone. He announced himself with a loud "Harrumph! Where exactly are we with this project, girlie?"

Girlie? It took everything she had not to correct him. Fontaine had obviously been a no-show for his own sensitivity training.

"I'm working on my report," Jillian said.

"When will it be completed? You're needed back here on the double."

Jillian took a deep breath, knowing that anything she said would sound like a bunch of excuses. "You gave me three weeks and there were some unforeseen circumstances. Hasn't Michael briefed you?"

"Suppose you tell me in your own words."

A long pause followed while Peter waited for her to elaborate.

"Well, first I hurt my ankle," Jillian said, "and there was the fire. Then a few days ago, guests came down with stomach problems that probably resulted from food poisoning. Since then, several have checked out."

No sympathetic noises on the other end. Peter finally said, "Despite these setbacks, you did manage to accomplish something?"

"That, I did."

Jillian could hear Peter sucking on his cigar. "Is the property in as bad a shape as I think it is?" he asked.

"There's certainly opportunity for improvement."

"Cut to the chase. What's your recommendation? Is the Bula worth pursuing or not?"

"At a fair price it would be. We'd have to spend a fortune on marketing, and there is that issue about the insurance."

"Not our problem. The bank's going to be all over Herrman. They have a considerable investment in the place. The resort will not be able to operate unless insurance is purchased and at a premium, at that."

"Good point. By the way where is Michael? I tried calling him earlier."

"I sent him off to scout out another property. Something you would be doing if you were finished there. So how long before you wrap up?"

Jillian waffled, "Well I don't know, that depends."

"Depends on what?"

"The competition."

Another HARRUMPH followed. "There's always competition, but few can take on Elite. We've got a name in the marketplace and the finances to make things happen. Spell it out for me. Do we need to worry?"

Jillian went on to explain what she suspected.

"Benjamin Fuller? I haven't heard that name in

some time. After the scandal, he pretty much fell off the face of the earth."

"What scandal?"

"Girlie, don't you keep up? A couple of years back, Benjamin Fuller was arrested for DUI and indecent exposure."

"That's impossible!"

Certainly not the fastidious, high-principled man she knew. Peter had to be pulling her leg.

"Jamison and Fuller paid big bucks to keep the news under wraps. Even so, everyone in the industry knew. The partnership was dissolved shortly thereafter, and that's the last anyone heard of the man."

"James Jamison is here on Taveuni," Jillian couldn't help blurting out. She was still reeling from the news. "He and Fuller seem tight."

"I'd hazard a guess they're more than friends. More likely they're business partners. When did James arrive?"

"Three days ago."

Another long silence followed. Peter's wheels were turning so loudly she could practically hear them through the airwaves. Finally he said what she was hoping for, "Don't you even think of leaving that place, girlie, until you find out what those two are up to."

"Don't worry, Peter, I won't."

When the connection was severed, Jillian exhaled the breath she didn't realize she was holding. Doubtful she would be pressured to come back to Chicago any time soon. She would also bet this would not be the last time Peter called her directly.

She picked up the receiver again and dialed. No modern phone system here.

"Franz Herrman," she demanded when a harried secretary answered.

"Who is this?"

"Jillian Gray of Elite."

A pause followed, then a too bright voice said, "Mr. Herrman is in a meeting and can't be disturbed. I can take a message."

Why was the owner avoiding her? Jillian would think, given all that had transpired, he would be dying to unload the place.

She emulated the woman's cheery tone. "I understand perfectly that Franz is in meetings. But you may want to mention that I called again. I am expecting a return phone call and not from another designee."

"Mr. Herrman wouldn't be able to return your call right away," the secretary said in her perky voice. "He's tied up for the day."

Jillian was sick and tired of Franz Herrman's avoidance of her. She no longer wanted to deal with Pollyanna and her lame excuses. Franz would see her.

"I'm free for a breakfast meeting tomorrow at seven o'clock. I'll be on the outdoor patio. I'll expect Mr. Herrman to meet me there." She slammed the phone down before the woman could say another word.

It was only ten o'clock in the morning and the whole day lay ahead. Jillian remembered Desmond Bailey's invitation and decided checking out his operation might not be a bad idea. Scuba diving was something she'd always wanted to do but never made the time for.

She grabbed a bathing suit and towel, stuffed them in a canvas bag and slapped on a jaunty straw hat before shoving on sunglasses.

It was a glorious day outside, not a cloud in the sky. Jillian made her way along a flower-lined path heading toward the ocean. She passed several guests who, judging from their attire and the gear they carried, were intent on enjoying a day at the beach.

Following the signs for SCUBA, she finally found Desmond's operation. It was a large clapboard structure painted in hot pink and yellow. A colorful mural depicted men and women outfitted in full dive gear. Jillian mounted three front steps and entered the building.

She was surprised to find the place teeming with people. The counter was practically mobbed. Off to the side, a group gathered around a dive master who gave them instructions, prepping them for an upcoming dive. Against one wall, a sign listed prices for renting equipment as well as taking a dive. There was no sign of Desmond Bailey or his partner, Keith. Impatiently she waited her turn in line.

"Playing hooky?" a deep voice said from behind her.

Jillian swung around to face Ben. For just a brief moment, she had difficulty breathing.

He was shirtless, his broad shoulders and tapered waist exposed. Dark curls with a hint of silver rimmed his solar plexus, then ran in a straight line down to as far as she could see. In his huge hands he held a dive mask and fins. Jillian drew in a deep breath and willed herself to break the electric connection.

"How're James and Ilya?" she asked, finding her voice. "Have they recovered?"

She hadn't seen Ben or his friends since she'd accompanied him to the lobby that night. They'd soon separated, pushed apart by the guests.

Ben's eyes never left her face. "Both are fully recovered and are tending to business in town. Desmond asked me to help out since he's short-staffed. Why don't you consider joining us?"

He gestured to the group that listened intently to what the dive master had to say.

Diving wasn't really part of Jillian's plan. She'd come to check out the facilities, think about the possibility, and maybe lie in the sun.

"I've never scuba dived," she admitted. "But I did

want to talk to Desmond about maybe snorkeling. That's a bit more my style."

"Where's your sense of adventure, Jill?" Ben nudged her in the rib with one elbow. "Come with us to the Great White Wall. Haven't you heard Taveuni has some of the world's best coral?"

She was tempted and reasoned it was all in a day's work. But the truth was she didn't want Ben to see her floundering around. She said, "That kind of dive sounds intimidating and not something a novice should try."

"Who's talking about diving?" Ben grinned at her, and his chipped front tooth reminded her of a little boy. She got a glimpse of a young man who'd probably broken more than his share of hearts.

"I'll give you lessons some time if you'd like. I'm PADI certified," he offered. "Come on. At least come for the ride."

There was still no sign of Desmond, or Keith, for that matter, and that took care of what she'd hoped to accomplish. The only thing she had planned for today was working on that infuriating report and prepping for her meeting with Franz. That is, providing he showed up.

"You've got a towel, and isn't that a bathing suit I see peeking out the top of that bag?" Ben asked, peering at the canvas bag she still clutched.

"Yes, but I was planning on getting a little sun and maybe sticking one toe in the water."

"You can do that on the boat." He tugged on her arm. "Come."

When Jillian resisted, Ben turned and called to the dive master, "Stan, do you have room for one more?"

The diver, who was lean and very Polynesian looking, stopped in the midst of his talk.

"Sure we do."

"That's settled then," Ben said, taking Jillian's bag from her and loping off to join the group.

He'd given her little choice but to follow. She trekked alongside him down a wooden pier and was helped into the boat that awaited the group. Jillian looked around as the eclectic mix of people boarded. One couple, by virtue of their accent, was most likely Australian. An Asian man clutched a camera and looked totally bewildered. Another couple, she deduced by their effusive greeting and drawl, was American. With them were a couple of long-haired twenty-somethings outfitted in retro gear. Bringing up the rear was a Polynesian man holding a bag of diving gear. She and Ben were the only two blacks.

The boat whizzed them across the Somosomo Straits, passing kayakers and windsurfers out enjoying the day. Floating in the clouds were a few brave souls determined to parasail.

Jillian sat back taking it all in. She enjoyed the wind whipping against her face and the sun beating down on her shoulders. Doing something so spontaneous was a good decision, she decided.

Ben draped a loose arm around her shoulders. She was immediately conscious of his suntan lotion commingling with his natural body heat. Together it was a heady concoction.

"Isn't this exhilarating?" Ben said to her. "What would you be doing in Chicago today if you were working?"

Jillian thought about that before admitting, "Probably stressing."

"On some level, you must enjoy that stress. Do you like what you're doing?"

She answered honestly, shouting above the noise of the boat's engine. "At times I do. Although I have to admit my life isn't that well-balanced. It seems to be mostly consumed by work."

"You're ambitious and driven. I could tell that from the moment we met."

Ben's golden eyes sparkled, taking the bite off his words. His shoulders were already a deep, burnished copper and she distractedly thought he might burn. He was enjoying teasing her.

"You could, huh?" she said, flirting right back.

"You must have a backbone of steel and an aggressive nature or you could never survive working for Peter Fontaine."

Jillian gave him a sideward glance. "Do you know Peter?"

Ben hesitated for a moment before saying, "Um hmm. I've come up against him a time or two. The man's a shrewd operator."

"Oh, come on now. Aren't you?"

That produced a chuckle, then Ben switched the subject. "What have you decided about the Bula?"

Jillian decided to be direct. She was conscious of the people around them trying not to listen. "Why do you want to know? Do you have some interest in the place?"

He dropped the arm wrapped around her and placed both palms on his thighs. Large hands, her wayward mind registered.

"Of course, I do. I live on the property. Naturally I have some interest as to what becomes of it. I'll have to look for another place and that's always annoying. If Elite takes over, you'll want to make changes. The Bula may even close temporarily for renovations."

"True."

"Okay, folks. We're here," the dive master called, stopping any further chatter. "Better start putting on your gear."

Jillian watched as those around her began slipping into suits and stepping into fins. Ben didn't move.

"Aren't you going to suit up?" Jillian prodded.

"Nope. Changed my mind. Think I'll sit here. Someone needs to stay aboard."

She looked at him sideways. "And that someone is you? Why?"

"Because I'd rather stay and enjoy your company."

"But you came to help out."

"And I am."

Jillian tossed him a puzzled look. She listened idly as the guide droned on, instructing the group.

"You'll swim down about twenty feet before you enter the tunnel," he said, "then you'll dive for another ninety feet. Depending on the current, you may only have ten or fifteen seconds to see all that beautiful coral, so stay alert or you'll miss the entire thing."

For a brief moment, Jillian regretted not being certified. She wished Ben would do what he had come to do and join the group in their dive. His proximity was most unsettling, and now she couldn't even think straight. Her gaze scanned the group already dressed in diving gear. Some had already taken their positions and were slowly lowering themselves over the sides. Soon the boat emptied out and she was left alone with Ben and the Polynesian, who hadn't been introduced.

"So when will you be heading home?" Ben asked. He handed her a bottle she thought was water before putting on sunglasses. Stretching out across the now vacant seats, he tilted his face to the sun.

The question came as a surprise. When in doubt, stick to vague answers.

"When I feel totally comfortable that I've discovered everything I need to know."

Ben's loud yawn forced her attention back to him. He had clasped both hands behind his head. "Why is this project so important to you?" Another yawn almost drowned out the last of his words.

Okay, he asked. *So, what the hell?* "My career hinges on acquiring the Bula."

"Care to elaborate, or is that best kept under your hat?"

There was little he could do with the information she was about to give him.

"Elite Corporation has resorts on every continent," Jillian explained. "For years, we've been trying to acquire property in the South Pacific. None of the negotiations ever came to fruition. Acquiring the Bula will be a major coup and will assure me a vice presidency. That's a huge accomplishment."

Ben's breathing had evened. For a moment, Jillian thought he might be asleep.

"What about the people you put out of work? Don't you care?"

"Anyone who's worth keeping will be retained. Franz wants to sell. Elite may want to buy. If we can work out a mutually agreeable arrangement, it will be a win/win situation for all."

"If you say so."

Ben was being much too blasé. She decided a full frontal attack was definitely in order. Ben was a captive audience after all.

"Sure you don't have some interest in the Bula?"

"Me?"

"Yes, you."

"As I said before, I live there. Naturally I have an interest." He smothered another yawn. "Don't mean to be rude but I'm taking a nap."

What an infuriating person. The nerve of him dismissing her. Ben had made it clear there would be no further discussion.

Damn the man!

Chapter 9

Ben lowered his lids and pretended to sleep. In the week or so since Jillian had been in Taveuni her outward appearance had changed. Her skin glowed and had turned an attractive shade of cinnamon. Her cropped hair had golden highlights, and overall she was more relaxed. Even the tension lines around her mouth had softened. And the ever present notebook, which had been a permanent attachment, was nowhere in sight.

Ben was trying to figure out why he found her so attractive. She was nothing like Karen in stature or outlook. Must be her intellect that appealed to him. Jillian's prime focus was business and he'd never once witnessed an emotional outburst. Unusual to have those qualities in a woman.

Surreptitiously he let his eyes travel the length of her. Yellow was a good color for Jill but he was sorry she'd chosen to wear capris rather than shorts. They hid most of her legs and those legs needed showcasing. What was the matter with him, lusting after a woman he barely knew? Ben's conclusion was that he'd been celibate for far too long. He didn't see that situation changing any time soon. He'd promised himself to get through his grieving. He would not come to another woman as damaged goods.

Not that Jillian Gray was the type of woman he wanted. Much as he admired her determination and drive, he needed someone less career-oriented, someone who would be content with his current lifestyle and who would not get bored with Fiji life. Jillian seemed to be slowly adjusting to the laid-back habit, but at some point island life would lose its luster and she would be chomping at the bit to return to the States.

Ben heard a commotion and sensed something was wrong. He scrambled into an upright position and at the same time heard anguished shouts. The dive master had surfaced carrying one of the hippie types. The man he'd been partnered with surfaced as well. They were yelling at the top of their lungs, words like, "Help get him up!"

The Polynesian man hung over the side of the boat. Jillian stood alongside him, her face ash gray.

"What's happening?" Ben asked, leaning over and peering into the water. Not waiting for an answer, he made his own assessment. "Dammit, a diver is in distress."

"Do something," Jillian screamed. "Call the coast guard. What if he drowned?"

Ben's first inclination was to jump overboard and render assistance. But he decided he would probably be more useful helping the huge Polynesian to bring the diver up. Below, the dive master, still carrying what looked like the semi-conscious man, finally made it to the anchoring line.

"Stay here, partner," the Polynesian man ordered Ben. "I'm going to need your strength. Stan needs my help. That guy's dead weight." He tossed Ben his radio transmitter and without saying another word jumped overboard.

Ben peered down at the water where several of the

divers had surfaced and were coming to the guide's aid. With some effort and an outburst of commands they managed to hoist the half-conscious man and his rescuer up the rope and onto a floating platform.

Ben took over. He got into a crouching position and began administering mouth-to-mouth resuscitation on the man. When the diver expelled water in Ben's mouth, he felt both repulsion and exhilaration. He turned the man on his side, freeing him to gasp, gag and gulp oxygen. When he retched again, Ben's insides threatened to spill. He swallowed his own bile and made sure the man's breathing was regular before turning him over to the huge Polynesian.

By then most of the other divers had climbed on board. A male voice, one he didn't recognize, was already radioing for the coast guard. Others covered the exposed man with bath towels.

Several of the divers stood around visibly shaken. Their adrenaline spent, and brawn no longer needed, defenses were raw. Others just stared into nothingness, in shock.

Nausea took over when Ben realized he still had the taste of the man in his mouth. He staggered to the side of the boat and began dry heaving. A palm settled on the small of his back, and a wet towel was pressed against his neck.

Jillian asked, "Are you okay? Maybe a little water would help."

He managed a nod, embarrassed that she would see him like this. Another wave of nausea hit him and he leaned over the railing and spat.

She continued to talk, ignoring the fact that he must be a pretty revolting sight.

"It was admirable of you. Mouth-to-mouth is not for the squeamish." All the while, she continued to press the ice cold compress against his heated skin.

Ben hated that she saw him with all his defenses

down and his emotions raw. But, dammit, what had started out as a picture perfect day had been spoiled. A man had almost drowned and might still be in grave danger. Quite possibly others surfacing too rapidly would need medical attention.

He emptied what was left in his stomach and gratefully accepted the chilled bottle of water Jillian held out. Taking a swig, he spat the liquid into the ocean, glad to be rid of the foul taste in his mouth.

Somewhere up above, he could hear the blades of a helicopter approaching. He placed both hands on the rails of the boat and forced himself to get it together.

"Why don't you sit?" Jillian said, her palm still on the small of his back.

"Because I'd rather stand."

She remained with him through the entire evacuation process, watching as the coast guard took both the impaired man, who seemed a bit disoriented, and those divers who'd surfaced too rapidly. All were given oxygen and then flown to a decompression facility for treatment.

Ben finally made his way toward a seat, reasoning that the boat's accelerated speed was the reason he couldn't regain his equilibrium.

Jillian sat alongside him, holding his hand. She didn't say another word for the entire journey until they pulled up to a pier mobbed with people.

Amongst the crowd were Marlon Hinds, Desmond Bailey and Keith Chan. Ben pulled himself together, clasped Jillian's hand, and charged off the boat, avoiding the local press, who shouted questions. He just wanted to get home and away from the mob.

Questions came fast and furiously.

"What's the status of the diver?" one of the local television reporters Ben recognized asked.

"Is the man alive?"

"How could something like this happen?"

"Mr. Fuller, were you a part of the dive?"

"No comment," a strong female voice snapped, one he recognized as Jillian's.

"And what exactly is your relationship to Mr. Fuller?"

"Call me a friend."

Jillian still held his hand as they maneuvered their way through people.

"Get out of our faces, ghoul," she shot at one photographer.

Golf carts were waiting and Ben headed for the first vacant one.

"We're going to Mr. Fuller's bure," Jillian ordered, getting in.

Ben tried to hide his surprise. It was the longest ride in history, but finally he was home and mounting his own three front steps, where Anna stood waiting.

"Mr. Ben, Mr. Ben, I heard what happened. It's all around town." The words rushed out of Anna in an accent so thick he almost didn't understand her. "I heard the diver ran out of air, began to panic and waited too long to drop his weight belt."

Jillian saved him from responding.

"Mr. Ben is exhausted. He's the real hero, Anna. Your Mr. Ben saved the day. Had he not stepped in and given mouth-to-mouth resuscitation, the outcome might have been very different."

"I need fresh air, lots of it," Ben said, wanting to turn the subject away from himself. "How about we sit on the verandah?"

He was still shaken. There was always the possibility the man who'd almost drowned could take a turn for the worse.

"Please bring Mr. Ben some water, Anna," Jillian ordered. "Maybe toast and soup if you have it. Something that will go down easily."

"I'll eat only if you join me," Ben interrupted. He

hated that she was treating him like an invalid. He sank into a wicker chair with comfortable looking pillows, leaned back and closed his eyes.

"Anna, make sure you bring enough for two."

"I wasn't planning on staying for dinner."

"You are now."

That shut Jillian up.

Anna, deciding she wanted no part of their skirmish, hurried off to do her boss's bidding.

"Thanks for staying," Ben said, eyes still closed. "You'd want to be here if Desmond and Keith phone with an update. That diver's regulator got lost somewhere along the way. I'm just hoping he's not brain-damaged."

"Didn't his dive buddy say he was able to reinsert the regulator?"

"Yes, but you never know how long he'd been breathing on his own."

Jillian's stomach growled. It made Ben realize neither of them had eaten in hours. He doubted he would be able to hold down anything solid, but he still needed to eat. Soup and toast were the obvious option.

"Are you sure you're not exhausted and would rather be in bed?" Jillian asked as a long silence stretched out.

"Sleep right now would be impossible."

Anna was soon back carrying a chilled pitcher of water. "You might want to watch the news, Mr. Ben, ma'am. Should I bring the television outside?"

"Yes, please, and I'll be happy to help."

Jillian got up and followed the woman inside. They returned bringing a medium-sized portable television out and setting it on the table. On screen, several people were being interviewed, most pitifully uninformed. All pretended to be knowledgeable of an event they hadn't even seen.

The scene on screen now shifted to the dive shop where a prominent sign declared the place CLOSED. There was no sign of Keith or Desmond.

Ben groaned, simultaneously shaking his head. "This is probably the biggest event that's happened on Taveuni, the newscasters will milk this disaster for weeks."

The shrill ringing of the phone interrupted further words. Anna hustled off to answer. She came back, receiver in hand.

"Sir, I think it might be a reporter."

"Tell the vultures I'm not here," Ben snapped wearily.

"I'll handle it, if you'd like," Jillian offered, retrieving the receiver from Anna. "I didn't think an island this size had this many reporters. There's a good possibility they'll be on your doorstep next."

Ben's colorful expletive gave a good idea of what he was thinking.

Jillian's lips twitched. In a cool voice, she spoke into the phone.

"Who is this?" She covered the mouthpiece with one hand and mouthed, "Who's Sara Grosvenor?"

Ben groaned, "A freelance correspondent and a first class pain in the butt."

"Mr. Fuller isn't able to come to the phone," Jillian said sweetly, speaking into the mouthpiece again.

"Why not?" came the retort over the phone.

"Because he's asleep. May I take a message?"

"Who are you?"

"I'm a friend."

"Were you the woman with him on the dive?"

Jillian slammed down the phone, cutting off the inquisition. She turned to them and said, "We better go inside while we still can."

Ben, wide awake and back to form, led the way. When they were seated in the kitchen, he said, "Given that Academy Award performance, you must be a pro at this."

Jillian hiked an eyebrow but otherwise didn't acknowledge the comment. "Prepare yourself. The horde is about to descend," she said.

Ben let loose with a deep-throated chuckle and Anna began setting out bowls.

"I've got frozen fish chowder," the housekeeper offered. Then noticing Jillian's frown, she added, "It's tasty. I made it myself."

"How about plain broth?"

"That I can manage, but it's canned."

"Canned will do just fine," Ben interrupted. He was sick to death of them fussing.

In less than ten minutes the broth was heated and triangles of toast set before them. They ate in silence but Ben didn't finish his food. He put on a good face, but his mouth still held the remnants of the diver's vomit.

When Jillian was done she pushed her plate aside. "I hate to eat and run," she said, easing out of her chair and beginning to pick up the plates. "I have a breakfast meeting to prepare for."

Ben frowned, "Hold on a minute. I'll see if I can get hold of Marlon and get an update."

He didn't want her to leave, at least not yet. Jillian sank back in her seat while Anna buzzed around making tea. Ben tried reaching Marlon but to no avail.

A loud banging on the door got their attention.

"They're here." Jillian announced. Anna looked like she was about to burst into tears. "I'll peek out the window and see how many we're dealing with."

Ben hung up the phone. "No answer from Marlon," he confirmed, rolling his eyes. "I'm in no mood for these people."

Jillian shifted the curtains, Ben at her side. "Some reporters and the usual voyeurs," she confirmed.

The banging continued, followed by loud shouts.

"We want an interview, Ben."

"Come on out and tell us your story."

"Is Florence Nightingale still with you? What's your relationship to her?"

Trust the local paparazzi to put their own spin on this.

And finally, "What do you have to say about the Bula's bad luck? First there was a fire, and then an outbreak of food poisoning; now there's been this diving disaster. The place seems to be jinxed."

Jillian and Ben exchanged looks. He draped an arm around her shoulders and she leaned in to him. What did "disaster" mean? Did it mean that someone had died?

Much as he wanted to acquire the resort, this type of publicity would not necessarily help. People tended to stay away from places plagued with bad luck. It would cost a small fortune to combat the type of PR that was rapidly building.

Ben placed a chaste kiss on Jillian's cheek. She did not tug away. Having her in his arms felt comfortable and right.

"Thanks for being here," he said, "and thanks for taking such good care of me."

"That's what friends are for," she said, running her fingers through his hair. It was an intimate gesture and completely unlike her.

He laced his fingers through hers, squelching the urge to kiss her the way he really wanted to. Instead he said rather benignly, "Is that what we are? Friends? I'd been hoping that we might explore something more. Jillian Gray, you are one helluva woman."

"And you are one helluva man."

Chapter 10

"Sorry I'm late," Jillian said, sliding into the seat Franz Herrman held out. "I overslept. It's been a rather rough night."

Franz Herrman removed his glasses and stood. The palm trees sheltering their table swayed and blew wisps of what remained of his once blond hair into a halo.

"No need to apologize. I heard the press was after anyone out on that boat. Thankfully, I have an electronic gate, which kept them out. That didn't stop the phone calls, though. Coffee?" Franz gestured to an attentive waiter.

"I'd love some."

Jillian allowed the waiter to pour. After sipping on the steaming hot liquid, she admitted, "I didn't make it back to my room until way after nightfall. I was trapped at a friend's. Finally, I was able to sneak through a back door. The reporters made it sound as if one of the men had died. It wasn't until I watched the news on television that I realized they were playing up the sensational angle."

Franz rolled his eyes. "You know how those people get. The journalists here don't have much to report, so this is big news. Anyway, it was a close call. The good thing is that the divers are fine. They were given oxygen, then flown to a decompression facility for treatment. I expect they'll be released some time this morning."

"That's a relief," Jillian said, meaning it. "I was under the impression they were all skilled divers. All PADI certified."

"That's one of our requirements. We would never take a novice out on that kind of dive."

"I'm a novice."

"But you didn't dive. The dive master would never have let you," he reminded.

Their waiter returned, handing them menus. After a brief scrutiny, Jillian set hers aside.

"You've decided already?" Franz asked. He hadn't even glanced at his.

"Not at all a difficult decision. Not when the coconut-battered French toast has my name written all over it. What are you going to have?"

"The same thing I always have. Egg whites, wheat toast and bottled water."

"That's too healthy for me." Jillian smiled, softening her words, then said graciously, "Now I see why you're so fit. You've also been quite busy."

Franz nodded but did not acknowledge the gentle chastisement. He stared out in the direction of a tranquil ocean where several guests were attempting an early morning swim. After a while he said, "This last week has been exceedingly trying. Comes with the territory. Nothing ever goes smoothly when you're running a resort. There's always one emergency or another."

"Yes, and there have been several," Jillian said, eyeballing him. "That seems unusually high."

"Not as unusual as you would think." He stroked his chin and assessed her carefully. "Accidents happen."

"But are these really accidents or is someone trying to scare me away?"

Franz set his coffee cup down. "Why would you say that?"

Jillian wondered if he was just playing things close to the vest. His raised eyebrows and the rivets around his mouth had deepened. She decided to needle him a little just to see what his reaction would be.

"It almost seems as if someone resents me being here. Maybe the idea is to make it look like acquiring the Bula is a bad proposition."

Franz seemed truly surprised. "Who would go to such lengths? There are pitifully few people interested in the property. And the few that there are, are well aware of the challenges."

When the waiter returned with their food, Jillian's brain went into overdrive. Her competition must be local then. She had a pretty good idea who it might be. Ben, having lived on the property, would probably know every irksome thing about the place. He'd know about blackouts, water shortages and recurrent maintenance issues. He'd even know about ongoing labor disputes. And he'd use this information to pick up the place cheap.

But would he and his friends do whatever it took to keep Elite from making an offer? Someone could have easily been killed. Why was acquiring the Bula so important to him?

No point in pussyfooting around the issue. She decided to ask.

"Does Ben Fuller have an interest in the Bula?"

She eyed Franz over the rim of his cup and watched his reaction.

The owner didn't bat an eye. "Why don't you ask him? I thought you two were friends."

"More like acquaintances."

"You were on a diving trip together," Franz said pointedly. "You were at his bungalow last night."

Did everyone know she had spent the day with Ben?

"He was simply being hospitable," she said. "He asked me to join him for a bite. I accepted. No crime in that."

"Shall we get down to business?" Franz asked, changing the subject abruptly.

Jillian went instantly on the alert. The German, typically no nonsense, wanted to cut to the chase.

"Elite is very interested in the property," she said, matching his business-like tone. "Rather than insult you, I'd like to hear what types of numbers we're talking about. What in your opinion would make this a fair deal?"

Franz named a figure.

Jillian jotted a note, then looked him squarely in the eye. "Surely, you couldn't be serious."

"Dead serious. I would be expecting something in that range. I'll need to cover my loan and make a profit."

She made another note in her pocket organizer, then tapped the Formica table with her capped Mont Blanc. "I'll need to speak to Peter Fontaine and see if he's still interested. He might not be."

Franz, appearing unperturbed, sipped on his coffee. "You're right. No point in either of us wasting our time."

Jillian wondered if the man was being delusional or playing hardball. She'd thought the German really wanted to sell. Now she wondered if he had another buyer in mind?

And she wondered if that buyer was Ben.

On the other side of the patio, Ben was having his own breakfast meeting with Ilya, James, and William Leone, the investment banker.

"Why would you want to take a gamble on the Bula?" William asked, looking truly puzzled. "The place has been a losing proposition for years. It will take money to regain the public's confidence. And even if you're willing to advertise, it may take years to recoup what you'll lay out. There are other properties up for sale."

Ben wondered what this was all about. He'd expected the man to be enthusiastic. This was almost a done deal. He now had all the financial backing he needed to make such a deal happen.

"Sure, there are other properties," he said. "But none has as much promise as this one. Few come with this much acreage plus a building that can be turned into a manufacturing plant. None have as many existing coconut trees."

William raised an eyebrow. "You've obviously done your market research. But there are several copra manufacturing plants on Taveuni. Why would yours be unique?"

While the man was clearly doing his job, Ben was tired of the third degree. He spoke slowly, enunciating every word. "I plan on bottling coconut water, not selling copra in the strictest sense. But I might use the jelly to make soaps and lotions. No one I know of has done that yet. The place will be locally owned and managed. Foreigners won't be imported to do jobs natives are eminently qualified for. Hundreds of locals will be employed. And the Bula will serve a dual purpose as both a hotel and manufacturing plant."

"Altruism is nice," Ilya interjected, "but I'd want to make a sizeable profit." Her smile took the sting off her words. "I'd need a return to make this worth my while."

"And you'll have it," Ben assured her. "Everyone's pushing the benefits of Fiji water but no one has marketed the therapeutic effects of coconut water. We're sitting on a veritable gold mine. Plus, we'll give back to the community in a meaningful way. People are much more willing to work when there's something in it for them. Your initial monetary layout will be returned tenfold."

"That smacks of spiritualism," Ilya said, sounding as if she didn't necessarily agree. She stroked his arm. "And here I was thinking that no blood ran in those cold veins."

Ben ignored the deliberate come on. He was not interested in the woman.

James, who'd been quiet so far, flashed him an amused look. He chose that moment to interject. "Ben and I owned and ran a business for fourteen years. He's got a nose for making a profit. I can't think of one property he picked that turned out to be a dog. You've done your homework, haven't you, Ben?"

Ben nodded and listened as James continued.

"Ben lives on the property and knows what's really going on. It's no secret Franz's wife is terminally ill. He wants to make whatever time she has left memorable. He wants to get her the best possible treatment, maybe travel a bit. All of that costs bucks."

"Does Jillian Gray know the full story?" Ilya asked, giving Ben a sly smile. "I got the impression you two might be getting cozy."

"What full story?"

Ben wanted to tell the obnoxious woman to mind her business but reminded himself he needed her. Not her, just the money she was willing to bring to the table.

"That Franz needs cash—and quickly."

"How would I know?"

"There's an expression. Lots of confidences get divulged during pillow talk."

Ben refused to take the bait. "Like I said before, I have no idea what Jillian knows or doesn't know."

"But weren't you out on a dive with her yesterday?" Ilya said snidely. "She was seen by reporters entering your cottage with you. To hear them tell it, she spent the night. My guess is she wasn't there to discuss business."

"Ben will do what it takes," James said smoothly, coming quickly to the rescue. "What better way to find out what you need to know than by socializing with the competition."

William began to look exceedingly uncomfortable, but he remained silent, jotting his notes. Finally, he looked up to say, "You'll call me with the names of the attorneys who are structuring this deal."

"Naturally, we will," James offered. "Ben already has that covered."

"Looks like our competition has the inside track," Ilya said in an overly loud voice. "Isn't that Jillian Gray and Franz Herrman having breakfast together?"

Ben's heart almost stopped, and it had nothing to do with the fact that Jillian had gotten one over on him.

He looked in the direction everyone was staring and right into the eyes of a very surprised Jillian Gray, who quickly recovered.

Ben raised a hand and waved at her. She waved back. He thought it was interesting that she hadn't mentioned last evening that she was meeting with Franz. He slid his chair back, excused himself, and headed off in their direction.

As he got closer, the expression on Jillian's face was priceless. She practically gaped.

Franz Herrman, spotting Ben, waved and rose.

"Hey, Ben," he greeted. "Join us."

Ben slid into the chair Franz held out, the one right next to Jillian.

"Hi, Jill," he said smoothly, knowing full well the abbreviation irked her. "How were things after you left my place last night? Were reporters camped on your doorstep?"

Obviously not pleased at all by Ben's inference that the two had spent a good part of the night together, Jillian glanced at Franz. The German's expression remained blank.

"Thankfully there were no reporters waiting. I was so beat I went straight to bed."

"I would expect no less after all that drama."

Franz now looked from one to the other. Seconds ticked by before he gestured to a waiter.

"Bring us another pot of coffee and a menu."

Jillian, too, didn't seem overly flustered, but Ben could tell by her tense posture that his presence had the desired effect. He intended to make her squirm.

"Is this breakfast business or pleasure?" he asked when the conversation lulled. "I would hate to interrupt."

"A little of both," Franz said amiably. "Now that all the hoopla has died down, and the divers are out of the woods, this was as good a time as any to meet with Jillian."

"You mean you two haven't talked before?"

Ben knew full well they had not.

Jillian recovered her voice and spoke up. "Franz has been busy, but I was left in good hands. Marlon has taken good care of me and he's been very informative."

"Speaking of which," Ben said, "where is Marlon today? I stopped by his office earlier to congratulate him on an outstanding performance. You did see him on the late news?"

"Yes, I did. He fielded the reporters' questions with his usual aplomb," Franz said affably. "As always he is the consummate professional. Whoever buys the property would be getting a gift."

What a sly dog. He was pitting them against each other.

Franz gestured to a hovering waiter, beckoning him to pour from the pot.

"Would Marlon want to stay on as manager?" Jillian asked carefully. "Change can be difficult. He might not like the way Elite does business."

Ben made sure to keep his expression inscrutable. Jillian was acting as if it were a done deal. He spoke up for his friend. "Marlon is very flexible. He'll work hard regardless of whether he likes the new owner or not."

One point in his favor.

Ben reached for the pitcher of cream and poured himself a generous dollop. He waited for Jillian's comeback.

"I should hope he would. But in my experience it's been better to clean house and start new. Having an enthusiastic and fresh team aboard is critical."

Ben wrapped his fingers around the hot coffee cup. Point two went to Jillian.

"Let's agree to disagree," he said benignly. "I believe loyalty and hard work should be rewarded. You can't put a price tag on supportive employees who won't rob you blind. So many are passive aggressive while undermining their boss."

"Exactly, which is why I recommend cleaning house." Jillian tossed him a wintry smile—one that was hard to interpret. Another point for her.

Refusing to make eye contact with him, she looked at Franz. "There are a few more questions I'd like to ask before we wrap up."

The message was clear. She was there to discuss business and she wanted Ben gone. Time to return to the people he'd abandoned. But not before he ruffled her feathers.

He deliberately took his time finishing up his

coffee. He sipped slowly and continued to make small talk. As the time dragged on, Jillian became quite visibly put out. One sandaled toe beat out a rhythmic rat-a-tat-tat.

Ben placed a hand under the table, stilling her knee. "That's rather annoying."

He thought she would jump out of her skin. Placing her hand over his, she pried it off her kneecap, all the while smiling at Franz.

"Shall we finish up then? I'm expecting a phone call from headquarters and I need to be in my room," she said to the owner.

The German nodded and Ben, having no other choice, stood.

"I'll leave you two, then. Thanks for the coffee." Raising his hand in a half salute, he took off.

Jillian had just made it sound as if she and Franz had come to some verbal agreement. Now all that was left was money exchanging hands.

It would be a cold day on Taveuni before Ben let that happen. And this wasn't anything personal in terms of Jillian Gray. He was in fact beginning to like the woman.

Chapter 11

Jillian held the phone away from her ear and took a deep breath. Peter Fontaine was practically yelling at her.

"I want you to wrap this thing up quickly. Elite wants this property and the Bula needs a buyer. So, why are you dragging your feet?"

"I'm not," Jillian said, speaking calmly and clearly. "I've had some difficulty getting an audience with Franz Herrman. There have also been a number of issues involving the property, as you know."

"Make it happen. That's why you're there. Give him a deadline to meet with you, and if he doesn't comply tell him we're no longer interested."

Why was Peter using the corporation as an excuse? "Elite" meant him. He wanted the property. It would be a personal feather in Peter's cap to acquire a resort in Fiji. He could then thumb his nose at the other conglomerates that, despite their efforts, had been unsuccessful. Most smaller islands resisted having an American chain, fearing the types of tourists they'd get.

"I've already met with Franz," Jillian said. "His demands are outrageous. I can't imagine we'd be willing to pay anywhere close to what he's asking."

"What is he asking?"

Jillian told him. Peter whistled. "The man's delusional. Our attorneys are already structuring the deal. The preliminary figures you've sent us regarding expenses and such give us an idea of the bottom line. We'll make a low bid."

"What about the competition?" Jillian asked. "What if they're willing to meet Franz's demands? Are we willing to counter?"

In other words, how badly do you want this property and what are you willing to do to make this deal work?

"Girlie," Jillian flinched at what she supposed Peter thought was an endearment. "If, as we suspect, the competition is Ben Fuller and his old partner, James, there's nothing to worry about. Those guys won't lay out a penny more than the place is worth. What's the occupancy level right now?"

"Practically nil. The place was pretty much cleared out after the food poisoning incident. And after this diving disaster, those guests that are left are looking to bail."

"That was no accident," Peter said sagely. "That was an intentional attempt on a man's life."

"Peter, I was out on that dive. I saw the diver being hoisted to the surface. He ran short of oxygen and failed to release his weight belt immediately. If his buddy hadn't gotten him out of that belt and helped him breathe until the master was summoned, the outcome would have been very different."

"You haven't read your newspaper this morning," Peter said too quietly. "The first thing even a novice in our business does is read the local paper."

What did he mean? Jillian had gotten up early with the express purpose of taking a brisk walk. The paper she'd decided to read later. She'd convinced herself that exercise would be a good start to her day and would help her clear her head. She'd planned on returning to put the final touches on her report and e-mail it to Michael, her boss, to be passed on to Peter.

"Suppose you tell me what I missed," Jillian said, refusing to let on that she hadn't yet seen the paper.

Peter subscribed to every possible periodical, and then some. It was said that there were members of the research department that did nothing but review the events in the most obscure places, lest they miss out on a good deal.

"Reread today's paper and then give Franz this message from me. Tell him to unload his albatross now, while I'm still willing to take it off of his hands, then get back to me."

"Peter, please let me do it my way," Jillian pleaded. "Franz finally met with me instead of handing me off to his general manager. We've established a good rapport. He's not a stupid man. He knows Elite's reputation and he knows that financing won't be a problem on our end."

"Then make the deal quickly. An empty hotel is not a profitable hotel. Assure him that we'll keep twenty-five percent of the locals on in some capacity, and the remainder will be given a decent package to go away."

Peter had never been this generous before. He was as tough as they come. Clearly he wanted this property badly.

"Are you sure you want to do this?" Jillian asked.

"If it will sweeten the deal and get you back here soon, then yes."

"What about Michael? I've left him several messages none of which have been returned."

Peter grunted. "I've told Michael you are reporting directly to me on this project. Besides, he's been traveling like crazy and international cell phones in foreign countries aren't exactly reliable. Your boss is picking up your slack while you're away, which is another reason I need you back."

What happened to take as much time as you need? Jillian got the distinct feeling she was being tested. Peter wanted to see for himself how she managed under pressure and a changed deadline.

He concluded the conversation with what Jillian considered a veiled threat. "A vice presidency is up for grabs, girlie. It would be nice to see an African-American woman in an officer's chair."

Jillian wanted to ask him why it had taken him so long to put one there, but refrained. Instead she demurely answered, "I understand perfectly, Peter, and I am the obvious person to be in that seat. I won't let you down."

The newspaper Jillian had insisted be delivered every morning at seven was nowhere to be found. She'd gotten used to it not showing up until later, and as had been explained to her by one of the workers, she was getting it earlier than most. This was considered delivery Fiji-time.

Jillian picked up the receiver again and dialed. She still couldn't get used to the fact there were no buttons to push. After at least seven rings a disinterested voice inquired, "What can I do for you, ma'am?"

"I'd like to have today's newspaper sent up right away," Jillian demanded.

"Your paper should be there by now," the woman said, sounding like a robot, as there was no inflection in her tone. "Check outside in the courtyard?"

Jillian hadn't thought to do that. She'd been expecting to find it on the steps where it usually was, folded and bagged to protect it from the elements.

"I'll call you back if it's not here," Jillian said, hanging up.

Outside, she scanned the yard. Nothing remotely looking like the paper was in sight. Jillian stepped gingerly between huge pots holding bougainvillea, orchids and trailing ferns. Finally she found the missing paper hidden behind a terra cotta urn. Some lazy person, rather than opening the door to the courtyard, had thrown it over the wall.

She retreated, paper in hand, to a tiny table shaded by a blooming frangipani tree. Then, thinking she could use another cup of coffee, she raced inside to pour from the pot made earlier.

Cup in hand, she returned and unfolded the paper with some trepidation. The disastrous dive had made front page news. Jillian scanned the article and, gasping, set it aside. Upon inspection of the diver's equipment, it was now thought it had been tampered with. That would certainly explain Peter's earlier call and his feeling that Elite needed to move in, and now. This was the perfect opportunity to offer an embarrassingly low bid as Franz might be desperate to unload.

It seemed so unethical and so predatory to take advantage of Franz's continual misfortune. Business was business, but this seemed more like extortion. The Bula had promise. Although Franz was asking an outrageous price, and she questioned if he really wanted to sell, if the place were spruced up a bit, room rates could be increased.

Jillian had made discreet inquiries and learned that the surrounding, better-maintained properties were asking at least a third more. So, even if room rates initially increased slightly, a gigantic profit could still be made.

She would finish her report and propose Peter offer a fair price for the place. She would attempt to set up another meeting with Franz and tell him about Peter's counteroffer. A guarantee of jobs for twenty-five percent of the staff was not a bad thing, plus Elite's willingness to absorb the cost of severance packages was an additional bonus.

Now she needed to find out if what she read was true. If the diver's equipment had been tampered with, then someone was deadly serious about acquiring the property and would let nothing stand in the way. It scared her that they might come after her next. Perhaps Peter was right, she needed to wrap this thing up, and quick.

Ben sat in the simple clapboard house listening to the man on the podium. At one time, he'd been a renowned surgeon but drinking had ruined his career. In a matter of fact voice he told his tale of how alcoholism had cost him everything, and how only when he'd finally hit rock bottom, he'd turned to Alcoholics Anonymous for help.

Ben attempted to make these meetings at least three times a week. He needed the fellowship and the support. Lately, he'd started coming more often, and that had a lot to do with his attraction to Jillian Gray. It scared him.

Up until September 11, Ben had always been a confident man, and one in total control of his life. But when his family was killed, it was as if life had spun out of control. Drinking had helped get him through the day. It had dulled his senses and his capacity to feel. Now his emotions were slowly awakening again and that was unnerving. He wanted a drink. Needed one to steady his nerves, especially when he was around Jillian Gray.

The kiss they had shared was still very vivid in his mind's eye. The passion that had been ignited had rocked the steady world he had built for himself and shaken him to the core. Ben cautioned himself to step back, rationalizing his reaction as to not having been with a woman in over a year.

He was not looking for a romantic dalliance nor was he the type of man who loved them and left them. Though admittedly, he'd done some pretty dastardly things when he was drunk—things he was now ashamed of.

Dazed, Ben watched a local woman step up to the podium. She was on the late side of fifty with graying hair, the grandmotherly type.

"My name is Keala," she began, "I am an alcoholic."

She began recounting her story about fighting bouts of depression when her husband had walked out, leaving her with five mouths to feed. She talked about drinking herself into oblivion, losing her children to foster care, and losing the job that had helped keep food on the table. Eventually she'd ended up on the street. Tears flowing down her face, Keala admitted that she had prostituted herself to have money for that next feel-good drink. She'd finally hit rock bottom when one of her tricks beat her up and left her naked on the street. She'd then ended up in the hospital.

When the tale concluded, Ben felt as if he'd just relived his own personal nightmare. He cleared his throat. Keala could so easily have been him. God knew he'd had his embarrassing moments, but he'd been blessed with supportive friends. Friends who loved him enough to take a stand. At the time, he didn't think James had done him a favor by severing their partnership. But it had been a gift, forcing him to take a vacation and look deep within himself. In Taveuni, he'd had time to examine his life, reflect and find spiritualism and a deep belief. He'd attained a certain sense of peace.

The thing he liked most about Fiji was that people didn't define themselves by their material possessions. Life for the most part was simple, uncomplicated and stress free. It had given Ben time to put his priorities in order and he'd become grateful and appreciative of the small things in life. Then along came Jillian Gray, rocking the safe world he had built.

One day at a time, Ben reminded himself, repeating

the familiar mantra. You can only stay drink free one day at a time. Only the shared experiences of his fellow alcoholics could keep him on the straight and narrow. He vowed he would attend these meetings more often. He needed it.

Ben sensed that he was being observed. Across the room he spotted Ricky Lohman, his volleyball mate and one of the local contractors. Ricky had been his sponsor at AA. He'd convinced Ben he couldn't do it alone and he'd encouraged him to get help. In so many ways Ben owed Ricky his life. He was determined to pay the man back. Ricky was the person he planned on hiring to renovate the Bula and turn a decrepit building on the property into a manufacturing plant.

When the meeting eventually ended, Ben was still thinking about Jillian and how grateful he'd been for her presence on that dive. She was a truly interesting woman and under the tough exterior was a kind and considerate human being. Under different circumstances they could easily have been friends. Maybe more than friends. Where had that thought come from?

Perhaps his grieving was over and he'd finally healed. But he'd vowed that he would never, ever put his heart on the line again. To love meant to lose, and he simply couldn't endure the pain. He'd already had a lifetime of hurt.

A slap on his back brought him quickly back to reality. Ricky's voice boomed, "Did you see today's paper? Who would ever have thought something like this would happen on Taveuni? It's getting to be like the States."

"What on earth are you talking about?" Ben asked. "I went for a jog early this morning and never did get time to read the paper."

"So, you don't know? They're saying the diver's

equipment had been tampered with, that's why he ran short of oxygen."

"Who would do something that despicable?" Ben said, speaking more to himself than Ricky.

Ricky shrugged. "Beats me, my friend. Maybe the guy had enemies."

"He was a tourist. Here to have fun."

"Maybe he pissed off one of the locals. I saw his picture on television. All that long hair made him look like a pothead. He could have stiffed some guy and didn't pay for his stash, that's bound to make somebody mad."

"You've got a vivid imagination," Ben said, used to Ricky's wild exaggeration. "I'll go and see if I can find Marlon and get the real scoop. When are you getting that estimate to me?"

"Next week. You'll be showing up for the volleyball game tomorrow?"

"Sure. It's been a while."

"Good. We need your killer serve."

Ben hadn't had time for volleyball lately. But since James and Ilya were leaving today, maybe he'd get back to the game he enjoyed so much. At the very least, it relieved tension and kept him in shape.

"See you tomorrow, my friend," Ricky said, sauntering off.

"Get me that estimate!" Ben yelled, heading off in the opposite direction.

Instead of taking a more direct path, Ben decided to stroll along the beach. He needed the time to clear his head and figure out what was happening. Deep in thought, and perplexed by what Ricky had just told him, he barely heard a female voice call to him.

"Ben!"

His heart raced as recognition dawned. Jillian, outfitted in a long skirt and a bikini bra, was heading straight toward him. It was the first time he'd seen her so scantily clad. His eyes lingered on her lean frame, then almost popped at the sight of her full breasts and tempting cleavage. He hadn't realized she was so shapely or so well endowed. He'd always been a breast man. Recovering almost immediately, he tried not to stare.

"Hey, Jill," he said.

Jillian pretended to glare at him. "The name is Jillian, remember? Where are you heading to?"

"Just taking a walk," Ben answered, keeping it light. "Care to join me?"

A second or two went by before she said, "I just might."

Ben fell in step with her and tucked her hand in the crook of his elbow. "You're awfully quiet."

"Just thinking. I read this morning's paper. If you can put any credence in what the reporter had to say, a man was almost murdered. His gear was rented and his airflow was deliberately blocked, despite the initial reports of running out of oxygen; it could have been anyone. That could have been you."

"Except for the fact, my dear, that I have my own diving gear and I am experienced. One of the first things I learned was not to kick furiously when I felt I was sinking. That increases the amount of air you deplete. The next is to drop your weight belt when your life is at stake."

She gave him a look, one he wasn't sure how to interpret. "There is a killer at large," Jillian said, now sounding shaken up. "I wonder if the next person he'll come after is me."

He sensed that she was speaking more to herself than to him. Using his free hand, he patted the hand at the bend of his elbow.

"I wouldn't let that happen."

And he meant every word.

Chapter 12

"Have you ever been married?" Ben asked, his fingers idly tracing a path across Jillian's arm.

"No. Haven't gotten around to it yet." He didn't need to know the details about how she'd sacrificed a love life for her career.

Ben pressed on. "What about a long-term relationship? Don't you want children?"

It was something Jillian hadn't given much thought to. There were no serious prospects on the horizon anyway. But truth be told, lately she was beginning to feel that something was missing.

"I have a few years to think about it," she said carefully.

"Don't think too long. You are in your thirties, aren't you?"

The implication was clear. Her biological clock was ticking; she needed to get busy.

After walking on the practically deserted beach, they'd flopped down on vacant deck chairs and Ben had found them an umbrella, which he'd quickly erected. He'd then flagged down a vendor and bought them both iced teas.

"What about you? Would you consider remarrying?" Jillian asked, turning the tables on him.

At first she thought he wouldn't answer. But finally he said, "I'm not sure I'd make that kind of commitment again."

"Why?"

"It's an emotional investment," he said somewhat brusquely. "I'm unwilling to go there again."

End of conversation.

Ben's shirt hung over the back of the deck chair. Jillian stared at his bare chest and broad shoulders. Both gleamed with the coconut oil he'd convinced her to lather on. Just looking at him made her feel good.

"You don't do emotions well, I take it?" she asked, raising an eyebrow.

"Do you?"

Touché. She'd never been the type of woman who got easily swept away. Her involvements had always been calculated and safe. Whenever she'd been tempted to get crazy she'd walked away.

"Ben," she said, changing the tenor of the conversation. "Do you have some interest in purchasing the Bula?"

There, she had come out and said it.

"Why?" he asked.

"Because I got the distinct impression from Franz that Elite's competition might be local, and I suspected it was you."

"Yes, I am interested in the property," he admitted. "Does that affect our being friends?"

Jillian thought about it for a moment. There was a part of her that wanted to believe that Ben was trustworthy. She liked him, and for the little time she had left, it would be nice to have a friend to spend time with.

It would not be the first time she'd been able to

maintain a friendship with someone on the other side of the bargaining table. In many ways, her business was similar to that of a lawyer. You did what you had to do to get the job done and you couldn't take anything personally. Except the stakes were high this time. She needed to win.

"Jillian?" Ben slid off his deck chair and was bent over her. The back of his knuckles brushed the side of her cheek.

"Yes, Ben."

"I think we should give friendship a whirl for whatever little time you have left here."

Her gaze locked with his. Did he read minds?

Ben's index finger now traced a straight line across her lips and she froze. Jillian cautioned herself to be careful and to keep a clear head. She was slowly losing that battle as Ben's finger continued to explore.

"Do you have lunch plans?" he asked, his voice barely a whisper.

Think, Jillian, think. Make some excuse.

Nothing came to mind. "I'm free," she answered in what she thought were measured tones.

"Good, then let me take you to a local joint. There's one on the other side of the island that has great food and a fun atmosphere. You can't go back to the States without having at least one local experience."

Ben now eased himself onto the same deck chair as Jillian and stretched out his legs. He threw an arm loosely around her shoulders. She slid closer to him, hoping that the chair, which was beginning to creak, was sturdy enough to hold them. All the while she reasoned this was what friends did, better not make too much of it.

Jillian was intensely aware of Ben's heat and the smell of the slick coconut oil she'd rubbed on him. Despite knowing that they were after the same thing, she felt safe with this man, and even trusted him to a point.

"We should go back to the hotel and change," Ben said, placing a kiss on her cheek. "I'll pick you up in, say"—he glanced at his watch—"half an hour."

"Make it an hour."

That would give her time to put the finishing touches on her report and send it off to Peter Fontaine. She could then play hooky with a clear conscience.

"Okay, an hour it is," Ben said agreeably. "Be sure to bring a hat, the afternoon sun can be brutal."

With that, Ben unfurled long limbs, extended a hand and helped her up.

An hour later, the blast of a car horn got Jillian's attention. Quickly scanning her e-mail attachment for the third time, she hit the SEND button. Rattan bag in hand, she went outside to meet Ben. He was already inside the courtyard and making his way to the front door.

"You're rocking," he said, his eyes sliding up her bare legs and then down again.

Jillian blushed like a teenager. She'd taken time with her appearance and had decided to wear walking shorts and a bright off-the-shoulder top. She'd even opted for a touch more make-up than she usually wore. What had happened to the cool, collected person she prided herself on being?

Ben helped her into the cherry-red Jeep Wrangler with the open top. He settled her comfortably in front before hopping into the driver's seat.

"We're off," he announced.

"What's the restaurant called?"

"It's a surprise," Ben said mysteriously. "Sit back and enjoy the ride."

Twenty-five minutes later, after being bounced down a series of rutted roads and up several volcanic inclines, they came to a stop in the middle of what appeared to be a rainforest.

Ben pointed to a gigantic tree. "We're here. What do you think?"

Jillian looked at him and then at the tree, her confusion evident. "Here where?"

"The restaurant."

"You're kidding. The restaurant is up that tree? How on earth are we supposed to get up there? Climb?"

Ben's rumbling laughter indicated she was right on target. Something about his boyish charm appealed to her. His chip-toothed smile made her want to do just about anything he asked. She could only imagine how many hearts he'd wrecked.

"There's your access," Ben pointed out. "Do you need a hand?"

"A ladder?"

It sure looked like a vine-covered ladder to her.

"Rungs carved into the trunk of the tree. You're athletic. Go for it."

Jillian rose to the challenge. Stepping ahead of Ben, she gingerly ascended the first rung.

Ben followed closely behind, his hands cupping her hips, steadying her. The heat from his hands conjured up erotic thoughts—ones she had no business entertaining.

At the top they stepped onto a level platform. A closed door wreathed in vines held a simple sign, "The Tree House."

From outside, Jillian heard muted music and the hum of conversation. Delectable spices wafted out, making her mouth water. "How many people does this place hold?" she asked Ben.

"No more than thirty. There are roughly about eight tables. The help is included in that count and so is the entertainment."

"Is that music I hear?"

"See for yourself," Ben said, capturing her hand in his and pushing his shoulder against the closed front door.

They entered what looked to be a cave. Moss seemed to grow off high ceilings and garlands of greenery and exotic flowers rimmed mocha walls. In hidden recesses, mini-waterfalls cascaded against volcanic rock.

A shapely hostess outfitted in a lei and grass skirt approached them. "Your table is ready, Mr. Fuller," she said, undulating toward the back of the room and gesturing for them to follow.

The table and chairs they were led to were no more than hewn-out trunks of trees, but the chairs were padded in colorful batik cushions, and were amazingly comfortable when Jillian sat.

"Your waiter will be by with your usual," their hostess said. "That means your coconut water is on its way." She winked.

"Would you rather have something else?" Ben asked Jillian.

"No, coconut water sounds fine to me."

Jillian realized much of the music was piped. But it made her shoulders sway and her feet tap to the beat. On a raised dais, a man and woman performed the intricate steps of the hula.

"I love it," Jillian said, charmed by the décor and the intimate setting.

"So do I."

Ben handed her a woven mat, which was in actuality the menu, with beautiful calligraphy written on the front and back. After scrutinizing it she handed it back to Ben. The choices were overwhelming.

"You choose," she said, knowing that his selection would be memorable and something special. So far every time they'd dined together he'd known exactly what she'd enjoy. Even the other night's simple but nourishing meal had been delicious.

When their waiter returned, Ben ordered shrimp and lobster puff pastries and a gigantic salad as an appetizer. Their main course was curried crab with a side order of white rice and fresh avocado. All tasted like nothing Jillian had experienced before. She managed to finish everything that was set in front of her.

"Room for dessert?" Ben asked, his eyes echoing his amusement at her empty plate. "You must at least try the fried ice cream."

When she looked about to protest, he frowned at her. But she noticed that at no time had he suggested they have wine.

"Don't you drink?" she asked, her curiosity finally getting the best of her.

"Not anymore."

That was that. No further explanation.

Recalling Peter Fontaine's words, Jillian wondered if there had been some credence to them. He'd mentioned that Ben had been arrested a long time ago for driving under the influence and indecent exposure.

It was hard to believe that of the man seated across from her. Ben was rarely out of control. She'd only seen him lose it once, on the dive, and who could blame him? She couldn't imagine he'd ever allowed alcohol to impair his thinking. But why would Peter lie?

"I'm an alcoholic," Ben confessed. "If I have just one drink it might lead to many."

So Peter hadn't exactly lied. Maybe bent the truth a bit.

"Thank you for telling me," was all Jillian could

find to say. She was pleased that Ben trusted her enough to volunteer the information. She longed to ask him if it was true that he'd actually been arrested. How could a man as confident and successful as he end up drinking? But asking would be intrusive and they didn't have that type of relationship. Not yet. Where did that come from?

"Do you think less of me now?" he asked, tuning in to her thoughts. Tawny eyes carefully scrutinized her face for a reaction. He reached for his glass and pretended to examine the clear liquid. Speaking more to himself than to her, he said, "This has become my beverage of choice. Coconut water is low in fat and calories and great for cooling the body down."

Determined to keep things light, Jillian said, "If it works for you, why not? How were you able to get a handle on your drinking?"

"With a lot of help from my friends." Ben smiled wryly. "I was too far gone to go it alone. The people of Taveuni took me under their wing. Ricky Lohman, one of the men I play volleyball with, is a recovering alcoholic. He insisted I attend an AA meeting with him. I owe him my life."

"Oh, Ben," Jillian said, covering his hand with hers. "I'm sure it was rough, but look how far you've come."

"One day at a time. I did many things when I was drinking that I'm not particularly proud of." He turned his hand over to link their fingers together.

"We all have our skeletons," Jillian said, liking him more and more. There was something about Ben Fuller that made you feel all your secrets were safe. She cautioned herself not to get too attached to him.

"I think we should try that dessert," she said.

Ben gestured to a hovering waiter. "You won't be disappointed. We'll have the fried ice cream, please, and some of those wonderful lichee nuts on the side." After the waiter left he admitted, "I'm surprised at how easily you accepted my confession. Don't you have questions, or has Peter filled you in on me?"

She decided to play dumb. "My guess is you and Peter aren't friends. Anything you want to tell me?"

"You're right. We're not friends. Ever since Jamison and Fuller grabbed a piece of property Fontaine was after, he's been out for blood. He holds a grudge."

Dessert arrived just then and the conversation ended. Jillian found it strange that Peter hadn't mentioned they were archenemies. Very strange indeed.

Ben paid the check and stood.

"How about we take a walk?"

"I'd like that. We need to walk off these calories."

They climbed down the precarious tree trunk and onto the ground again.

Holding Ben's hand, Jillian followed him through an overgrown path leading into the rainforest. He helped her climb over uprooted trees and they walked deeper into the forest. The temperature grew cooler and the sunshine had almost disappeared. Jillian heard the rustle of what she thought might be animals in the undergrowth and that made her grip Ben's hand tighter.

"What you heard was a mongoose," Ben said, with a sly smile. "I haven't run into a skunk yet, but there's always a first time."

"Peeeew!"

Jillian punched his shoulder playfully. It felt good to be outdoors and carefree, walking amidst greenery she'd never seen before, and smelling the damp yet delectable scents of the forest. For a brief moment she wished that life was always like this, and she didn't have the type of career that came with responsibility or stress. It would be nice to make time for camping and hiking, things she never seemed to be able to do.

"Did you see that?" Jillian practically jumped into Ben's arms as a slithering, green monster with a triple chin and a tail that rivaled a dragon skittered by.

Ben slid an arm around her waist and tried his best not to laugh. "Did I see what?"

"The Loch Ness monster. That Godzilla thing."

"Oh, you mean the iguana. They're harmless. They're more afraid of you than you are of them."

"It doesn't look harmless to me."

Jillian had never seen a lizard quite that large before. The thing had to be at least four feet long.

She cowered against Ben and his grip around her waist tightened.

Then suddenly he was kissing the sides of her mouth and she was letting him, the oversized lizard forgotten.

"Make sure it doesn't come back," she whispered breathlessly when he let her up for breath.

Ben stamped his feet to scare the iguana off. The green monster disappeared into the nearby bushes.

Then Ben dipped his head again and gave her a heart-stopping kiss, demanding more than she was willing to give right now. His persistence paid off when his tongue circled her mouth and Jillian matched him move for move. She felt dizzy and a bit unsteady when the kiss ended. The truth was she was over the moon.

Ben had come to a full stop. He drew them down to sit under a shady tree. Forgetting all about Godzilla and the slimy creatures that might be hiding out in the bushes, Jillian leaned her head against his shoulder, letting him kiss her eyelids and the bridge of her nose.

It seemed natural when Ben eased her onto her back. Then she was lying down beside him, staring at the leaves up above. Jillian ignored the twigs poking at her back and arms. Even the thought of poison ivy couldn't end this moment of total insanity.

Jillian was too caught up in the smell and feel of this man. She was wallowing in a heady experience; it was totally new for a woman who seldom deviated from her plan. It felt surreal to be sequestered in a fantasy world, with no scheduled meetings or hectic deadlines.

Ben's arm circled her neck. She rolled onto her side, twining her arms around him. He blew a soft breath against the hollow of her throat, and when he kissed her again, the safe little world that she'd been cocooned in shattered. Emotions too new to examine surfaced. Caution was thrown to the wind and Jillian went with the flow.

Her hands kneaded Ben's broad back and his finger traced a path across her clavicle. She wanted to leap out of her skin and let this man have every inch of her.

Ben's legs hooked around her ankles, trapping her. It was a vise she enjoyed being in. Leaves crunched under her back and an earthy greenness filled her nostrils. She was on sensory overload, overdosing on this man who lay practically on top of her.

Ben ground himself into her and Jillian arched her hips until they fit. His rough palm slid into the opening of her shirt and cupped one lace-covered nipple.

That simple touch was her undoing. Rough, warm and calloused fingers slid below the delicate barrier and found skin. Jillian nipped at his neck and Ben's lips tugged at her earlobe. The little noises coming from her throat couldn't possibly be hers.

"I want to make love to you," he said, his raspy voice sounding as if the wind had been knocked out of him. "I'd like to take you home with me to a comfortable bed."

Common sense kicked in. Jillian slid out from

under him. There were hundreds of reasons why making love to Ben was a bad idea.

Sleeping with him would only complicate matters. Already she was whirring out of control.

A voice that couldn't possibly be hers said, "I want to make love to you, too. Please take me home."

Ben was up in an instant, extending his hand.

As if it was the most natural thing in the world, Jillian fit her hand into his and they headed back to the Jeep.

Chapter 13

"Anna is visiting relatives, she won't be back until tomorrow," Ben said when they pulled up in front of his bure.

Now it really sank in, she'd agreed to go home with a man she had no relationship with. And it would just be her and him.

"Throw caution to the wind," the same naughty voice that had whispered in her ear earlier said. "Think of this as giving in to indulgence. You deserve to have fun."

But this wasn't about fun. She was beginning to care about Ben. And she hated to think that he might have intentionally set out to seduce her. What if he'd figured getting her into bed would soften her up, and make her divulge Elite's plans?

Ben had to know she was smarter than that. Plus she was cold sober. She would simply take this for what it was worth, with no expectations that it would lead to anything more. Maybe Ben Fuller was exactly what she needed right now—a little diversion.

"You've still got the forest in your hair," he said as they entered his front door.

Jillian began brushing at her head frantically. Ben reached over, plucking a handful of leaves free and

An Important Message From The ARABESQUE Publisher

Dear Arabesque Reader,

I invite you to join the club! The Arabesque book club delivers four novels each month right to your front door! It's easy, and you will never miss a romance by one of our award-winning authors!

With upcoming novels featuring strong, sexy women, and African-American heroes that are charming, loving and true… you won't want to miss a single release. Our authors fill each page with exceptional dialogue, exciting plot twists, and enough sizzling romance to keep you riveted until the satisfying end! To receive novels by bestselling authors such as Gwynne Forster, Janice Sims, Angela Winters and others, I encourage you to join now!

Read about the men we love… in the pages of Arabesque!

Linda Gill
PUBLISHER, ARABESQUE ROMANCE NOVELS

P.S. Watch out for the next Summer Series **"Ports Of Call"** *that will take you to the exotic locales of Venice, Fiji, the Caribbean and Ghana! You won't need a passport to travel, just collect all four novels to enjoy romance around the world! For more details, visit us at www.BET.com.*

SPECIAL OFFER! 4 BOOKS FREE!

ARABESQUE

BET BOOKS
www.BET.com

A SPECIAL "THANK YOU" FROM ARABESQUE JUST FOR YOU!

Send this card back and you'll receive 4 FREE Arabesque Novels—a $25.96 value—absolutely FREE!

The introductory 4 Arabesque Romance books are yours FREE (plus $1.99 shipping & handling). If you wish to continue to receive 4 books every month, do nothing. Each month, we will send you 4 New Arabesque Romance Novels for your free examination. If you wish to keep them, pay just $18* (plus, $1.99 shipping & handling). If you decide not to continue, you owe nothing!

- Send no money now.
- Never an obligation.
- Books delivered to your door!

We hope that after receiving your FREE books you'll want to remain an Arabesque subscriber, but the choice is yours! So why not take advantage of this Arabesque offer, with no risk of any kind. You'll be glad you did!

In fact, we're so sure you will love your Arabesque novels, that we will send you an Arabesque Tote Bag FREE with your first paid shipment.

* PRICES SUBJECT TO CHANGE.

YOU'LL GET 4 SELECT ROMANCES PLUS THIS FABULOUS TOTE BAG!

ARABESQUE

Visit us at:
www.BET.com

THE "THANK YOU" GIFT INCLUDES:

- 4 books absolutely FREE (plus $1.99 for shipping and handling).
- A FREE newsletter, *Arabesque Romance News*, filled with author interviews, book previews, special offers, and more!
- No risks or obligations. You're free to cancel whenever you wish with no questions asked.

FREE TOTE BAG CERTIFICATE

Yes! Please send me 4 FREE Arabesque novels (plus $1.99 for shipping & handling). I understand I am under no obligation to purchase any books, as explained on the back of this card. Send my free tote bag after my first regular paid shipment.

NAME _____

ADDRESS _____ APT. _____

CITY _____ STATE _____ ZIP _____

TELEPHONE (___) _____

E-MAIL _____

SIGNATURE _____

Offer limited to one per household and not valid to current subscribers. All orders subject to approval. Terms, offer, & price subject to change. Tote bags available while supplies last.

Thank You!

AN075A

ARABESQUE

Accepting the four introductory books for FREE (plus $1.99 to offset the cost of shipping & handling) places you under no obligation to buy anything. You may keep the books and return the shipping statement marked "cancelled". If you do not cancel, about a month later we will send 4 additional Arabesque novels, and you will be billed the preferred subscriber's price of just $4.50 per title. That's $18.00* for all 4 books for a savings of almost 30% off the cover price (Plus $1.99 for shipping and handling). You may cancel at any time, but if you choose to continue, every month we'll send you 4 more books, which you may either purchase at the preferred discount price. . . or return to us and cancel your subscription.

* PRICES SUBJECT TO CHANGE

THE ARABESQUE ROMANCE BOOK CLUB
P.O. BOX 5214
CLIFTON NJ 07015-5214

PLACE STAMP HERE

sniffing them. "Smells like you," he said, tossing her a heart-wrenching smile. "Smells wonderful."

"Does not." She punched his arm playfully.

"Come here, you."

Jillian entered Ben's open arms. He carefully and methodically removed the last signs indicating her earlier slip into insanity.

"Want something to drink?"

"Yes, water would be nice."

His arm still around her waist, Ben guided her into the kitchen.

Jillian perched on one of the stools and watched him remove two bottles of water from the refrigerator.

"Coconut?" she quipped.

"How did you guess?"

He slid into the v of her legs, so close that she could smell his male scent. He rested a chilled bottle against her cheek and she closed her eyes.

"Feels good," Jillian mouthed.

Then he set the bottle aside and began kissing her again. The last remnants of ambivalence dissolved. Practically pulling her from her seat, he linked an arm around her waist. Together they walked up the hallway.

Ben's room was bathed in a golden hue from the rays of a setting sun. Jillian stood in the circle of his arms, trying to regain her equilibrium and get her senses back. Planned or not, Ben had turned her orderly world completely upside down. It was a foreign feeling for a woman who'd made order a career.

Ben's hands began massaging her shoulders. He kissed the sides of her neck. Then he pulled away from her and quickly began to undress.

She heard the sound of something metallic clang across the wooden floors; it sounded as if coins had spilled from Ben's pockets. Jillian stared at Ben's perfect body, unable to believe how muscular his arms were, and the incredible breadth of his chest. There wasn't an excess ounce of flesh on the man. She wanted to run her fingers through the dark hair covering his torso and sink her lips into all that bronze skin.

Ben had one finger hitched at the waistband of his black undershorts. He was staring at her in a most mesmerizing way.

"Get out of those clothes, darling, or I'm coming over to undress you," he said.

Jillian slid out of her shorts and tugged off her top. Ben watched her every move. He appeared openly pleased by what he saw. Then he crossed the short distance between them and took her into his arms.

This time Jillian kissed him back with a passion she didn't know she possessed. He was peeling off her panties and unclasping her bra. Naked, he lowered her onto the bed and covered his body with hers. The heat coming off of him warmed her more than any blanket ever could.

A myriad of sensations converged as Jillian opened her eyes and looked up at the vaulted ceiling. Ben's hand swept her breasts, tugging at one nipple. A finger of the other hand settled into her bellybutton, making circles. He nipped at her earlobe and used his knee to part her legs.

"Do you have a condom?" she breathed.

He groaned, rolled off of her, and fumbled through the drawer of the nightstand. After taking the time to position the thing in place, he returned to her.

Jillian arched herself up to meet him and wrapped her legs around his waist. Soon they were so close they were melded together.

Blood pounded in her ears and the throbbing at her core was unbearable. He was moving rhythmically now, entering and exiting her. Oh, the sounds he made, the feel of him. It would only be seconds before she imploded.

Lovemaking felt right, better than right. Jillian's hands grasped Ben's back, nails digging into his flesh. When he gave a deep thrust, she spiraled out of control. The ceiling receded to be replaced by shooting stars and fireworks

"Ben!"

"Jillian!"

More shallow breaths. Then, in perfect synchronicity, they hurled over the top.

It took at least ten minutes before Jillian came down. The evidence of their coupling lay all around: crumpled sheets and the pungent smell of sex. What had she done? She'd just slept with the enemy and there was no turning back. She needed time and space to think. She needed to go home.

Jillian untangled herself from Ben's limbs. He seemed to be sleeping the sleep of the dead. She found her clothes and stepped into them, almost stumbling over a metallic object that looked like a pen. Bending over, she reached for it.

She picked up what looked to be a Mont Blanc pen. She'd seen its mate somewhere before. It dawned on her that it matched the pen she'd found in front of the burned-out cottage. Pocketing the instrument, she decided to head home.

At the same time a horrendous thought began to percolate. Had Ben Fuller been the one responsible for the fire? Had she just slept with an arsonist? God, she needed time to think.

Ben woke up shortly thereafter. For the first time in a long time he felt content and perfectly relaxed. He'd just had the most amazing dream. He had a family again, though not one he recognized as his.

Reaching out an arm for Jillian, he encountered emptiness. Puzzled, he turned onto his side.

"Jill," he called, hoping that the nickname she despised might elicit a response.

No answer.

Glancing at his watch, Ben realized it was still relatively early, not yet dinnertime. Where was Jillian?

"Babe, are you there?"

Just silence.

Nude, and growing more concerned by the moment, he jumped out of bed and set off to find her. Ben checked every room, then searched for a note. It soon became apparent that Jillian had left him.

He threw on his clothes, deciding that he was not going to let her off that easily. They needed to talk.

Less than ten minutes later, he entered the courtyard and loped up the walk. Banging on her door got absolutely no response. He debated what to do next. He could walk around the property, doubtful that she'd left. Jillian had no means of transportation.

A curtain shifted, catching his eye. He banged on the door again, this time calling, "Jillian, I know you're home. Open up."

Several minutes elapsed, then he got angry. What kind of crazy game was she playing? They were two consenting adults who'd willingly taken their friendship another step. It had been a gigantic leap for a man who hadn't slept with a woman in over a year—not since he'd acknowledged that the flings he'd had when he was drunk were hurtful to women, who were expecting more than he was capable of giving at that time.

If he had to hazard a guess, Jillian wasn't given to climbing in and out of bed with any man who presented himself either. So why had she run off? Could the intense passion they'd shared scared her?

"I'm going to break the door down. If you don't open up," Ben threatened, banging like a madman.

The door flew open and he took a step back. Jillian stood barring the doorway with one arm.

"Is there a problem?" Her voice was icy cold.

What had happened to the warm, wonderful woman who'd made love to him less than an hour before?

"Suppose you tell me?" Ben answered. "Now move aside and let me come in unless you'd rather the entire resort hear our business."

His comment got the necessary result. She dropped her arm and he brushed by her.

"Okay, so what is it you came to say?"

There was no invitation to take a seat.

"Why don't we both make ourselves comfortable?"

"Why?"

Ben stared at her, unable to believe what he was hearing. What had brought this on?

He decided to address it head on. "Did I do something to offend you? A short time ago we were in bed together. When I opened my eyes you were gone."

"You were fast asleep. I assumed you needed your rest."

Was that what this was about? She was ticked at him because he'd fallen asleep and maybe snored. Women. He would never understand them.

Ben took a step toward Jillian, softening his tone. "I'm sorry, my falling asleep was no reflection on you." He reached out, caressing her arm.

She stepped back, making sure they were in no way connected.

The whole thing made no sense. "Okay, give it to me straight," Ben said. "Why are you mad?"

Jillian circled the room before heading for the desk. She picked up what looked to him like a pen and shook it at him.

"Is this pen yours?"

Things were getting crazier by the minute. "No, I don't own a Mont Blanc. What does this have to do with what we're discussing?"

"Everything." She fumbled through her purse, found what she was looking for, and held up the mate. "This pen was found at the site of the burned-out cottage."

"So?" She wasn't making sense. Ben threw his hands wide in a frustrated gesture. "You're losing me. What does one have to do with the other?"

"I found this pen at your home. It fell out of your slacks and rolled onto the floor."

"And that's why you're angry? That's why you left?" It took Ben several seconds to make the connection. "You think I am somehow involved? That I set the fire deliberately? Why would I do that?"

"You're after the same thing I am," Jillian said bluntly.

Ben's temper snapped. It had been a long time since he'd lost total control. He'd just spent the majority of the day with this woman. They'd had a good time, or seemed to, he'd thought. And they'd just made incredible love. Now she was accusing him of something so totally despicable that he had to wonder if she'd used him. He certainly hadn't used her.

"Okay," he said, enunciating each word. "You found a pen at the site of the burned-out property. You found another that looked like it at my home; a fully furnished time-share that I rent. And rather than asking me about it, like any sane person would do, you made an assumption and fled."

Jillian had the grace to look ashamed. Ben was too angry to back off now. "I didn't lie to you, Jillian. When you asked, I admitted I was interested in acquiring the Bula." He bit down hard on his lower jaw, trying to rein in his temper. "Maybe it was a good thing something like this happened. Now I know what you're all about. There's only one thing you are interested in, getting that property. And clearly you don't trust me."

"Ben," Jillian said, taking a step toward him and holding a hand out. "I'm sorry, perhaps you're right. Maybe I jumped to conclusions. Maybe we should talk this out."

He was much too angry to be conciliatory now. It had been a mistake to come here. Maybe they both needed a good night's sleep.

The urge to have just one drink became all-consuming. He needed to put space between them and just think. When he felt like this it was time to call his sponsor. Ricky Lohman would talk him through temptation. He'd always been his rock.

"I'm sorry, Jillian. I'm no longer in the mood to talk," he said, backing out of the room.

"Oh, Ben, please reconsider. I admit I just might have been wrong."

Ben closed his ears to her pleas. Jillian's actions clearly indicated she didn't trust him. Sleeping with her had been a mistake. One he didn't plan on repeating.

Chapter 14

"You'll need to knock down the entire structure and start from scratch," Ricky Lohman said to Ben. "That's my professional recommendation."

Both men circled the abandoned building that a long time ago must have been a distillery. Ben had earmarked it as his coconut manufacturing plant.

"This project is getting more expensive by the minute," Ben muttered. "Something here must be salvageable: a wall, windowpane, door?"

Ricky shook his head, at the same time looking around at the crumbling building. "Not in my estimation. The place should be demolished. It's unsafe and has been abandoned for as many years as I've lived here."

"I'll need to think about new construction instead of reconstruction then," Ben said, more to himself than the contractor.

He and Ricky, who was also his sponsor, had spent the last couple of days meeting. They'd devised a plan as to how to get the coconut manufacturing plant up and running in a relatively short time. It had kept him busy and taken his mind off Jillian and drink. Ricky, who'd struggled with alcoholism since he was a teenager, had been a rock.

Now Ben turned to the burly Rotuman. "How much is this going to run me?" he asked.

Ricky's brow furrowed. "I'll work the figures up and get back to you."

"I need them like yesterday. I'm meeting with Franz and I don't want to offer him a penny more than the Bula's worth, especially if this is going to be an expensive project."

"You speak as if this is in the bag. What about Elite?" Ricky's shrewd eyes examined Ben for a reaction. "The corporation has deep pockets. What if they counter and you can't meet it?"

"I plan on countering right back. Franz's wife is a local and very well-connected. The Bula used to be owned by her father. When he got ill Cathy and Franz bought him out. Trust me, she's not crazy about seeing the property fall into foreign hands."

"Technically you're foreign," Rick pointed out.

"That may be so, but I'm planning on living here for the rest of my life. Cathy knows that I'd restore the Bula to its old charm. My employees would all be locals. And you should know that the people of Taveuni could use the work."

Ricky grinned from ear to ear and slapped Ben's back. "Just testing you, bro. So when exactly are you going to make this offer?"

"When I meet with Franz."

Ricky circled the decrepit building again and made notes on his clipboard. "What's with you and her anyway?"

His question took Ben by surprise. Was his interest that transparent? Then he remembered nothing was sacred on an island this size.

"I'm not sure what you're getting at?" Ben said, keeping his expression blank.

Ricky's brown eyes narrowed. "Word has it you two have something going on."

"Word is wrong."

"You turn down most of the island women and you take a newcomer out on a dive with you. Then you take the woman to a remote area for lunch and then you take her home."

Ben clapped a palm on Ricky's chest, sending the Rotuman stumbling back. "Does everyone know my business on this damn island?"

"You know they do," Ricky said, prying Ben's fingers off his chest and flashing him a knowing smile. "I think she's good for you. She's a bit uptight but maybe you need stuffy. She might help you get your priorities in order and maybe even mellow you out a bit."

"I don't need mellowing," Ben said, glaring at Ricky. "And I certainly don't need a woman in my life. My focus now is on making this deal happen. Why would I put any effort into connecting with a woman who'll be leaving for the States in a few days?"

"You could have fooled me," Ricky said, scribbling on his pad. "Look, I have to get going if I'm going to make my other appointment. I don't want to be late."

"You will get back to me with what it's going to cost to fix this place up?" Ben said as Ricky hurried off.

"Sure will."

Ricky hopped into his truck. "See you at the meeting later," he said over his shoulder.

"Count on that." Ben's parting wave was lost in the billowing smoke of the man's truck.

He stood frozen for a moment, looking around the old distillery and wondering what the renovation would cost.

* * *

"Ms. Gray, I have a message for you," called the woman manning the guest relations desk the moment Jillian emerged from the back offices.

She'd gone there hoping to find Marlon. Peter had e-mailed her with a number of questions after reading her report. They were questions that seemed ridiculous and somewhat premature. He wanted an itemized list of things like bedding and cutlery and the current inventory on hand.

Jillian accepted the note the smiling receptionist handed her. Everyone had become overly friendly and ingratiating these days. Clearly the staff had been briefed that she was there for a purpose, and all wanted to ensure their jobs.

Opening the note with some trepidation, she felt a twinge of surprise. Michael had called, and she'd missed him. It had been some time since they spoke. Now he'd left a message saying it was urgent that she get back to him. The number he'd left wasn't his cell phone and was one she didn't recognize.

As Jillian hurried back to her bure she wondered why the sudden urgency. Up until now, Michael had been the perfect boss. Basically he left her alone, but it had been ages since she'd dealt with him directly. Peter Fontaine had taken over and Michael had been shoved aside.

She'd viewed her dealings with Peter as a good thing. It was her time to shine. Now she wasn't so sure. Michael had been a nice buffer. He'd been terrific to bounce ideas off of. Not so with Peter, who viewed waffling or indecision as a major weakness. Jillian had simply e-mailed her report, outlining the pluses and minuses of buying the Bula. She'd recommended Elite offer what the place was worth. She already knew Peter wanted the property and even though it had been let go, she could see why he did.

Outside, in the privacy of her courtyard, Jillian

used her recently charged international cell phone to call the number Michael had left her.

A New Zealand hotel operator, with a clipped accent, fielded her inquiry for Michael Rosen, and then transferred her to his hotel room.

He came on the line relatively quickly.

"Hey, you caught me just in time. What took you so long to get back to me?"

"You're one to talk. I left you several messages."

"I don't recall getting any." His voice had taken on a serious tone.

"Peter kept telling me that you've been sent out of town. You do know he's been dealing with me directly."

"Yes, yes, I heard. Initially Peter asked me to step out of the way. He wanted to see what you were made of. Since this is taking unusually long he's asked me to get involved again."

"How involved are you planning to become?" Jillian asked, her blood boiling. She didn't recall asking for help.

"Involved enough to hop a plane and come to Taveuni. In fact I'm leaving for the airport shortly. Peter wants this whole thing wrapped up quickly so we can move on to other things."

"And a male presence would do that?"

Michael grunted an affirmation.

Jillian took umbrage at that. "That's the most chauvinistic thing I've heard in a long time. Just because I've had a few setbacks, he's sending you in? This place has been plagued with problems. The key decision-makers haven't been available. Everyone is on Fiji time."

"Peter wants you back in Chicago," Michael said firmly. "My instructions are to make the deal and bring you home with me. He's given us four days."

"What about the three weeks that I was promised?" Jillian shouted at him.

"Once our boss's mind is made up, there's no changing it. You know how that is."

Jillian bit back the words on the tip of her tongue. She was not at all happy about Michael charging in. At times he could be headstrong. The Fijians didn't operate on Chicago time, nor would they take kindly to a high-handed approach. All that aside, she was getting the message loud and clear: Peter thought she wasn't competent to see the deal through, Michael was coming to rescue her. But she'd be damned if she let him take over.

What was the point in getting emotional? She would simply be labeled a hysterical woman.

"We'll need to move quickly then," she said, moving in to professional mode. "Meetings will need to be set up soon."

"That's all been taken care of," Michael said. "We're meeting with Franz Herrman tomorrow at ten."

"What about the legal and financial aspects? All that will need to be ironed out."

"Once we get a verbal agreement from these people then we'll hightail it back to Chicago and let the attorneys do the rest. Contracts can always be couriered over and it's on to the next project."

"When will you be arriving?" Jillian asked.

"Later this evening. I've got a car picking me up."

Jillian hung up feeling as if she'd just had the rug pulled out from under her. These last few days had been the worst she'd ever experienced. Ben had been studiously avoiding her, and she'd felt so alone.

Now she needed time to strategize. Her promotion to vice president had hinged on her securing this deal. Michael being dispatched to save her indicated it wasn't locked in.

Jillian had wanted—no, needed—to show her

parents that an African-American woman could achieve success in a lily-white corporate world. She'd wanted them to be proud of her and to know that there were positions other than nanny, housekeeper, nurse, or teacher where a black woman could excel.

She decided to walk around the property and clear her head. Arms pumping, she maintained long strides. She would have to handle Michael's arrival graciously and she would be professional if it was the last thing she did.

Her walk took her off the beaten path and into an area that was secluded. After spotting what appeared to be an abandoned building, she headed over to explore.

The structure was run down and served no useful purpose that she could see. It probably should have been torn down because in its current dilapidated state it really was an eyesore.

A massive door dangled off rusty hinges. Jillian managed to ease the door open and entered what appeared to be an abandoned warehouse. The interior smelled foul. Droppings on the floor signified that this might be some wild animals' haven and soiled rags were scattered on the floor.

She spotted a man with his back to her. He circled the floor, snapping the occasional photograph. Why in the world would anyone want to take pictures of an abandoned, decrepit building? Hearing her footsteps, he turned. Jillian found herself face to face with Ben, the last person she expected. It was too late to run off now and there was no place to go.

It had been three whole days since she'd seen him last. She'd spent those three days feeling guilty and out of sorts, wondering if she'd falsely accused him of something he hadn't done.

"Hello, Ben," Jillian said, because there really was no other choice.

His eyes swept over her, assessing her and at first she thought he wouldn't answer. Then he said, "Hello, Jillian."

She felt strangely disappointed that it hadn't been "Jill." The pet name was starting to grow on her. It signified camaraderie and the bond they'd had.

"Ben," she began. "I've been meaning to stop by and apologize to you, but it's been hectic these last few days."

"I've been home."

He held the camera between palms that were both calloused and gentle, hands that had sent tremors running through her body. They'd certainly awakened the woman in her.

"I was afraid you wouldn't take my call," she admitted.

"That's a bunch of bull and you know it," he growled, his golden eyes never leaving her face. "If you really wanted to talk to me, you would have made the time."

Jillian didn't want to argue, not in her current state of mind. Their little disagreement seemed insignificant now and Ben Fuller was the closest thing she had to a friend. She needed to speak with someone who had sound business acumen. She needed this man.

"You're right," she said humbly. "My behavior has been inexcusable. I should have made the time. But the truth is I was embarrassed."

"As you should be," Ben said, not cutting her any slack. "You pretty much accused me of masterminding all these mishaps. The only thing you didn't do was call me a murderer to my face."

Jillian thought he might turn away and return to whatever he'd been doing. She reached out and grabbed his wrists.

Ben seemed to debate whether he should pull out of her grasp, but she maintained a strong hold.

"What are you doing?" he gritted through clenched teeth.

"Stopping you from walking away from me. I need an opinion. You know how the corporate world works. I need your advice."

Maybe it was the tone of her voice, or maybe it was the expression on her face, that made him pause. His stance changed and he was the gentler Ben she remembered—the man who'd taken her to bed. Taking her arm, he headed for the door.

"We'll talk outside," he said. "Where the air is fresher."

The sun shone brightly overhead as he led her up a path lined with greenery. Brambles reached out, scratching her face and tugging at her hair. It reminded her of the other day when they'd wandered through the rainforest, and she'd reflected on what it might be like if it were just her and him.

They walked for a good five minutes before Ben stopped in front of what looked like an uprooted coconut tree. He brushed debris off the trunk and gestured for her to sit. It was so quiet that for a moment she forgot there was an outside world. At last he'd given her private time.

"So talk," Ben said, giving her the opening she needed.

And Jillian did, the words coming out in quick bursts. She explained that her boss, Michael Rosen, was on his way to Taveuni. And she shared that she feared Peter Fontaine thought she was in over her head. But something stopped her from telling Ben that a promotion was at stake.

He listened quietly until she'd completed her tale.

"You may be overreacting," he said, in even tones. "Peter was confident in your abilities or he would not have sent you to Taveuni. Why do you think something might have happened to make him change his mind?"

Ben's squinted eyes and tightly clenched lips indicated he was examining all the possibilities. He'd just echoed everything she'd thought.

"Peter knew this was going to be a delicate negotiation," Jillian admitted. "He reads the newspapers and knows of all the problems."

Ben's fingers worried his forehead. "I was surprised that Elite sent you here to begin with. They're not big on minorities, and certainly not in important positions."

What Ben said was true, but Jillian had always been treated with respect. She'd never had reason to think of Elite as a racist company.

"I've done a good job so far for the company," Jillian said, defending herself. "I've worked like a dog, and I've closed every huge deal I've been assigned. My competency has never been questioned."

"Hmmm, but this is different. Peter is obsessed with obtaining this property. I wonder why."

Jillian didn't answer him. She didn't want to divulge any information Ben could use against her. A little voice reminded her Ben wanted the property, too. Could he be trusted to be objective?

"How would you play it if you were me?" Jillian asked, switching the conversation.

His eyes focused on her again and she was lost in their midst. "You're a team player. Let Michael think you're grateful to have his assistance."

"What?"

"You don't necessarily have to be ingratiating," Ben said soothingly. "You know how to stroke him a bit? Simply outline everything you've done so far. Let him see the written report. Then the two of you can approach Franz as equals."

Jillian thought about it.

"Do you have another meeting set up with Franz and Marlon?" Ben asked.

"Yes, Michael already set one up."

"Be smarter than Michael then. You conduct the meeting and treat him as reinforcement."

Again he'd echoed her thoughts. She was on the right track. Jillian knew the kind of money Elite was willing to spend. Barring any nasty surprises, she could easily close the deal, though closing the deal would mean leaving Taveuni and ending her friendship with Ben.

She reached out her hand and took his. "Thank you for listening and thank you for your advice. I really am sorry about the other day. I never should have made such unfounded accusations."

"Apology accepted," he said. "If the tables were turned I might have thought the same thing. You'll have to trust me, the pen isn't mine. No more Mont Blancs for me, fake or otherwise, and there haven't been for quite some time."

Ben sounded so sincere, she wanted to believe him. Deep down she'd sensed he was a nice man. What if they'd met under different circumstances? What if Ben still lived in the States?

Maybe they could have taken this friendship further. No, God forbid. Perish the thought.

Chapter 15

"When exactly is your colleague arriving?" Ben asked, offering Jillian his arm and helping her up from the fallen tree.

What had prompted the question? Mere curiosity, or was he simply assessing how much time they had left together?

"Michael mentioned he was catching a flight from New Zealand later this evening," Jillian answered.

"Maybe you should find out what time he's coming in and meet him at the airport."

She shot Ben a puzzled look. What was he getting at? "Why? Michael hardly needs a babysitter. He's ordered a car and is perfectly capable of getting to the hotel on his own."

Ben touched her arm. "My advice to you is to make sure you're the first person he encounters. It'll give you time to bend his ear a bit and fill him in. If he's been instructed to call your bastard of a boss on arrival, your being there will circumvent that."

"You are shrewd," Jillian acknowledged, a comprehending smile on her lips.

They'd left the main compound behind and

entered into an area densely populated by coconut trees. After climbing a pebble-strewn incline, they stared down on the lush valley. A turquoise ocean provided an enchanting backdrop and reminded Jillian of something she'd seen on a movie set.

"This truly is paradise," Jillian said, a hitch in her voice. "It's so peaceful and so serene. I've always dreamed of having one of these houses on a cliff overlooking the ocean. This would be so perfect."

"Funny that you should say that," Ben answered, an enigmatic expression on his face. "I'm having a home built on the other side of the island with a view much like this. I discovered this place on one of my walks. This acreage is all part of the Bula, but I am sure you know that."

She didn't know that, but nodded her head anyway. Let him think that she was well acquainted with the site map. Ben didn't have to know that she'd only made a cursory glance of the map so she could figure out where the buildings and leisure activities were located. Let the reconstruction team and architects do the rest.

"I envy you," she said, sighing. "You made the choice to simply drop out of life. And you were blessed with the wherewithal to make that dream happen. This, in my opinion is the perfect escape."

It must be all this rest and relaxation that was making her think like this. She'd loved being a wanderer, loved the adrenaline high of flying into a strange country, meeting the people, assessing properties, and then hightailing it out of there.

"You would think," Ben said, as if forgetting that she was still there with him, "that Franz would have taken advantage of this wonderful view. Think of the price cottages away from the main thoroughfare could command. Let's walk around and explore a bit." He pointed to the velvety green valley below.

Accepting the hand Ben offered, Jillian followed him down another overgrown path. They walked with the sun's rays beating down on their faces, inhaling the salty ocean air. They passed trees that Ben said were banana, breadfruit, and soursop. He pointed out plants neither could name.

"What's that?" Jillian asked, spotting a willowy bush with leaves shaped like hands with missing fingers.

Ben stopped to examine the bright green leaves. He sniffed at them and frowned.

"Is there something wrong?" Jillian asked, disturbed by the expression on his face.

"Cannabis," Ben snapped. "Lots of it." He gestured to the field that they were passing, where an abundance of the stuff grew.

"Canna— what?"

"Cannabis. Marijuana."

Jillian still wasn't getting it. Sure she knew what marijuana was, though she'd never indulged.

"Why would anyone choose such a beautiful and desolate area to grow a hallucinogenic drug?" she asked, shaking her head in wonder.

Ben's look clearly indicated that she wasn't quite grasping his full meaning. Simultaneously, a whirring noise up above got their attention. A helicopter was circling the area, looking for an appropriate place to land.

"Know what I'm thinking? We better make ourselves scarce." He whipped an arm around her waist and pulled her with him into the nearby bushes. "Let's see if my suspicions are about to be confirmed."

The whirring-clacking sound of blades came closer. The noise made Jillian cover her ears. The copter was so close it looked like it might land on their heads and she could feel the breeze.

Two men emerged from somewhere and began waving to the pilot. The aircraft circled again and then landed in a nearby clearing. The men, who from their appearance seemed to be natives, raced toward the bird, dragging two burlap bags with them. The bird's blades were still going, making the bushes close by sway. The two bags were quickly exchanged for an envelope and the whirlybird took off again.

Ben sat holding Jillian tightly. She huddled into his arms thinking that this was all surreal. Finally she broke the silence.

"Tell me we're dreaming."

"You're wide awake, babe. We've just witnessed a drug deal."

Babe? Better not to dwell on that endearment. Better to focus on the fact he'd confirmed what she'd been thinking.

To cover her disconcertment, Jillian spoke quickly. "Who would have thought?"

Ben's eyebrows winged upward. "Does make you wonder if Franz knows this type of illegal activity goes on on his property?"

"Would he condone it?"

Ben shrugged. "Hard to tell. There's big money in drugs. People get greedy."

"Why would he need to sell the property, if he's making money on the side?"

"Perhaps he's gotten all he needs. Maybe what he's looking to do now is improve the quality of family life. His priorities might have shifted. Illness will do that to you."

"I'm sorry. I don't understand," Jillian said, stopping. "Is Franz sick?"

Ben explained the situation, telling her that

Franz's wife Cathy had been diagnosed with terminal cancer.

Jillian felt for the man. She'd always thought of Franz Herrman as the consummate business type, cool and very distant. He'd courted Elite with such urgency. Jillian simply figured he'd thought a foreign enterprise might be more willing to pay the Bula big bucks.

"I had no idea it was a personal situation forcing this sale," she said carefully, reminding herself to tread lightly. In a relatively short space of time she'd found out quite a lot.

What she'd learned she planned on using to her advantage. No, Elite's advantage.

"Maybe we should start back," she suggested after a while. "Do you have an update on the divers and the tampered equipment? Has anyone fessed up or been caught?"

Ben shook his head. "Not really. Just that they've been released and given a clean bill of health."

She was about to scramble out of the bushes when his fingers clasped her forearm. "Stay put for another couple of minutes, just until those guys leave. We wouldn't want them to know we saw them."

Jillian had almost forgotten about the men hidden in the underbrush. She and Ben had been sitting so close they were practically welded together.

Another five minutes passed before the men reappeared. This time they were counting bills and arguing loudly.

"I keep telling you," one of them said. "We should up our take."

"The boss gives us what he gives us. We just collect."

"I say he's selling this stuff way too cheap."

"If we cut him out, what do you think we could make?"

One of the men named a figure. The other whistled.

"You might have something there. We're the ones placing ourselves in danger. We do all the work. He gets most of the money. Doesn't seem right."

"I've been telling you that," the shorter of them said. "Gonna be late for work if we don't move it. We'll talk again after our shift. Meet you in the usual place."

The other man grunted and together they skulked off through the underbrush.

"Recognize any of them?" Jillian asked. Ben shook his head. "I wonder who the boss is?"

Ben, still holding onto her arm, whispered, "My guess is it's someone in a fairly high position."

"Must be Franz or Marlon then? But isn't Marlon your friend? Why would he get himself involved in something so sordid?"

"Friend is not the term I'd use to describe my relationship with Marlon." Ben was gazing around, making sure the coast was clear. "More like acquaintances." He glanced at his watch. "I need to get back. There's a meeting I don't want to miss."

Jillian's guard went back up. Why all of a sudden was Ben in such a hurry? Was he looking to find Franz and make his own deal? Was he planning on one-upping her before she and Michael could have their own meeting? Hesitant to voice her fear, Jillian allowed Ben to lead her out into the opening.

Five minutes later, she touched on the topic again. "What do you think we should do about what we just witnessed?"

Ben's clenched jaw indicated he too was contemplating the next course of action. "I'm not quite sure how to proceed. I'll think about it."

"I'm going to talk to Michael," Jillian said, coming to a decision. "Elite can't afford any negative publicity."

Ben suddenly stopped walking. He looped an arm around her waist. "Why don't we wait a day or two. We'll come back here tomorrow around the same time and see if there's a repeat of today's activities. That'll give us time to scout around and ask a few questions, find out what capacity these men are employed in."

What Ben said made good sense. Two days in a row of repeated activity would give credence to their story. It wouldn't seem as if they'd overreacted because a couple of native men were enterprising and out to make a quick buck.

As they walked by the abandoned warehouse again, Jillian noticed the front door was wide open. The first thing she thought of was that maybe someone had sought refuge there. Ben noticed, too, but he hurried past, announcing, "I don't have time to check out who's inside. Are you okay to find your way back from here?"

Then he dipped his head and gave her a heart-stopping kiss—a kiss that left her head spinning and her body wanting more. A kiss that was filled with promise.

With a quick salute, he loped off. Jillian resisted the urge to follow him. There was something about Ben that made her want to follow him to the ends of the earth.

"Jillian, you look wonderful and rested," Michael said the minute he spotted her. He hugged her to him and in his breezy way said, "Are you sure you've been working?"

Was that a dig? She wasn't sure how to take his comment. Jillian came back with, "And you look tired. Peter must really be working you."

Michael did look tired. Tired, stuffy and out of place in Taveuni. He was still dressed in his crisp white shirt and conservative pinstriped suit. He stood out like a sore thumb among those more casually dressed in the restaurant. Even his navy silk tie still held a perfect knot.

"It's been hell since you've been gone," Michael admitted, motioning over the waitress and taking it upon himself to order coffee for two.

His flight had been delayed and Jillian had not been able to get concrete information about his arrival. Knowing that he would eventually contact her, she'd ignored Ben's advice and remained at the hotel.

Jillian was still staying in the bridal suite because the hotel was now practically vacant. She'd spent considerable time reading and rereading the report she'd already sent off to the home office. She'd critiqued her own words, wondering how she could have made improvements. And she'd jotted notes, adding her comments about what she'd witnessed earlier. She'd also mentioned Franz's wife, Cathy's illness.

Jillian had debated whether to send the updated report to Peter or wait to discuss the situation with Michael. Then she'd decided she was making too much of the whole thing and had done nothing at all.

"Okay, tell me everything," Michael said, breaking into her musings. "Start with your arrival in Taveuni."

She'd just been given the perfect opening she needed.

"What specifically would you like to hear?"

"Why this deal hasn't closed?"

Based on his comment, Jillian wasn't sure whether he was on her side or not. Peter had to have filled him in on the numerous setbacks the Bula had experienced. Surely he'd told Michael guests were leaving the resort in droves due to the bad publicity. Michael had to know the decision-makers, the people she needed to meet with, had been inundated with all that going on.

Jillian answered his question with one of her own. "Michael, why are you really here?"

Her boss's smile shot up a megawatt. She knew that smile well. It was the one he used to disarm others and make them comfortable. It would not work with her.

"I'm here," he said, "because Peter wants you in Sao Paulo, and we need to wrap up this deal quickly."

"But this is my project. I've invested quite a bit of time and energy already. Now I'm getting the feeling Peter doesn't trust me, which is why he sent you here."

The waitress returned with their coffee and the conversation ceased temporarily. Michael poured them two cups.

"I wouldn't exactly say he doesn't trust you," he said carefully. "Peter suspects Ben Fuller has his sights on the property. He doesn't want him pouring on the charm and bamboozling you. Fuller's made a home here and probably has powerful contacts. I came to offer reinforcement and provide a male presence."

Jillian set her cup down so hard liquid spilled over the sides. Her eyes never left Michael's. "So, what you're saying is that Peter doesn't think 'his girlie' is capable of going up against Ben Fuller."

Michael grabbed her hand across the table. "The guy's no fool, Jillian. He has a long-standing reputation for moving in on what he wants, and taking it, and the consequences be damned. He's done that to Peter more than a time or two over the years. There's no love lost between them."

For a moment, Jillian thought there might be a double meaning behind his words, a subtle warning that she was not to trust Ben with her heart. But how would he know about the sexual tension between them? Who would have told him?

"Elite has a similar reputation," she came back with. "Ben's been a decent guy. Our relationship has been cordial."

"So you've met him then?"

"Yes, I have." Jillian's stomach went all quivery at the image of Ben she'd just conjured up. Michael should only know she'd done better than meet Ben. "I happen to like the man," she said.

"Talking about me again, Jill?" A deep male voice said from behind her.

Her stomach quivered like Jell-O and she swung around to greet the man she was daydreaming about. Ben had a beautiful native woman, young enough to be his daughter, with him. She clung to his arm.

Jillian felt as if she'd been stabbed. She returned Ben's heated gaze and tried to ignore the sour taste in her mouth.

"Aren't you going to introduce us, Jill?" Ben asked, staring directly at Michael.

Jillian's boss stood, while she remained frozen, thrown back to a time in elementary school when she'd been taunted. She could still hear the voices.

"Jack and Jill went up the hill to fetch a pail of water. Jack fell down and broke his crown, and Jill came tumbling after, panties down."

Jillian pulled herself together. "Yes, of course." She

made the introductions and when she got to the young woman, she paused.

"This is Simone, Anna's daughter," Ben said, pushing the young woman forward.

Simone's attention seemed to be concentrated solely on Ben. Was it Jillian's imagination or had her grip on his arm tightened?

"So this is *the* Ben Fuller I've heard so much about?" Michael said, clasping Ben's hand in a firm grip.

"And you are Michael Rosen, Jill's boss. She's mentioned you a time or two."

"Would you like to join us?" Michael asked, his hand making a sweeping gesture toward two vacant seats.

"No, thanks. Simone and I are here for a heart-to-heart and then we're leaving."

Did leaving mean that he and the housekeeper's daughter were heading back to his place? Did she live in the cottage out back with Anna? The thought was a disquieting one to Jillian. Even more upsetting was thinking that she'd been used to fill a void. She didn't know Ben's reputation and she'd slept with him, telling herself to have no expectations. So why did she want to throttle the woman with him?

"Hopefully we're still on for tomorrow," Ben said, looking directly at her. "Same time. Same place." He winked, and taking Anna's daughter with him, set off to find a table.

After he was out of earshot, Michael looked at her questioningly. "What was that about?"

"Nothing."

"Nothing, my foot. The man couldn't take his eyes off you, and to paraphrase him, tomorrow you and he have a date."

"Hardly the type of date you're thinking," Jillian grunted, refusing to meet Michael's gaze. "In case you haven't noticed, Ben seems to have already been spoken for."

Jillian looked over in the direction of where Ben and Simone were seated. Their heads were inches apart and she felt another stabbing twinge in her gut.

Business. She had to focus on business.

"I get the feeling you being here means my promotion is in jeopardy?" she said to Michael. "You would tell me, wouldn't you?"

Michael's index finger worried his eyebrow. "Look, I've never lied to you before, and I won't lie to you now."

"Just tell me."

"I'm not sure you want to hear this, but I'll be as straight as I can with you. No, your promotion isn't assured. If I were you I'd start looking around."

The cup Jillian held fell, shattering on the terrazzo floor.

It was the last thing she'd expected Michael to say.

Chapter 16

They were crouched down in the same bushes as yesterday—so close, Ben could smell Jillian's shampoo. The delectable scent filled his nostrils and reminded him of an exotic garden.

Time ticked by and they grew increasingly more uncomfortable. Beads of sweat settled on Ben's forehead and trickled down his chest.

"God, it's hot," he said to Jillian, blowing what he hoped was cool air on her neck. She was hunkered down next to him in what had to be an uncomfortable position.

"That feels good," she said, turning her head slightly.

Ben blew out another breath and Jillian sighed. "I wonder if they'll show up?"

"Let's give it another ten minutes." He nuzzled her neck with his nose. "You've been so quiet. Anything wrong?"

He wondered if Jillian was upset because she'd seen him with Simone? The child—and he did think of her as a child—was only seventeen and desperately needed a male role model. Anna had given birth to her at age sixteen and out of wedlock.

Ben did the best he could, when he could, but his

role in Simone's life was limited to her infrequent visits home from boarding school. It was the only expense the father, who was very much married, shouldered.

Jillian's shoulders stiffened, but she remained quiet.

"Come on now, spit it out. Something's obviously bothering you."

"I need to close this deal. A lot hinges on Elite acquiring the Bula," she answered.

And to think he'd assumed she was jealous of Simone and that in some small way he mattered.

His voice was gruffer than he meant it to be when he responded. "Surely Peter Fontaine has had his share of deals fall through. He may pout a bit, but he'll eventually move on. What are you worried about? Becoming the fall guy?"

Jillian swiveled around to look him fully in the face. Ah, he had touched a nerve.

"Hardly," she snapped. "I suppose you think you've got it in the bag."

"Did I say that?"

This was crazy; she was so clearly spoiling for a fight. She'd been distracted and edgy since they'd met.

Holding her by the shoulders, Ben turned her around to face him.

"Come on, Jill, ease up. Elite and this acquisition shouldn't be the beginning and end of your world. It's just business, nothing personal, babe."

"This is my world." She surprised him by admitting it in a stiff, no-nonsense tone. "I've built my entire life around my career. My parents are lower middle class. They had few expectations for me. I'm determined to show them that that being black doesn't mean settling for menial positions. You should have higher aspirations, be somebody."

"And you think your parents are nobodies?" he

asked, his fingers making circles on her back. "Jill, look at me. You're lovely, intelligent, and you have a lot going on. You're also driven, maybe too driven. Corporations suck the life out of you. They take everything you have and give back very little—unless of course you're fortunate enough to be the owner."

The noise of whirring helicopter blades stopped Ben from saying more.

"Do you hear that?" Jillian said. "They're back."

Ben parted the leaves and peered out. "It sure sounds like it. But where are our men?"

He'd barely gotten the words out when the two men scurried out of the bushes directly opposite them and raced toward the clearing. The helicopter hovering above landed. Again two bags exchanged hands. The shorter of the men pocketed an envelope. Then, without looking around or conversing, they raced off.

"So yesterday wasn't a fluke," Jillian said, her voice filled with wonder. "This is a regular operation."

"Sure looks like it."

"I'm bringing this up when Michael and I meet with Franz and Marlon," she said, her voice filled with fervor.

"When is that?" Ben asked carefully.

"Tonight. We're having dinner."

That didn't give him much time. Elite was moving fast and he needed to move faster. He'd worked too hard to have his dream slip away.

"Let's say Franz accepts Elite's offer. When will you be leaving?"

"Shortly thereafter. I'm being sent off to South America on another project."

He felt strangely let down, as if he was about to lose a good friend. "Do you think Fontaine will hold onto the Bula if he's lucky enough to get it?" he asked, focusing on business again and determined to make the strange mood go away.

Jillian's response took a while coming. "Hard to say. Elite has nothing in the South Pacific right now. Restoring the property and flipping it might be the way to go."

Ben's fingers now kneaded the tense knots in her back. He switched the topic. "Do you ever take vacation? Put your feet up and relax?"

Jillian groaned. "Vacation? What's that? These past few weeks are the closest I've come to R&R."

"Then take a week off if it's owed to you. Stay here and spend some time with me."

Jillian fixed those serious brown eyes on him. "Why? Aren't you otherwise involved? Besides my life is in Chicago and yours is here. Foolish to pursue the impossible."

Ben chuckled. So she was jealous, and maybe just a little bit interested in him. He felt better.

"Simone is seventeen years old, jailbait in the States, if that's who you're referring to." His fingers again circled, squeezing her shoulder blades. "Come on, think about it. We owe it to ourselves to explore the possibilities."

He was pushing and knew it. But Jillian fascinated him in a way no other woman had since his wife's death. He'd never quite met anyone so focused, and who in many ways reminded him of himself. She pushed emotions to the side to be dealt with later. But why was this job so all consuming and so important to her? Was it the prestige thing? Money aside, it was a helluva life, always on the road, and at the beck and call of a tyrannical boss.

"We should be going," she said, when his fingers made contact with her bare skin where shirt and slacks had separated.

"Not until I do this."

A TASTE OF PARADISE 163

He bent his head and claimed her lips. At first she resisted; then his tongue probed and she loosened up. The kiss turned into an intimate dance.

Jillian opened up, allowing him access into the recesses of her mouth. Her arms slid around Ben's neck and he pressed his advantage. Twigs scraped his face and he forgot about everything except the fact he was able to feel again. Jillian smelled like a woman who'd taken a bath in citrus. It was heady and alluring. He pushed her shirt up toward her neck and she settled firmly against him.

She wasn't the kind of woman he wanted to take in a bush. She belonged in a comfortable bed, stretched out alongside him. But he didn't want to break the mood, sensing that if he stopped, any possibility of lovemaking would be over with.

Ben's hands circled her lace-covered breasts, found the clasp and popped it open. Jillian's firm breasts spilled into his hands. He kneaded the nipples and laved her neck with his tongue. She made little gasping noises. They needed to get out of the bushes and quickly. He slid his hands under her buttocks, squeezed, and lifted her up. She wound her arms around his neck, and spotting a tree in the shade, he settled them under it.

Jillian lay on top of him. Ben worked a finger under the waistband of the cotton drawstring slacks she wore.

"Take them off," he ordered.

She sat up, undid the string, and slid out of them. Ben took off his own slacks and practically tore off his underpants. Jillian did likewise.

"Protection. Did you bring anything with you?" she asked.

He scrambled up, found the foil package he'd optimistically placed in his wallet and sheathed himself. She lay on her back now, and he raised her legs up, settling himself on top of her. Entering her slowly, she arched upward and grabbed his back. Ben's fingers splayed across her buttocks, pressing her into him. She nibbled on his ear and her breathing grew shallow. He was caught up in the moment. Caught up in the smell and feel of her.

"Oh, baby," he said. "Oh, baby."

They were moving in tandem. She circled. He thrusted. Sensations he'd forgotten existed came to the fore. Ben nibbled the sides of her neck. Jillian gasped loudly. His knee nudged one leg even further apart and he dove into her sweetness.

"Ben," Jillian screamed. I'm going to . . ."

"I'm coming with you, baby. Arrrgh . . . I'm coming."

With what he had left, he gave a final thrust. When he let go, the entire world went black.

He came to slowly, his fingers stroking Jillian's back. The urge to have a drink was overpowering. This woman had left her mark on him in a relatively short time. He wondered if being lonely had something to do with it. No hotel or coconut manufacturing plant, bad as he coveted them, could ever make up for the feeling of a woman in his arms. Not just any woman. Jillian.

She stirred under him. "Ben, maybe it is time to go." She sounded so relaxed he wouldn't have recognized her voice. "Michael and I have a few things to discuss before our dinner engagement."

That was it. Her mind was never far away from business. So where did that leave him?

"Yes, it is getting late. We should go," he agreed, kissing her on the temple and starting up.

They gathered their clothing and quickly began to dress. What he didn't tell Jillian was that he had a meeting of his own.

Let her be surprised. In some ways he was as focused on business as she.

"Elite is prepared to make an offer," Michael said, splaying his long fingers across the mahogany table.

He'd positioned himself as the man in charge and Jillian resented that he'd taken over.

Franz Herrman seemed amused by the power play. He stroked his chin and appeared to listen intently to what Michael had to say. His expression gave nothing away. Cathy, his wife, sat beside him, a stunning Polynesian with beautiful eyes and a haunted look on her face.

Tonight Franz had pulled out all the stops. He was using his private dining room, a place that was amazingly European in design.

Around the dark mahogany table sat six people: Franz, Cathy, Marlon, Michael, Jillian, and a British gent who'd been introduced as Lucas, legal counsel for the Bula.

On the far wall, a gilt smoked mirror distorted everyone's reflection. Catty-cornered to that wall, a gigantic sideboard held chafing dishes and cutlery. A maid outfitted in full uniform, including cap, scurried back and forth fetching drinks and coffee and whatever the guests requested.

Jillian had worn a demure black business suit to the meeting. It felt rigid and restricting and made her feel mousy and unattractive. But it was what Michael expected, and what Elite considered appropriate for a business meeting.

"And just what kind of offer is Elite prepared to make?" Franz challenged. An unlit cigar waited at his fingertips.

"The Bula needs some refurbishing, that's going to cost," Michael countered, stalling. "Jillian's been here over two weeks and she's witnessed your problems. There's been a mysterious fire that some suspect an arsonist caused. Next was a bout of food poisoning, followed by a diving accident, which according to the investigators wasn't an accident at all. As a result, most of your guests have checked out."

"And your point being?" Marlon quickly interjected.

"My point being that bad news travels fast. Your occupancy rate is at an all-time low. You need this deal to stay afloat."

"You haven't answered my question," Franz reminded him. "How much money is Elite prepared to offer?"

Michael flicked an invisible speck off the cuff of his sleeve. Then in slow motion he slid the paper he'd been holding across the table toward Franz.

The German stopped its progress with a clap of his hand. He made a huge production of reading it, before shoving it Marlon's way.

"This is insulting." Marlon whizzed it back the way it had come.

Michael's fingers drummed the table. "It's exactly what the property's worth, maybe even a bit more than current-day value."

"What if I told you we have a better offer—an offer which comes with a guarantee that our employees wouldn't be tossed out on the street. We're assured the property wouldn't be sold once it's been fixed up."

Jillian froze. Ben had sold her out. He'd taken her off the cuff remark earlier and shared it. It was a snakish thing to do.

"I can't imagine a reputable company would be willing to pay more than we're offering. You've got quite a bit of debt," Michael said smoothly.

"That might be so, but the Bula's name and

reputation stand on their own," Franz snapped back.

"The property's run down, the service abysmal," Jillian offered. "As for the Bula's reputation, that's debatable. You've lost a star in the last year or so. Guests expect service. They want to be pampered."

"We've made an offer, take it or leave it," Michael countered.

"We'll leave it." Franz beckoned the maid over and ordered her to bring him a hefty glass of Scotch.

Jillian had thought the German wanted to unload this albatross. And she'd also thought Ben had the inside scoop when he'd mentioned Franz's wife's illness. Maybe that was a bunch of bull also. Franz's wife, though looking a bit wan, seemed fine to her.

She was beginning to smell a big fat rat. That rat had Ben Fuller's name written all over it. She wasn't about to cave, regardless of whether thinking of Ben made her go warm all over. Admittedly, she had a wicked physical attraction to the man. But that aside, she'd invested too much of her time to relinquish a coveted prize.

"So I take it you have a better offer," she interjected, before Michael could think of a quick comeback.

"We do," Marlon said benignly. He removed a pen from his shirt pocket and scribbled down a figure. "Now if you can meet this, then maybe we can talk." He slid the paper across the table again.

Jillian's eyes were riveted on the pen he was holding. It matched the one she'd found at the burned-out site, and the one she'd seen at Ben's home.

"Where did you get that pen?" she asked.

She'd gotten everyone's attention now. The attorney scowled at her.

"Would you like one?" Marlon asked, "There's plenty where these came from. I give them out as incentives to the staff."

Jillian's mind quickly went into overdrive. To think she'd suspected the worst of Ben. The pens were a dime a dozen. Maybe she'd have to rethink the whole thing.

"I'd love to have one as a little memento," she answered, softening her tone.

The maid returned holding two heaping platters of meat that smelled quite delectable. She set the plates down and minced off to the kitchen.

More dishes were brought out and the group began helping themselves. When coffee and a soufflé were served they returned to the business at hand.

"You'll need time to think this over," Franz said. "But don't wait too long. We are prepared to accept the more lucrative offer."

"Would that be from Ben Fuller?" Jillian asked.

The men all seemed stunned.

"Ben told me he was interested in the Bula," Jillian explained. "But I thought he would be reluctant to make an offer until the matter of the drug trafficking on the premises was addressed."

"What drug trafficking? Jillian, you'd better explain." This came from Marlon.

Everyone's eyes were on her again.

"Ben and I were taking a walk when we found a field with marijuana plants. A helicopter zoomed out of nowhere and two men who claimed to be employees handed over bags. Money was exchanged."

"Why didn't you come to me immediately?" Franz asked, his face taking on a waxen look.

The attorney, Lucas, seated next to him made a choking sound.

"Because we thought it might have been a one time thing," Jillian answered. "But it happened again."

"And neither of you mentioned it, until now," Marlon sputtered, sounding totally outraged.

"Ben didn't tell you?" Jillian said.

Franz and Marlon exchanged looks. "No, he didn't."

"And he went ahead and placed his bid even though he knew illegal transactions were taking place on the grounds?"

"And so did you. Here's your offer," Marlon tapped the paper that remained in the center of the table.

"Jillian, how long have you known about this?" Michael asked.

She knew she'd surprised him by bringing it up. But she'd needed leverage. Ben's offer was being considered seriously. Elite had to get back into the race.

"What exactly is Ben offering that we can't match?" she asked. "We've given you a fair price and we've told you we are prepared to pay severance packages to the employees who are let go."

"Ben gave his word that no jobs would be lost. He wants to employ more locals," Cathy interjected for the very first time. "The vision he has for the Bula is in line with Franz's and mine. He's a man of his word."

"So why are we here then if you've made up your mind?"

Michael shot up and Jillian stood with him.

"You have exactly twenty-four hours before Elite withdraws its offer," Michael said in a hard, cold voice. "We were prepared to pay cash, not a bad offer."

Michael stalked out of the room, Jillian trailing him.

Behind her, Jillian heard all hell break loose. She smothered a smile.

Chapter 17

"Way to go, Ben." Ricky slapped Ben's back. The contractor's dark hair was slicked back by perspiration. He used the towel draped around his neck to wipe the rivulets streaming down his cheeks.

Ben's team had won the volleyball game. Now the remainder of the group huddled around planning which watering hole to go to celebrate.

"What are you doing for the rest of the day?" Ricky asked as the others continued to chat. "I'm going to take a quick shower, then take a look at the warehouse again. I've got some ideas about how I can make the place work without costing you a bundle."

"I'm considering heading home and doing the same—showering, I mean. Then I'm going to try to find Marlon. I'd like to find out if Franz has considered my offer."

"And if he hasn't, what then?"

"I'll lick my wounds over several glasses of coconut water. Why don't you come over to my place and we'll talk after you're done."

"I might just do that," Ricky said, preparing to take off. "By the way, there's another hotel on the other side of the island that might interest you. It's got acres and acres of coconut trees. And the old man really wants to sell." Over his shoulder Ricky added, "Simone's home from school, so that's another incentive to visit you."

"She's too young for you," Ben admonished, pretending to give Ricky a stern look.

Ricky's crush on Simone was obvious. He followed her around like a little puppy dog with its tongue hanging out.

"Hey!" Cyndi, another of the volleyball players, came up to him. "You can't leave. We've got some celebrating to do." She punched Ben's arm.

"If alcohol is involved, I'm out of here."

"You're no fun." She placed a hand on her hip. "We're beginning to think you're anti-social, or is it that you'd rather spend your time with that Elite woman?"

Ben simply gave her a blank look. Amazing what everyone thought they knew. Spotting Marlon heading his way, Ben excused himself and loped off to meet him.

"What brings you to the beach?" Ben asked the manager.

"I was hoping to find you here. Do you have time for a cold drink?"

"Sure, if you make it nonalcoholic."

They found a table with a shady umbrella, ordered two glasses of passion fruit juice, and sat back and people-watched.

"So what's going on?" Ben asked after a while when Marlon didn't seem keen on initiating conversation.

"Why didn't you tell me you'd discovered drug traffickers on the premises?" Marlon began.

"Who told you that?"

"Jillian mentioned it at yesterday's meeting."

"What?" Ben gasped, truly taken aback. Jillian had promised not to bring it up. He'd thought they'd had an agreement. Now Marlon was sitting back waiting for him to offer an explanation.

The two glasses of juice were set before them. The waiter, assured that they needed nothing further, disappeared.

Marlon's hands circled his glass. "I've suspected for a while something was going on," he said.

"Then why didn't you act?"

"Because I couldn't prove it."

"What does Franz have to say about all this?"

Marlon thought for a moment. "He took it in stride. We've interviewed the staff and offered a bonus to anyone who knows anything. Eventually someone will come forward. Money talks."

Ben was tempted to ask if the manager suspected that Franz might be involved. But he wisely kept his own counsel. "Has Elite made an offer?" he asked.

"Yes, they have, and that's all I can say."

"And will a decision be made soon?" Ben probed.

"I'm guessing in a day or two."

"What's the holdup?"

"I don't know."

Ben decided to play his ace card. "If this isn't wrapped up in a day or so, I'm making a similar offer to the guy across the street."

"You're interested in Plantation Acres?" Marlon asked, sounding shocked.

"Why not? The property has promise. The Bula may be my first choice, but Plantation Acres means less work, and they're close to foreclosure and desperate."

"B—ut I thought you had your heart set on the Bula."

"I did, but this is taking too long. I may even consider withdrawing my bid."

"You'd let Elite walk away with the property?"

Marlon sounded truly outraged, as if he had a personal stake in it.

"If I have to," Ben said, standing and remembering his invitation to Ricky Lohman to stop by. "I have to go. Thanks for the drink."

Let Marlon mull over what he'd just said, convey his threat to Franz if necessary. It wasn't that he'd lost interest in the resort. His heart just wasn't into making this deal anymore. Not since he met Jillian. Their involvement, if that's what you could call it, had made him realize that as important as the property had once been to him, it wasn't worth creating an irreparable rift.

It hit Ben with a sudden force. He wanted this woman, more than he'd ever wanted any brick-and-mortar building, even more than his constant desire to have a drink.

And he was going after her, even though she'd broken her promise. He could not, and would not, let her leave for Chicago without declaring his intentions. He could only hope that she would have him.

"Okay, Ben," Marlon said, also standing. "You know I'm on your side. Let's hope there's something to tell you soon."

"Let's hope so," Ben said, his mind still on Jill.

Three hours later, Ricky Lohman still hadn't shown up. Ben had used the time to think. He'd decided if it were that important to Jillian, he'd let her have the property. There were others on Taveuni that would serve the same purpose. He'd concentrate his efforts on Plantation Acres, and if that didn't work out, then he'd explore the opportunity Ricky mentioned.

Ben paced the floor and decided that whiling away the time at home analyzing why Jill broke her promise served no purpose. He would find the woman and confront her. They would have a frank talk and he would tell her what he thought of her.

He poured himself a glass of coconut water and gulped it. The drink, much as he loved it, was a poor substitute for alcohol. He dismissed the thought. He'd come too far in his sobriety to take a step back. Taking several deep breaths, he splashed water on his face and decided to let the element of surprise be on his side.

Before he could change his mind, he was out the front door and heading for the bridal suite.

A gray sky and heavy billowing clouds signaled that rain was imminent. Ben let himself into the courtyard and loped up the walkway. Not giving it a second thought, he pounded on Jillian's front door.

He was forced to take a step back as the door flew open. Jillian stood glaring at him, hands on her hips.

"What do you want?" she snarled. He'd never seen her quite this angry.

Something was wrong. He was the one who should be angry. Furious actually.

"Is Michael here with you?"

"What does it matter?"

There was a rumble of thunder, followed by the harsh crack of lightning.

"I'd like to talk to you alone, so better let me in. It's about to pour." Ben placed a foot in the doorjamb before she could slam the door shut.

"I don't want you in here," she sputtered.

"Well, that's too damn bad. I'm in."

Jillian stood facing him, arms crossed. "You've got a helluva nerve."

"I could say the same of you."

She actually flinched. "You're the one who sold me out, now you have the audacity to show up at my door."

Ben took a deep breath; maybe there had been a misunderstanding after all. Although communication was the key, he couldn't, and wouldn't, confess his true feelings to an angry woman.

"Let's sit and talk," he said, crossing over toward one of the wicker chairs.

"I prefer to stand."

"As you wish. Now why are you so mad?"

Jillian's chest heaved. He watched her try to get back in check. Meanwhile he resisted the urge to gather her into his arms and kiss her senseless.

"I trusted you," she said in a tight little voice. "Yet you used an off the cuff comment against me."

Ben was truly puzzled. "What did I say?"

Jillian's breasts and shoulders continued to heave as she struggled to gather her composure. Outside, the rain was coming down in heavy sheets and the thunder made it sound like the heavens were falling.

"Yesterday I mentioned that there was the possibility Peter might fix the Bula up and sell it. You set up a meeting with Franz and Marlon before I could, and you used my words against me."

"I did not," Ben said, taking a step toward her.

Jillian took a step back.

"Then how did they know? Those words were practically thrown at me in the middle of negotiations."

Ben shook his head, tossing Jillian an outraged look. "Hasn't it occurred to you that your boss has a sharkish reputation in this business? He's known for making a quick buck and damned be humanity."

"The same could have been said about you a few years back," Jillian tossed right back at him. "I'm not sure you've changed."

Memories he'd prefer to forget surfaced. She'd pushed a dangerous button and he exploded.

He shook a finger at her. "Just wait a second. If anyone violated anyone's confidence it was you. You promised not to mention what we had witnessed. We agreed we would let it go a day or two."

"And I kept my promise," Jillian hissed, "I let a day

or two go by. I only used that information after I learned that you'd stabbed me in the back."

"God, woman, you kill me." Ben's palms clapped both sides of his head. Things had gotten way out of control and he didn't know if he could salvage them.

Jillian glared at him. Ben took another step forward until they were so close he could smell the Garden of Eve scent he associated with her. This time she did not move. He placed his hands on her shoulders. "If you want the Bula, honey, it's yours. I'm backing off."

"What?"

He could feel her body tremble beneath his hands. The phone jangled behind them. Dammit.

After five rings Jillian said, "I better get it."

Ben watched her pick up the phone and press the receiver to her ear.

"Yes, Michael. Sure I can meet you in the restaurant in five minutes."

She hung up and swung around to face him. "I don't understand. I thought you wanted this hotel. It seemed to mean everything to you."

"At one time it did," Ben admitted. "But that was before I fell in love with you."

Despite the heavy rain, he turned and left her.

Five minutes later, braving the deluge outside, Jillian made it to the restaurant. Michael was nowhere in sight. She took a seat and waited, thinking about what Ben had just admitted. His admission had thrown her into a tailspin.

Still, she was determined to focus on the business at hand. Michael had sounded serious, as if trouble were on the horizon. Better brace herself. She was in no mood to hear bad news and she sensed this discussion would not be good.

Spotting Michael, she waved.

He flung himself into the seat across from her. "You were right," he said, stripping off a dripping wet raincoat.

"Right about what?"

"Right about the fact that there's a huge drug operation going on on the premises. Two of the employees have just been arrested. It's made the news."

"Just what we need, another scandal," Jillian mumbled.

"I've already called Peter. His instructions are that we should walk away from this deal. He wants us to let things settle down a bit and then maybe revisit, making an offer in the next few months. You and I are catching a flight to Sao Paulo first thing tomorrow."

Jillian had been unprepared for this. Too much was happening, and way too fast. She was not prepared to leave.

"I don't even get to go back to Chicago for a day or so?" she asked, dazed.

Michael shook his head. "There's already a vice president in place to handle your part of the business."

That made her shoot out of her seat. "What do you mean?" She practically shouted. "You told me that Peter wasn't sure if he wanted to create another position. That he felt there were already too many layers in the organization. And you advised me, off the record, that is, to start looking at other companies that were a bit more liberal."

When Jillian had said her piece, blood roared in her ears and the veins at her temples throbbed. She'd done all this hard work and would be left with nothing. Not even the promotion she so badly coveted.

"Calm down," Michael said. "Take a deep breath and pull yourself together."

"Where did this person come from?" Jillian demanded.

Michael shook his head at the hovering waiter. "Not now," he admonished. He waited until the man left before saying, "She was wooed away from Lyndon and Wales."

"Peter hired Veronica Sabatino?"

"I'm afraid so."

"But she doesn't have the credentials I have," Jillian shouted, "and she certainly hasn't closed any deals that I know of."

Michael didn't say a thing but Jillian knew that he agreed with her. Veronica was a woman she had come up against a time or two. She was all show and little substance. They hated each other.

It was much too humiliating. Michael was expecting her to return to a job with her tail between her legs. Now she would have lesser responsibility. No way.

"Am I to continue to report to you?" Jillian asked. Something told her she already knew the answer.

Michael's expression told her there was more. "No, the reporting lines have changed. I wasn't supposed to tell you this, but you now report to Veronica."

"What!" A rather nasty expletive followed.

As far as Jillian was concerned the decision was made for her. "Tell Peter I quit," she said in a much calmer voice. "You're on your own tomorrow. Have fun in Sao Paulo."

She turned to leave. Michael was up like a flash, blocking her way. "Don't be too hasty. Another opportunity will come along. You'll get the next promotion. You know our company thinks highly of you."

"I no longer work for our company," Jillian said, flouncing off. "And incidentally," she flung over her shoulder, "if Peter really wants the Bula, it's his. Benjamin Fuller has withdrawn his offer."

She walked away, leaving Michael gaping.

Chapter 18

Three days and a great deal of angst later, Jillian had checked out of the Bula. She'd jumped into a taxi and asked the driver to take her as far away from the resort as he could, some place where she could find inexpensive lodging.

After making the rounds she'd managed to find a cute rental cottage overlooking the Pacific. The couple who owned it were British and currently on vacation.

Ignoring protocol, Jillian had e-mailed her resignation to Peter Fontaine, making it effective immediately. She'd then ignored his subsequent calls and his promises to ensure her a future promotion.

She'd also been up front with Marlon and Franz when she'd left, telling them that she'd quit Elite and was taking a vacation. Any questions could be referred to Michael, who was available by cell phone.

Now it felt good to spend time alone, but strange to have no meetings or obligations. Jillian had spent the last few days seated on the back deck, staring down at an azure ocean. During that time she'd done a great deal of soul-searching. She had enough saved up to live on for about six months and was certainly in no rush to get back to Chicago and her empty life.

Her one regret was not saying goodbye to Ben before she'd left. But she'd reasoned that time and space would help sort out her crazy, mixed-up feelings about him. She'd never once doubted his sincerity, though his professions of love had come as a shock and had left her even more confused.

Even so, in the last few days she'd had little time to reflect on his words or even examine her feelings. All of her adult life she'd been wrapped up in work. Romance, if that's what her brief encounters could be called, had taken a back seat. She'd let her career take over. It was how she defined herself, and now she didn't even have that.

Still a huge burden was lifted. She was finally free to do nothing but sit, swim and wander into the local restaurants. She didn't even have a phone. Her international cellular was turned in to Michael. For a woman who'd always stayed connected, she was suddenly disconnected.

Deciding that too much sitting around had already taken its toll, Jillian considered that a brisk walk would help burn off all that pent-up energy and clear her head. She'd exhaust herself so that sleep tonight would come easily.

Without bothering to check herself in the mirror, Jillian set off wearing the same crumpled pair of shorts and T-shirt she'd thrown on that morning. She carried a basket and headed for the shopping arcade where she meant to buy some groceries.

When she arrived, the little store was closed and there was no sign indicating when it would open.

What to do now? Next door there was a bar, maybe they would know the store's schedule.

* * *

"Hit me again," Ben said, waving his empty glass at the bartender.

He'd stopped at a tiny bar off the beaten track and, for the first time in a year and a half, had a drink.

One drink had led to several. Now he could barely feel the pain spiraling upward from his gut to settle in his chest. As his brain shut down, he wallowed in the mellow feeling, refusing to let guilt take over.

"Sure you want another one?" the bartender asked, the bottle of rum aimed at the glass and ready to pour.

"As sure as I'll ever be." Ben ignored the voice in his head telling him he was teetering on the brink of la-la-land. "Hit me."

Somewhere in the recesses of his brain he recognized he needed help and should call Ricky Lohman. Too late now, or was it? Screw Ricky, he decided.

Jillian's sudden disappearance had brought him here. She'd left without saying goodbye, a fact he'd learned from Marlon. It had hit him then that he'd lost the opportunity to really get to know her and explore any possibilities of "them."

"Is someone driving you home?" the bartender asked, his face blurry.

"What does it matter?"

"Matters to me."

The bar had been almost empty when Ben walked in. There were only a few local men perched on stools and well on their way to inebriation. He'd recognized the signs. Yet he'd ordered his first drink, belted it down and demanded another.

"After this one I'm cutting you off," the bartender said, capping the rum bottle.

"Oh, come on, Leo, give the guy a break," a man on the far end of the bar yelled.

"You live in walking distance," the bartender growled.

"I won't have your death on my hands. The most you can do is trip and break your nose."

"Been broken before," another of the patrons yelled.

Ben had no plans to get involved in the discussion. He sipped on his rum and coconut water, refusing to think.

"What can I do for you, young lady?" he heard the bartender ask a new arrival.

A voice he thought he recognized answered, "I was wondering whether the market next door is closed for the day." There was a long pause followed by a gasp. "Ben, is that you?"

Defiant, he picked up his glass and took another sip, tossing over his shoulder, "Who wants to know?"

"Jill. What are you doing here? And why are you drinking?"

Jill's name had a sobering effect. Ben set down his glass and squinted at her.

"You're still in Taveuni?" His words came out slurred.

"Where would I be?" she asked, facing him.

"Chicago. Hell, who knows?" He set down his glass, wiggling his fingers at her.

"You're drunk," Jillian said, getting directly in his line of vision.

Fuzzy or not, she was still the most beautiful woman he knew. Those long legs of hers had kept him up more than a night or two.

"I am not," he argued, though he was already having a hard time determining whether there was one or two of her.

"Please don't serve him anymore," she said to the bartender.

"You're not my mother," Ben slurred. "You got what you wanted, baby, and you hightailed it out of here without even saying goodbye. Now you're chastising me."

"Come on, Ben," Jillian said, tugging on his arm. "I'll drive you back to the Bula."

That gentle tug practically toppled him off the barstool. He stood and at the last minute found his balance. He crossed his arms.

"Keys, please," Jillian said, sticking out her hand.

"I'm perfectly capable of getting myself home."

"Just turn them over."

He shook his head but even that effort made him dizzy. Propping an arm on the bar, he steadied himself.

Jillian came closer. "Put an arm around me," she commanded.

A gruff male voice yelled from somewhere in the recesses of the room. "You heard the lady. Hand over your keys and put your arm around her. She's taking you home."

A very large man came out of nowhere. He towered over Ben.

"Who the hell are you?" Ben asked.

"Nobody you know. You're drunk and obviously this lady cares, or she wouldn't be offering to drive you home. Now turn over those keys or I'll take them from you."

"It's okay," Jillian said, quickly inserting herself between them. "I can handle him."

Glowering, Ben looked up at the towering giant. He had the presence of mind to recognize that he would never win a fight against this man, not that he'd ever been a brawler. But he wasn't a wimp either.

"Get out of my face," he said, jabbing a finger at the giant.

One of Jillian's hands patted his pockets. "Ah, there they are," she said, sliding her fingers in the space where his pocket gaped and fisting his keys.

"Way to go, lady," the giant bellowed as she removed the ring holding an assortment of keys. She placed an arm around Ben's waist and he didn't resist.

"How much does he owe you?" she asked the bartender.

"Tab's paid and here's his change." The bartender slid a stack of Fijian currency her way.

"Consider it your tip," Ben remembered to say.

Jillian took a tentative step, practically carrying him with her. Unsteadily, Ben tried his best to follow.

Outside, a blast of humid air hit him squarely in the face. Bile reached up to settle in his throat.

"I'm going to be sick," Ben said, pushing out of her hold. "Where's the bathroom?"

"There's none that I know of out here. You'll have to make do."

Jillian didn't sound the least sympathetic. Ben stumbled toward the curb, missed his footing and sat. He was aware of people around him, heard the buzz of passing conversations, and hoped that the world around him would stop spinning.

He clapped his hands to his head hoping that action would keep it upright, then dry heaved into the street. The scene registered that he was an embarrassment. Then a cool cloth was pressed against his forehead and a comforting hand rested on his arm. "Are you all right?" Jillian inquired.

He was not all right. He couldn't even see straight. But he was glad that she was sitting near him with one arm around his neck. The other held the cool handkerchief pressed against his head.

How long he sat there he didn't know. But eventually the objects around him steadied and he thought he might be able to get up.

"Where's your Jeep?" Jillian asked as soon as he showed signs that he might be able to move.

"On a side street."

The voice that answered was recognizably his.

"Which side street?"

Ben pointed in the direction where he thought he might have parked the vehicle.

"I'm going to find it and I'll come back to get you," she said, getting to her feet and heading off.

Ben didn't trust himself to follow her. He remained seated on the curb, ignoring the whispers of passers-by who hissed loudly, "Look at that drunk. Disgusting!"

He was never so happy to see a vehicle pull up. Jillian leapt from the driver's seat and quickly approached.

"Do you need help to get in?" she asked.

He'd be damned if he wouldn't make it there on his own.

Unsteadily, and after several tries, he managed to maneuver his way up and inside. Seated now, he suddenly felt very tired and was rapidly sobering up. The enormity of what he'd done finally hit him. He squeezed his eyes shut. He didn't want to think of it. Not now. He'd wait until he was fully sober.

"Don't you dare fall asleep on me," Jillian snapped. "I'll need directions to get you home."

She'd already put the Jeep in gear and was easing away from the curb.

Ben opened an eye. "Just follow the directions for resorts and it'll get you there." Then he burped.

"Disgusting! Hang your head out of the side window and hold on. I'm pulling over."

Ben was determined that even if he had to choke on his own bile he would not get sick in front of her.

"You know what?" Jillian said, making a quick U-turn and making his stomach turn over. "I'm taking you to my place."

"You have a place?" he said woodenly.

"I've rented a cottage."

"And the job that meant everything to you?"

"I'm unemployed."

She couldn't be serious. He stared at her. Jillian's face was slowly coming into focus.

"Marlon didn't tell you I quit?" she said, as if it wasn't any big deal.

"No, he didn't. He just said that you'd checked out of the resort."

They'd pulled up in front of a tiny cottage perched on the edge of a cliff.

"We're here," Jillian announced, stuffing his car keys into the bag she carried.

Ben got out and followed her up a dimly lit pathway and into the house.

Inside she asked, "Coffee?"

"Water, please."

"How are you feeling?"

"Like an eight-wheeler ran over me."

"Good." She pointed to an overstuffed couch. "Stretch out."

He didn't want to stretch out. He wanted to call Ricky Lohman. He needed his sponsor.

"Where's your phone?" he asked gruffly.

"I don't have one."

He had to get out of that house. The sight of Jillian in casual clothing, limbs exposed, was much too tempting. In his inebriated state he was bound to do something stupid.

"I need you to drive me back to the Bula," Ben said, coming to a sudden decision. "Just give me a few minutes to wash my face. Where's your bathroom?"

Jillian pointed up a hallway.

Ben did what he had to do and returned to find Jillian in the kitchen, fixing what looked like a salad.

"You need something in your stomach," she said without looking up.

"I need my sponsor more than I need food. I'm an alcoholic. I fell off the wagon and I need support."

Jillian just continued doing what she was doing. "Plates are in the cabinet above," she said. "Cutlery in the drawer."

Ben set the table, watched her pick up the salad bowl and bring it over.

"After we eat, I'll take you back to town," she said.

It suddenly hit him he'd never loved another woman as much as he loved Jillian. What he admired about her most was that she was able to stand up to him.

Chapter 19

"Why didn't you call me the moment you knew you were going to have that first drink?" Ricky Lohman demanded, getting right in Ben's face.

Jillian had dropped Ben off at the contractor's home instead of his cottage.

"You're drunk and you smell," Ricky said, taking a step back.

His sponsor's lack of empathy made Ben feel worse than ever. But then Ricky enveloped him in a gruff bear hug. "So why did you do it?"

"Stress, I guess."

"Stress!" Ricky shot him a dubious look. "You're used to stress. The Bula isn't the first property you've bought or sold."

"True. But it's been a while since I've come up against a major corporation. All that stuff happening on the property, dealing with Elite, was too much."

"More like that Elite woman, Jill, that got your tail in a spin. You fell for her hook, line and sinker."

Ben flinched. Ricky had always had the uncanny ability to see right through him. He didn't mince words either.

"I did," Ben admitted. "And what did it get me?"

"Sit," Ricky ordered, waving him to the sofa. "Let's talk this through. You walked away from a deal because you fell in love with the woman. She didn't go back to the States, that sends a mighty powerful message. Shouldn't you decide what you're going to do about her?"

"That's all I've been thinking about. And frankly, I don't know."

"Better do something quick. She's not going to remain on Taveuni forever. Can't have you popping into some bar every time you miss her."

Ricky was right, he needed to try to salvage whatever might be left between him and Jill. But first he needed to get back on track. Tonight's events were a huge setback and one he could not afford to repeat.

"I'm going to the first early AA meeting there is tomorrow," Ben said, making up his mind.

"Good idea. And I'm coming with you," Ricky said, slapping him on the shoulder. "Don't beat yourself up too badly, bro. You gave in to a weak moment and had a drink. Now move on and make sure it doesn't happen again."

Ben nodded. Remorse and guilt were eating him up. He was determined that he would never again give in to the urge to drink.

Realistically he knew that would be a tough challenge.

Jillian had just returned from the beach and was considering taking a shower when there was a knock at her door.

"Florist," a male voice announced.

She frowned, and thought for a moment. What would a florist want with her? No one knew where she was, except Ben.

"Are you sure you have the right address," she shouted through the closed door.

"I've got the correct address, ma'am."

She grabbed a cover-up and opened the door a crack. The delivery boy was partially hidden behind a gigantic arrangement of orchids, bird-of-paradise, exotic flowers, and ferns.

"Where shall I set these down?" he asked.

Jillian gestured to the coffee table, which held a stack of magazines.

"Over there, please."

The young man placed the urn on the table and turned, preparing to leave.

"Wait, let me tip you." She found money in the purse she'd left on the kitchen counter. The young man thanked her and left.

Jillian dug through the greenery, searching for a card. Could Peter Fontaine be making a last play at getting her back? It would take more than an elaborate floral arrangement to soften her up. She was not interested in working for a company she could not trust.

At the base, she found an envelope and withdrew the simple white card.

Thank you for coming to my rescue last evening.
Thank you for being you.
Ben

How sweet of him to send a tangible acknowledgement of his appreciation. Ben was a complicated man; tough as they came on the outside, but sensitive and vulnerable as well. All the components were very appealing.

Jillian buried her nose in the flowers, inhaling their cloying scent. She would have to find a way to thank Ben. In so many ways she'd been wrong about him. It had taken incredible selflessness to step aside and basically hand her the Bula. It also took guts to admit that he loved her, and what had she said? She'd left the man dangling.

Making up her mind, Jillian decided that later she would drive to his cottage and thank him in person. Maybe they could start over and try being friends.

Franz Herrman sat on Ben's verandah, a cup of coffee in easy reach. This afternoon the German did not appear his usual confident self.

"I'd like you to reconsider buying the Bula. I'm ready to sell," he said.

Ben, still suffering from an awful hangover, kept his expression neutral. He decided to play hardball.

"I'm no longer interested. I'm looking at other properties that would serve the same purpose."

Franz took a sip of his coffee and set his cup down. "This is hard for me to admit but I need to sell. I'd like you to buy the Bula, Cathy feels most comfortable with you as the owner."

Thank you, lord. "Your wife is a lovely lady," Ben answered.

"Yes, that she is. But her cancer's no longer in remission. She may not have long."

"I'm sorry, Franz. So sorry."

At least Franz was being given the opportunity to prepare. Ben's loss had been sudden. He'd been given no prior warning. Wham, bam, a plane had gone down. There'd never been closure. Memorial services didn't cut it.

Ben wanted to reach out and touch Franz's arm but he knew better. Franz wasn't the kind of man you got warm and fuzzy with. Cathy, even-tempered as they came, had brought out the best in him. It was said she kept her husband ethical.

"Okay, suppose you sell me the Bula, then what?" Ben asked. "Are you exploring any kinds of experimental treatment?"

"I'm thinking about it. But first I take Cathy on a long vacation, then we go to Switzerland and see what the doctors say."

"Okay, if I agree to what you're proposing. What about the marijuana situation on the property?"

Franz looked at Ben through weary blue eyes. "You probably already know two of the kitchen staff were arrested."

"Yes, I did hear. But I would imagine they were not acting alone. They must have been hired by someone on your staff."

The German shrugged. "If that's the case they're not talking."

"And if I am still interested in the Bula, how much are you willing to take?"

Franz named a figure. Ben sat up. "Did I hear you correctly? That's a lot less than your original figure."

Franz's shoulders were bowed. "I have no choice. I need to get out quickly. At this point I would even consider a small down payment, maybe even signing over the mortgage. But we'll talk."

Ben pitied the man. He'd always been arrogant and it was almost embarrassing to see him so humbled. But the offer was one only a fool would refuse.

"Okay, you've got a deal," he said, making up his mind quickly. "How soon can we make this happen?"

Franz sighed his relief. "I'll contact the bank and get hold of my attorneys. I'll push for later this week. Will that work for you?"

"Works for me."

The two men shook hands. Ben watched the owner of the Bula, who'd aged a decade, get into his car. After he left, Ben sat sipping on the cooling coffee and reflecting on how much he had to be thankful for. Good health for one, and a second chance to give back to a people who'd welcomed him with open arms and made no judgments.

He'd been blessed. Life was a fragile thing and way too short. Ben made a silent promise. No slip-ups again. He was an alcoholic, but that shouldn't stop him from living. His focus now had to be on this business. If Jillian wanted him she would have to come to him.

Decision made, he picked up the coffee cups and went inside.

Jillian rapped on the front door of Ben's bure and sucked in a breath. She was fairly certain he was at home because the red Jeep was parked out front. She took another deep breath, tamped down her trepidation, and waited.

Raising her hand, she was prepared to knock again, but the door swung open.

"What brings you here?" Ben asked, a wide smile on his face. He moved aside, allowing her to enter.

Jillian took a tentative step inside. She looked at the man beaming at her with such open admiration that she could not help smiling back. Today he was back to form. He wore walking shorts and a short-sleeved Polo shirt, giving a tantalizing view of his muscular arms. He looked nothing like the disheveled man she had rescued last evening.

"I came to thank you," she said, her eyes never leaving his face. "The flowers are beautiful, but certainly unnecessary."

There was a twinkle in Ben's eyes when he answered. "So you got them. It was the least I could do. You went out of your way to help a disgusting drunk. Frankly, you deserve more than a few pitiful flowers."

Jillian placed a hand on his arm. "Hardly pitiful.

They were beautiful and cost you a bundle." She smiled impishly at him. "No headache today?"

"Headache's gone," he admitted sheepishly. "Chased away by two aspirins. But seriously, I really am sorry that you were forced to witness the unpleasant side of me. Alcoholism is a curse and a disease that's hard to shake."

"That you recognize that is admirable," Jillian said.

"Nothing admirable about that." Ben took her arm. "Why don't we sit?"

They sat alongside each other on his comfortable couch, Ben's fingers making circles on Jillian's knee.

"I've been dying to ask you something," she admitted when the silence dragged on.

"Ask away."

"Did you once get arrested for DUI and indecent exposure, or was that something Peter made up?"

Dangerous territory. Jillian felt him tense up.

"Guilty of all of the above," Ben said.

Shocked, Jillian looked at him. She'd been so certain it was a Peter fabrication.

Ben went on to explain. "I was going through a horrific time. I'd lost my family and could barely think straight. Alcohol was the only thing that helped ease the pain—at least that's what I thought. I was drunk that day and I'd behaved inappropriately at an earlier meeting. I walked out and decided to go home. I badly needed to use the bathroom so I pulled off the highway. I didn't see the cop behind me. The rest you can imagine."

It wasn't funny, but Jillian did see the humor in the situation. Not the humor of Ben being drunk. She'd conjured up this image of a disgusting drunk exposing himself, not some man caught with his pants down in the process of emptying his bladder. Laughter rippled out.

"What's so funny?" Ben's expression indicated he was reliving the pain. "It cost my company a bundle.

I was forced to attend traffic school. Since it was a first offense and no one was injured, I got off with just having my hand slapped."

"I'm sorry," Jillian said. "I didn't mean to make light of it. It must have been embarrassing and disastrous when it happened. But look, you're no longer the man you were then."

"You couldn't tell by last night."

Ben grunted. Jillian could tell he regretted his fall from grace. He was still beating himself up. She slid off the couch, realizing he might need space. "Look, I won't hold you. I'm sure you have things to do."

Ben clamped a hand on her arm. "Actually, I don't. And there's something I need to tell you."

His touch made her heart rate accelerate. Treacherous hormones be damned.

"What is it?"

"Let's go for a walk."

A walk would be good. They'd be out surrounded by other people. Temptation would be held at bay. Only time would determine if her attraction to Ben was purely physical or if it was much more.

Jillian strolled alongside Ben through the almost deserted resort. Their walk took them by the abandoned warehouse.

Ben stopped abruptly in front of the building. Jillian shot him a quizzical look and asked, "Why are we here?"

He placed a foot on the crumbling concrete step leading to the entrance. "Franz Herrman visited me today."

"And?"

"He made me an offer I couldn't refuse. I'm buying the Bula."

It didn't come as a shock. She no longer cared what happened to the place. She had nothing invested.

"It's what you wanted." Jillian touched his arm. "It's all you wanted."

Ben fixed his tawny eyes on her. "You're dead wrong." Jillian felt the irresistible pull, a yearning to get next to him. She could not tear her gaze away. "It's what I thought I wanted, until I met you."

"Ben," Jillian answered. "I'm not sure I'm ready for this. I'm recovering from the loss of my job. I can't think clearly, and I'm not ready to commit."

"I'm not asking for a commitment. I am simply asking you to give us a chance. Can you do that?"

She thought about it, then began hesitantly, "We've only known each other a couple of weeks. That's not a long time."

Ben's arms wrapped around her. "Don't run away from me, Jill. Take the time. Let's get to know each other."

The sound of footsteps coming from inside the building caused them to freeze. Ben placed a finger to his lips, grabbed her hand, and practically shoved her into the nearby bushes. They remained there as the minutes ticked by.

The door of the warehouse eventually creaked open, and two Polynesians emerged, followed by the resort's elderly doctor.

"We're moving the operation," Dr. Charles said. "Your contact will arrive by boat. Go to the dock at midnight and be sure that you have the stuff."

"We'll be there, boss. But who's going to pay us?" a young woman Jillian recognized as a waitress asked the elderly doctor.

"Come to my bungalow right after, and there will be an envelope waiting for you under the doormat."

Nodding her understanding, the waitress took the hand of the man accompanying her and headed off.

Oblivious to being overheard, the doctor shuffled by them. They waited until he was gone.

"Are you thinking what I'm thinking?" Ben asked, straightening up.

"Seems pretty obvious to me. Dr. Charles is the one heading up this operation. Now who would have thought?"

"There was always something slimy about the guy. I could never quite put a finger on why I didn't trust him." Ben linked his fingers through hers. "Let's go inside and look around. I've got a feeling that this place is being used as a storehouse."

"You just might be right," Jillian said, following him in. "And if that's the case they've just been busted. I think we should go to the dock tonight."

Chapter 20

If anything, the inside of the warehouse smelled mustier than Ben remembered. One window on the far side of the building let in light. Ben sidestepped what looked like debris that had fallen from the ceiling and turned to Jillian.

"Be careful," he admonished. "Stay close to me."

She obliged by holding on to the back of his shirt. Ben wandered through the area, looking for signs of illegal activity.

"Over there," Jillian whispered, pointing. "I don't recall seeing tarpaulin before."

Ben didn't remember seeing it either and he'd been through the place plenty of times, and so had Ricky.

Gingerly he made his way to the far corner. Jillian was still holding onto his shirt. Something slithered across his foot and he kicked out.

Jillian screamed and clutched his shirt, almost ripping the fabric from his back.

"It's only a rat," Ben explained, watching the rodent skitter across the floor and slither under a pile of debris.

"Just a rat. I hope there aren't more where that came from."

A TASTE OF PARADISE

Ben chuckled, amused that she'd actually shown signs of being scared. They continued through the warehouse without further mishaps.

In the corner, a paint-stained drop cloth blended in with the floor. It looked like it might have been sitting there for ages, and would normally not be noticeable amid the junk.

"Do I dare pick it up?" Ben quipped. "What if it's home to the rodent's family?"

Jillian thumped him on the back. "Tell you what. I'll go stand over there"—she pointed to the window—"and you can do what you have to do."

True to her word, she let go of his shirt and headed for the window where the late afternoon sun streamed in, splotching the filthy floors.

"Jillian," Ben hissed. "Get over here. You'll never believe this."

He pointed to several burlap bags that had been cleverly hidden. It wasn't hard to figure out what they held.

Jillian was beside him quicker than he'd expected. Without saying another word, Ben pointed to the bags that looked like they were full to bursting.

"I think this is the stash," he said. "We'd better call the police."

Jillian crouched down and reached out a hand. "Let's make sure. It would be embarrassing if it turned out to be something else."

"Don't touch them!"

She turned around as if stung, giving him a quizzical look. "We'd look awfully stupid if we called the police and they held nothing incriminating."

"Then let me do it. Let my fingerprints be on those bags."

Gently he moved her aside and knelt down. Turning his head he said, "It may not even be worth opening, I can already tell by the smell."

An ancient voice came from behind them. "What are you doing? And what are those bags?"

Dr. Charles, the resort's doctor, hovered above. His skeletal physique appeared frozen as he stared at them in obvious shock.

Ben catapulted to his feet, facing the doctor. "What is it you think we're doing?"

The doctor stretched his lips, attempting to smile. "I don't have a clue. I just know that no one ever comes to this out-of-the-way place."

"You're here."

"I was taking a walk as I often do. I thought I heard voices."

If Ben hadn't overheard the previous exchange and seen the doctor, he would have thought nothing of his comments.

He decided that playing it dumb was the best course to take.

"We were walking by as well, thought we heard a noise, and decided to investigate. When we found these bags we guessed a vagrant might live here. Those bags probably hold his things."

Dr. Charles appeared uncomfortable. His rheumy eyes moved back and forth. "I keep saying the government should do something about the homeless. Now you've uncovered the poor sap's hiding place. You'll probably turn him in, and where will he live?"

"Oh, Ben, that would be terrible," Jillian said, playing along. "Let's just forget you ran across these bags and let's continue on our way."

Relief flooded the doctor's face, but there was still a noticeable glint in his eye. Ben sensed the moment he and Jillian turned their backs, those bags would definitely disappear.

"Doctor," Ben said, striving for affability and slapping the gaunt man's back, "it's a good thing we ran into each other. Did you hear I'm taking over the Bula? Can we find some place to have a private chat?"

Dr. Charles gawked at Ben. His face was now pasty white. "You're buying the hotel?" he asked, his voice high pitched and shrill in his dismay.

"That's right. There are just a few formalities to wrap up and it's mine." Ben winked at Jillian. "Will you be okay getting back to your place? Dr. Charles and I will need to find a quiet place to have our discussion."

Before Dr. Charles could say another word, Ben grabbed his elbow and maneuvered him out the door.

Left alone, Jillian wondered what to do next? Should she go to the lobby and call the police, or try to find Franz or Marlon?

Her instincts told her that she should not leave the warehouse. But Ben had Dr. Charles safely in tow and that should buy time. If she didn't do something about it, someone could return to haul away those bags. They might not be as frail as the doctor.

Jillian thought about all of the things that had gone down since her arrival. It would take only a few minutes to run over to the lobby, find a phone, and call the police. She raced to the entrance, pushed on the rickety door, and almost bumped into a man.

Jillian screamed.

"Hey, take it easy."

The man standing on the steps about to enter was someone she'd seen around the complex. He carried a bundle of rolled up papers under his arm.

"Is Ben in there?" he asked, his thumb jutted in the direction of the decrepit building. "And are you okay?"

Jillian was breathing more normally now. "He was,

but had to leave unexpectedly. He may be somewhere on the complex."

"You're sure you're okay?"

He seemed harmless enough. And sometimes you just had to trust.

"No, I'm not. Can you remain here until I get back? Make sure no one enters the building."

With that she raced off, heading for the lobby of the Bula and a phone.

Inside the large Tikki hut serving as a lobby, she scanned the area. The guest relations representative, recognizing her, nodded.

"Can I use your phone?"

"Certainly, Ms. Gray."

The phone was handed over, and Jillian quickly dialed the operator.

"Put me through to the police," she said quickly.

She was connected in an amazingly short time and greeted by a harried male voice.

"Sergeant Lin."

Jillian's words came out in a rush. "Please send the police to the Bula. There's an abandoned warehouse on the property being used to store marijuana."

"Who are you?"

A predictable question, and one she was not prepared to answer. Did she really want to get involved?

"That's not important. What's important is that you get over here as quickly as you can."

She hung up, thanked the hotel attendant, who'd been listening shamelessly, and retraced her steps. With any luck, Ben would be back.

Luck was with her. She spotted Ben holding an animated conversation with the man who'd agreed to stand watch. He waved to her.

"There you are. Have you two met?"

She shook her head, not sure she was in the mood for banalities.

"Jill, this is Ricky Lohman, my sponsor. You dropped me off at his home last night."

Jillian managed to give the man a curt nod. "I called the police," she blurted out. "They should be here any moment."

Ricky visibly gaped.

"Did you stop by to see Marlon and tell him what's going on?" Ben asked.

"Should I have?"

"Probably, but then again we don't know how far reaching this is."

"Where's Dr. Charles?" Jillian asked, her eyes scanning the surrounding area. "Tell me he didn't go back inside."

Ben shrugged. "Don't know and don't care. He may have gone looking for Franz. After I said my piece, he took off looking most unhappy."

"Speak of the devil," Ricky interjected, his attention riveted elsewhere. "Franz and reinforcements are here."

A group of people, Franz and Marlon among them, came hurrying up the path.

The Bula's owner swept up to them. "All right, you two, what's going on? If Inspector Watanabe hadn't clued me in I would still be in the dark. He was kind enough to drive over here himself."

Hearing his name, a rotund man with bobbling chins stepped forward. He nodded at them and stretched his lips into what was supposed to be a smile.

Franz continued, "One of his men mentioned a woman called to report drug trafficking on the premises. That woman would be you, Ms. Gray?"

No point in denying it, she'd been found out.

"Yes, I did," Jillian said.

"And the thought never entered your head that Marlon and I should be consulted?"

"Whoa," Ben said, raising both hands and coming to her defense. "Before you start beating up on Jill, go inside and look around. There must be enough pot on the premises to keep every resident in Taveuni high for weeks."

Franz grunted and led his entourage right by them, entering the crumbling building.

Ricky, Ben and Jillian followed closely behind.

Inside, Franz sniffed the noxious air, leaving Marlon to stroll the length of the room. The inspector busied himself poking about corners.

"Try the area to the far right, under the tarpaulin," Ben suggested.

The beefy inspector actually sprinted toward the area. For a man his size he moved quickly. Using his staff he lifted the edge of the tarpaulin.

"There's nothing here," he announced.

"What!" an ugly expletive came from Ben's direction.

"How could that be? I was only gone a moment," Jillian said. "Ricky, you were here. Did you see anyone enter or leave this place?"

"Not that I'm aware of."

Jillian's gaze swept the room; for the first time she noticed the open window.

"Look," she pointed. "That's where they made their escape."

Everyone charged toward the open window.

"What are we supposed to see?" the inspector demanded after he pretended to scan the area.

"Evidence that we are right. Someone had to have entered and left in a rush," Jillian explained.

"A number of someones," Ben added dryly. "It would have been impossible for one person to have removed the number of bags we saw."

Inspector Watanabe looked at them dubiously. "Perhaps you better start from the beginning."

Ben and Jillian exchanged looks. It was hard to determine whose side the policeman was on. He might be in cahoots with the drug lords for all they knew.

Ben began to explain what they'd uncovered weeks before, but omitted mentioning what they'd witnessed between Dr. Charles and the workers. He clearly didn't trust the inspector, and didn't seem sure about Marlon or Franz either.

"Well, this has been a complete waste of my time," Inspector Watanabe said, after Ben was through.

Franz stopped him in his tracks. "Wait, inspector, wouldn't it make sense to do a search of the property? If you're too busy, send around a couple of your men."

Watanabe grunted. "I'll see who I can spare."

"Why aren't you taking this seriously?" Ben demanded. Turning, he appealed to Marlon. "I've never been an alarmist but this is ridiculous. Two employees were arrested recently for drug trafficking, and we just uncovered where the drugs were being kept, yet we're being treated as if we're insane."

Marlon shrugged, seemingly unconcerned. "Inspector Watanabe doesn't seem to think it's a big deal. Besides there's no evidence."

That apparently did it for Ben. "Let's go, Jill. Coming, Rick?"

The two of them followed Ben to the door. A metallic object got her attention and Jillian bent over to pick it up. She shoved the pen in her pocket.

Four hours later she was still at Ben's cottage. Ricky Lohman had remained with them until Simone showed up, then he'd left, following Simone like a lovesick puppy.

After Ricky disappeared, Jillian said, "I should be heading home." She slid off the couch, stood up and stretched.

"Why don't you hang out for a while? We'll go to the docks and see what happens, then I'll take you home."

Midnight seemed a long way away. The thought of being alone with Ben, tempting as it was, scared her to death.

"I've monopolized enough of your time. I'm sure you have things to do."

"You're afraid to be alone with me," Ben stated. "Makes me wonder why."

His eyes never left her face and she schooled herself not to react. She would not give him the satisfaction. "Because," Jillian answered, striving for the truth, "whenever we're alone, you and I end up in bed."

"And that scares you. I must be losing my touch." Ben laughed, and Jillian found herself laughing with him. "How about you and I drive over to the Bouma Waterfall to watch the sun set?"

She'd been dying to see the waterfall in Heritage Park. Since it was only a fifteen minute drive, she gave in to temptation. "Okay, you've made me an offer I can't refuse. Let's go."

Ben quickly placed an arm around her and steered her toward the door.

Chapter 21

"It's twelve-thirty, do you think anyone will show?" Jillian asked, smothering a yawn.

For the last forty minutes she and Ben had been hunkered down in one of the fisherman's skiffs that had been left abandoned on the beach waiting to see if anyone would show up.

"Let's give it another ten minutes and then we'll go," Ben answered, his fingers kneading her neck.

Above, an orange-red moon illuminated white-on-white sand. Forty minutes had gone by slowly. During that time Jillian was enjoying being seated in the v of Ben's legs. He had both arms looped around her neck and they'd been talking quietly.

Ben blew a breath against her nape, then kissed the spot. "Tired of being with me, already?"

"Tired, period. It's been a long day."

"And about to get longer. Look, there's a boat pulling in."

Ben watched as two men jumped off and tied the boat to the dock. The men stood looking off into the distance as if awaiting someone's arrival. A few minutes later there was the crunch of footsteps on sand. Three shadows emerged carrying what looked like sacks on their backs. Muffled conversation followed as the sacks exchanged hands.

"Recognize anyone?" Jillian whispered.

"No, no one."

"What do we do now?"

"Stay put and listen. Maybe we'll learn about their plan."

The boat's engine had started up again. The three men, having successfully completed their transaction, were back on the dock.

As they walked by the skiff, Ben placed a finger to Jillian's lips.

"Better go collect our money," one of the men said.

"Yes, and better do it quick. The old doc says the envelope will be waiting under his front doormat."

They loped off in the direction of the bungalows.

Ben waited several minutes to be sure they had left. "I think we should follow," he said to Jillian, helping her up.

Hand in hand they walked through the deserted complex and toward Dr. Charles's bure.

The area was ablaze in lights when they arrived and surrounded by people. Three men were being stuffed into the back of a police car, and the ancient doctor was being handcuffed.

Marlon stood off to the side talking to policemen.

Grabbing Jillian's hand, Ben decided to make themselves known.

"Hey, what's going on?" he asked, approaching Marlon.

Marlon shaded his eyes and took a step toward them. "Ben, is that you?"

"Yes, it's me and Jillian. Why is Dr. Charles being arrested?"

"Looks like he headed up the drug ring. All three men pointed their fingers at him, now he's being taken down to the station for questioning."

Marlon began to explain that one of the men previously arrested had also implicated Dr. Charles. Franz had been insistent that undercover cops stake out the doctor's premises.

"Do you have enough to make charges stick?" Ben asked.

"The police think they do. Those three people you see being taken away told the police he was the one they reported to."

Jillian spoke up for the first time. "I wonder what made him do it?"

"Money. Greed."

"I thought he had plenty of that."

"Regardless. The more you have the more you want," Marlon said wryly.

Ben confided what they'd witnessed earlier. "We just came from the docks. A boat pulled up and bags were unloaded. We followed the men here."

"That information needs to be given to the police," Marlon said. "Officer, we've got two witnesses," Marlon called, without waiting for them to agree.

After that, things moved quickly. Ben and Jillian had no choice but to go to the station where they were questioned and filled out their statements. It wasn't until after five o'clock in the morning that they ended up in their respective beds.

Four days later, Jillian had just come back from a run. She was bone weary but at the same time energized. She booted up her laptop and noticed she had an e-mail from Michael. For a moment she sat debating whether to open it. Hearing news about Elite would only be depressing, she wasn't sure she was ready for that. Curiosity finally got the better of her and she clicked on the link.

Michael's message was unbelievable and unexpected. If anything it got her adrenaline flowing.

I just wanted to touch base with you and let you know that I've tendered my resignation. I've been offered a position as Senior Vice President at Rowan's International. How would you feel about coming aboard as acquisitions vice president?

It was a dream come true, an answer to a prayer. All she needed to do was click the reply button and say, "Yes." But Jillian hesitated. She'd been feeling more relaxed than ever this last week or so. There were no knots in her stomach and even the tension lines around her mouth had softened. Now what to do?

Jillian was not unfamiliar with the company. Rowan's International had established a reputation in Europe. And now the organization was slowly making inroads in the United States. They were becoming a force to be reckoned with. From everything she'd heard, the company paid well. And the added bonus was that she enjoyed working for Michael.

What was the problem then? She'd been enjoying her downtime. Forced to slow down and think, she'd readjusted her priorities. For years her identity had been linked to her job, and she'd worked hard to fight a stereotype. It had been a personal mission to show her family that being black didn't necessarily mean being poor and downtrodden, and she'd already proven that.

She would have to think about Michael's offer.

Think. What's there to think about? a little voice whispered in her ear. *You're nuts. This is what you've always wanted.*

A knock on the door got Jillian's full attention. She left the laptop running and hurried to the door.

"Who is it?"

"Ben."

"I'll be right there."

Jillian hadn't seen him since the drug bust. She'd assumed he'd been busy with his plans to take over the Bula. She smoothed her hair, gave a quick glance in the mirror, and decided she would have to do.

Ben greeted her with a hug. "Hi, stranger. Figured I'd stop by and take you to lunch. I want to discuss a business proposition with you."

She narrowed her eyes, gazing at him. What sort of business could they possibly have to discuss?

"You'll have to give me a few minutes to get myself together," she said, waving him to a seat.

She raced into the bathroom, her heart still thudding and took a quick shower. Now what to wear? Thumbing through the closet, she found linen shorts and a matching blouse, and quickly climbed into them. She added a touch of make-up for good measure, and raced back.

"Okay, I'm ready," Jillian said, a lively spring in her step.

"I'd say."

Ben's eyes traveled the length of her, settling on her legs. Jillian found herself blushing. She was doing that and a lot more, especially when she was around him.

Seconds later, they were seated in the Jeep and heading for a local restaurant that Ben assured her would be a treat.

Ben pulled up in front of a tiny house with several colorful umbrellas out front. Almost every table held people sipping colorful concoctions and sampling the fare of the day—barbecued shrimp on a skewer.

"This is really charming," Jillian said, following him up a shell-strewn path with twinkling white lights woven through the shrubbery. Large cages held squawking parrots and birds she wasn't familiar with.

"Eve's is special. This is where the locals eat."

"Ben," a petite middle-aged woman greeted. "You

haven't been by in a while. I wondered what happened to you." She looked expectantly at Jillian.

"This is my friend, Jill, Eve," Ben introduced, taking Jillian by the elbow and moving her forward.

Eve beamed at Jillian. "Welcome. What's your preference for seating? Inside or out?"

Ben looked at Jillian.

"Your choice."

"Out, if you can find us a table."

"Give me a minute and we'll have one cleared and ready." Eve gestured to a young boy who looked like he might be in his teens. "Get table four set."

While they waited, Ben led Jillian around back to a pond where huge lily pads floated and lazy goldfish swam. In minutes, Eve was back, ushering them to their table.

Seated, and coconut water poured, Jillian broached the subject. "So what did you want to talk to me about?"

"I've reached an agreement with Franz. Come next week, the Bula is officially mine. I'm going to need to make changes."

"Congratulations." She meant it. She was happy for him. Ben had wanted that property from the very beginning. Jillian took a sip of the chilled water and waited. He obviously had something on his mind and would eventually get to it.

"I'll need someone with business acumen to help make the transition," he continued. "My goal is to have the place restored to its old self and that will mean renovating. I want the hallmark to be gracious service but I want to retain the charm. You'll make that happen. I'll give you free rein."

"You're offering me a job? Why?" Jillian stared at him, not totally comprehending. She barely registered that menus were being set down before them.

"Because you'd be perfect," Ben said, smiling at

her and sending her heart rate soaring. "You've got the experience. You've seen world-class resorts. You can operate behind the scenes, mentor the local management staff, and make it happen. My time would then be devoted to the coconut plant, making sure it's up and running."

Jillian's fingers played with the napkin before her. What Ben had just proposed was preposterous. She'd always lived in a big city and immersed herself in corporate life. She doubted he would take kindly to any changes that she would implement. She'd want to update and provide services rivaling those of upscale western establishments, and she'd want to attract clientele that paid big bucks.

Michael's offer was more viable. It came with the kind of salary that she was used to, not that Ben had talked to her about money. And Chicago was home. All of her worldly possessions were there. Still she couldn't dismiss Ben's proposal, her opportunity to put her personal stamp on the resort. It was tempting and different, and she'd get a chance to work alongside Ben.

"I'll have to think about it," she answered, her attention focused on the menu now, a menu that was beginning to blur. Ben's presence had that effect on her.

"I'll need an answer shortly," he said, picking up his own bill of fare and perusing it.

"What if I agreed?" Jillian asked carefully, "And what if my vision is vastly different from yours?" She eyed him over the top of her menu, waiting.

He didn't disappoint her, diplomatic soul that he was. "We'd discuss it, and hopefully come to a compromise. Ready to order?"

He made it sound so easy, as if staying in Taveuni would not be a huge life change.

Jillian placed her order, reflecting all the while.

She'd been offered two options, both vastly different, but appealing in their own way. But could she give up her dream of a high-powered position, and the fast-paced life she'd built for herself? Could she walk away from her expensive high-rise and the trimmings of success? Was she willing to cast her lot with a recovering alcoholic, regardless of how good-looking and caring he was?

She had a lot to think about. And whatever decision she came to would require that she put emotions aside.

Chapter 22

"I'm thinking you could salvage the basic structure if you placed reinforcements here and here," Ricky Lohman said, circling the circumference of the warehouse again, Ben at his side. He pointed to several spots in the old building that needed obvious repair.

"Hmmm," Ben said, nodding his agreement. "That's certainly an alternative that would be less costly, but I am not looking for a temporary fix. I need something that will withstand time."

Ben had never actually done the grunt work in construction but he knew Ricky was giving him sound advice. The contractor had always looked out for his interest, professionally and personally.

"I've got two sets of numbers for you," Ricky said. "I've got pricing for an entirely new structure, and I've got figures for working with what we have. The foundation is sound and a few beams are salvageable. The rest, well who knows? My men are willing to throw in a few man-hours of labor each day for free. Shouldn't we get started?"

Ben continued to walk the circumference, scrutinizing the place from every angle. He would like nothing better than to get started on his beloved project, but there was so much that needed to be done at the hotel.

"I'll look over the numbers tonight and get back to you," he said. "Sorry it's taking this long, but I've been dealing with all sorts of problems. This manufacturing plant's been put on the back burner until I can get a handle on the hotel. Marlon has quit. He gave me two weeks notice."

"That's a bummer. I thought he would definitely want to stay now that you have taken over." Ricky whacked him on the shoulder with one of his rolled-up blueprints. "What's the deal? Wasn't your woman supposed to step in and manage that aspect of the business, leaving you free to focus on this project?"

Ben smiled wryly, "My woman, as you put it, has not gotten back to me. She's still mulling things over, trying to decide whether she's accepting an offer from the big guns in the States, or staying in Taveuni and working with me."

Ricky eyed Ben curiously. "Didn't she quit that highfalutin job with Elite when they screwed her over?"

"Yes, but she's had an entirely different offer."

The night Ben had shown up at Ricky's place drunk, he'd told his friend all about Jillian and how much he loved her. He'd also mentioned that he would like nothing better than to have her work alongside him.

Now he shamelessly admitted, "I peeked at Jill's laptop when she was out of the room the day I was over. I saw an e-mail from her old boss offering her a job."

"So?" Ricky said, a sparkle in his eye and a teasing expression on his face. "Why hasn't she hightailed it off to the States? Maybe you should turn the fabled Fuller charm up a notch. It works with all the local women."

"Because I can't match the kind of money a big

corporation would offer. What I can offer is a secure and challenging job."

"Money isn't always everything," Ricky said sagely. "Have you tried telling the woman how you feel about her?"

"I handed her the Bula. She must know how I feel."

"Shucks, I expected more of you. If Simone were to give me one bit of encouragement, I would be strewing roses in her path. I'd be telling her how much I loved her, not letting grass grow under my feet."

Glad for the switch in conversation, Ben said, "Simone needs to finish college. And you, my friend, if you are at all serious, need to develop discipline and patience."

"Who's talking about discipline and patience?" Ricky raised an eyebrow. "Move this romance forward. It's going around in circles. Neither of you are seventeen."

Ben pretended to glare at him. He recognized what Ricky said was true, but he didn't know what else to do. He'd told Jillian he loved her, he'd handed her his precious hotel. The only thing he could do now was wait and see.

"Thanks for the lecture. I've had just about enough of this place for today," Ben said smoothly. "Let's go see what's happening at the cricket game, unless you have something better to do."

They headed over to Mallory Square where a lively cricket game was underway. The Barbadian team had an awesome bowler and though the Fijians were losing hands down, you couldn't tell by their loud cheering.

"Isn't that Jillian over there with Desmond Bailey?" Ricky said through the side of his mouth.

Ben looked over at the makeshift bleachers where Jillian and Desmond were seated. When the Fijian bowler knocked all the wickets down, the couple were on their feet, embracing, jumping up and down.

There was a tug at the base of his gut and he felt his

chest tighten. So this was why there hadn't been a word from Jillian. Desmond was keeping her busy.

"Ben," Ricky called, astute as ever. "Don't let the sight of them get to you. It could be innocent, just two friends passing time with each other."

"Well, this old friend is going to take a walk over and see what's going on. Coming?"

Ricky chuckled. "'Course I'm coming. I wouldn't miss the entertainment for the world."

Ben and Ricky sauntered across the field and toward the bleachers where the couple sat. Desmond and Jillian appeared oblivious to their arrival. Their eyes were glued on the game. Ben, with Ricky following, climbed the bleachers, and slid into the vacant seat beside them.

"Hey, you two," Ben said the moment he was seated.

Jillian gaped and set down her paper cup beside her. Ben could smell the acrid contents. Beer.

"This is a surprise," she said, smiling.

"Is it?"

Desmond, who had his arm around Jillian's shoulders, nodded at them.

"Hey," he said. "Isn't this exciting? Too bad our boys are getting a severe whopping."

Ben grudgingly answered, "Well, the Barbadians are tough to beat. They're pros at the game."

Jillian remained silent, shifting uncomfortably. Good, let her squirm. Ben kept his eyes on her.

"Do you have plans for after the game?" he asked impulsively. He was aware that Ricky was totally tuned in and found the whole exchange amusing.

Desmond nudged Jillian. "Do we, hon?"

Hon? Why was Desmond acting like he owned Jill? And when did all of this happen? What did he miss?

Ben pressed on. "Ricky and I are thinking of hitting the Beach Shack afterward. The old lady who runs the place serves huge portions. Why don't you join us?"

"You're on," Desmond answered without consulting Jill. She tossed him a murderous glare to which he seemed oblivious.

"Maybe some other time. I've got a few things to do," she quickly interjected.

"They can wait until tomorrow." Desmond ran a hand across Jillian's bare shoulders. She was wearing a strapless top exposing flawless cinnamon skin. "You can take a couple of hours off to have a meal."

"Yes, Jill," Ben said, forcing a smile. "You won't want to miss more Fijian home cooking. It's not like we'll be there all night."

A huge roar came from the crowd around them. Ben's focus returned to the field. One of the Barbadians up to bat was running. Screams and whistles penetrated the air and there was no point in continuing the conversation.

"Way to go," Ricky whispered, jabbing Ben in the gut. "Better move in quickly and stake your claim. That Desmond has always been a sly one."

An hour later, all four were seated at a table on the beach watching the sun set. Jillian didn't seem to have much to say. She sat silently gazing out at the ocean. Desmond remained at her side, an arm loosely thrown around the back of her chair.

Under the table, Ben nudged Jillian's foot. She blinked at him. But at least he'd gotten her attention.

Desmond seemed at ease and kept initiating conversation. "So," he said. "What's the story with these guys who got arrested? I'm beginning to think that all the stuff happening at the Bula might be in some way linked. I mean the resort was up for sale, so they probably knew that someone would uncover their operation. Why not do everything in their power to drive the buyer off? My feeling is that old fool Dr. Charles couldn't have acted alone."

That thought had crossed Ben's mind more than a time or two. But he couldn't imagine who would have partnered with Charles. Not Marlon, that was for certain. He'd often confessed to Ben he didn't know why Franz kept the old man on.

Ricky was the one who answered. "My guess is you're right. Dr. Charles wasn't the only one involved. The man can barely walk and he's lazy. How would he have discovered fields of marijuana plants and set up an intricate operation requiring a helicopter or boat? There's got to be a heavyweight behind this."

Ben kept his eyes on Jill, only the slight ticking of her right eye indicated she was uncomfortable. Good. He hoped his presence made her squirm.

Desmond continued to ramble on. "You're not suggesting the current Bula management is involved? Wasn't Franz the one pushing the police to investigate? And Marlon as far as I know is squeaky clean. Hey, Jillian what do you think? You haven't said a word so far."

"I'm sorry," Jillian said. "What do I think about what?"

Ben, now feeling quite smug, winked at her. "Everyone seems to be speculating that there's a big cheese behind the marijuana operation, and that Dr. Charles wasn't acting on his own." He leaned across the table and fixed his attention on her escort. "So has Jill told you the good news? I've offered her a job."

Desmond reacted by picking up Jillian's chair with her in it and holding it up high.

"Yes," he said, pumping the chair up and down.

Ben wanted to throttle him.

Jillian screamed, "Put me down!"

"You've made my day," the owner of the scuba diving franchise said, setting Jillian back on the concrete patio floor again. "That means you're staying here. When do your duties officially start? And what will you be doing?"

"I haven't agreed to anything," Jillian said crossly. "Ben and I need to talk. Will you excuse us?"

It was just what Ben had hoped for, time alone with Jill. And she'd made it easy.

Ben crooked a finger at her. "Good idea, babe. Let's take a walk."

Without another word, they headed for the beach and away from the others. At one of the older broken-down piers, Ben stopped and took Jillian by the shoulders. "So what's going on between you and Desmond?" he asked.

"Nothing. I ran into him a couple times at the beach. We talked. He asked me to go to the game and I accepted."

Ben didn't know what to believe. Desmond made it look as if he and Jill were pretty close. It didn't look to him like this was their first date.

"I thought we had an understanding?" Ben said, looking directly at Jillian.

She bit down on her lower lip, looking at him as if he spoke a foreign language. "You're jealous. You have no reason to be."

"Why not? I haven't heard from you in days, then you show up at a cricket match with him."

"Desmond and I are friends."

"Friends don't call each other 'hon.' The man seems to have a rather proprietary attitude where you're concerned."

"And that's got you bent out of shape. Come on, you're a grown man."

Ben groaned. Did he have to spell it out? What was she not getting? "Woman, you're making me crazy. I've told you how I feel about you. I've offered you a job you have yet to say yes to. I don't know what more I can do."

"And I told you I would think about it. Ben, I can't make you any promises. You're offering me a whole new life—a life that is foreign. This type of decision can't be made overnight. We need to go back. We don't want to be rude; the others are waiting."

"As you wish," he said, releasing her abruptly. Jillian's step faltered. Regaining her balance, she turned and began retracing her steps to the restaurant, leaving Ben with no choice but to follow.

Ben was angry with himself. He'd allowed his emotions to take over and he'd botched this up real good. He'd meant to tell Jillian how much he cared for her. Instead, he'd come across like a bully, and a physically abusive one at that.

Jillian strode ahead of him, not even looking back. She headed for the table where the others were still seated.

She pasted a smile on her face and announced, "We're back."

Desmond held out her chair. As Jillian slid into it Ben heard him whisper, "Is everything okay, babe?"

Four days later, Jillian was sitting down in front of her computer accessing her e-mails. Michael had written to her again, as he'd done almost every day.

I need an answer from you or I'll have to start contacting headhunters. Is there something more I can do to sweeten this deal? Rowan's International is offering you stock options, an expense account and car allowance. What else can we do to make this happen?

Jillian drummed her fingers against the Formica desk. The company was offering her everything she wanted, so why couldn't she make up her mind?

Ben, that's why. Drat the man and his very tempting offer. She was letting her feelings for him—confused as they were—prevent her from making an intelligent decision. Ben was upset with her but surely he should understand her dilemma.

She found a blank sheet of paper, searched through her pocketbook and found a pen. Jillian looked at it blankly, finally remembering where it had come from. It had been lying on the warehouse floor.

Marlon had said he gave these pens out as incentives and there were plenty where this came from; probably no big deal.

Focusing, she began to list the positives and negatives of accepting Rowan's International's offer. Then she listed the pluses and minuses of staying on Taveuni and working for Ben.

Afterward she perused the list. The positives were all in Rowan's favor. Clearly it was a no-brainer and it made practical sense. Before she could change her mind she began typing her response to Michael. Rowan's International's offer was what she'd always dreamed of. It came with the right money and title and she wouldn't have to uproot her life.

Her little vacation was over with. Time to get back to the real world and resume her life.

Chapter 23

"I'm sorry," Jillian said. "Yours is a very tempting offer, but I've made my decision."

Ben simply stared at Jillian, his large hands splayed across the desk, his jaw muscles working.

Turning Ben down was turning out harder than she'd thought possible. She was walking away from a man she really cared about, leaving him for a job and a title she coveted. Jillian had convinced herself it was for the best.

She looked around the spacious back office noting the subtle changes Ben had already made. He'd rearranged furniture, hung ferns, and posted an action plan on the recently painted walls. Timelines were highlighted in neon, ensuring that his goals would be met.

Jillian's eyes watered. With a concentrated effort she blinked back tears and pulled herself together. Why was telling Ben she couldn't work for him this difficult? It was for the best.

Ben looked tired, tiny lines fanned out around his eyes and bracketed his mouth. He left the safety of the barrier separating them, a gigantic chrome and glass desk.

"Not as sorry as I am," he said, advancing. Jillian stepped back, taking a calming breath. Ben closed the space between them. "I can't say I am not disappointed." The pad of his thumb grazed the side of her face and she shivered. "When will you be leaving?"

"Probably in the next day or two. I'll need to firm up reservations. Michael expects me to start the job next week."

Jillian's hand covered that thumb, pressing it against her flesh, liking the warmth and feeling of the rough texture against her skin.

"In that case, let's have one last dinner together. Shall I pick you up?"

"Thank you, but I've rented a Jeep."

She hoped that Ben wouldn't notice the moisture on her eyelashes and how much her telling him she was leaving had hurt.

"I'll let Anna know that this is a farewell of sorts," he said. "She'll make something special." He picked up the phone. "See you at my bure at say, seven tonight."

"I'll be there."

No longer trusting herself to talk, Jillian left him.

Ben, for whatever reason, was disgruntled and irritable. "What about flowers, candles, a nice tablecloth?" he snapped at Anna.

His housekeeper, never one to get riled, smiled at him. "Don't you worry, Mr. Ben. I have it all under control. All you have to do is sit and talk to Ms. Gray."

Easy enough for her to say. Ben absent-mindedly ran his fingers through hair that was getting longer. This evening had to be perfect, better than perfect. Memorable. Perhaps Ricky was onto something. Maybe he should just go for it and be honest.

Jillian would be there in half an hour and he still

had to shower and dress. He'd use that time to compose what he planned on saying.

"What's for dessert?" Ben hurled over his shoulder as he walked away.

Anna's serene reply followed him. "Pineapple upside-down cake and vanilla ice cream."

Twenty minutes later, he was ready. Ben had opted for comfortable but casual. He'd chosen black. He wore midnight slacks, a black T-shirt, and he'd even moussed his hair.

He took one last walk through the house, making sure everything was perfect. Anna had outdone herself. She'd set a beautiful table using an immaculate linen cloth she'd found somewhere. She'd filled a crystal vase with red roses and orchids and placed it in the center, and she'd laid out china. Scented candles had been lit and placed in hidden alcoves. The smells coming from the kitchen had Ben's mouth watering.

As seven o'clock approached, Ben grew more nervous, he squelched that ever present urge to have a drink. And never one to articulate feelings or express deep emotion, he was again tempted to leave things as they were. He'd always operated under the premise *I'll show you, not tell you*. The truth was, communication had probably been the only problem between him and his late wife, Karen.

Ben followed the mouthwatering scents to the kitchen. There he opened up one of Anna's huge pots.

"Go away," she said, playfully swatting him with her spoon. "Go stand on the verandah and wait for your lady."

He retraced his steps, went outside and began pacing the length of the verandah, rehearsing again what he would say. He doubted whatever he said would make much of a difference. Jillian's mind was made up. But at least when she left he would have a clear conscience. He could at least say he'd spoken his mind.

A black Jeep pulled up. Jillian climbed out of it carrying a bright red shopping bag and wearing those silly Jimmy Choos. Ben hid a smile. Jillian's stride had bounce to it now. She waved at him—a far different person from the prissy, overbearing woman who'd charged onto the island determined to have her way.

"Hi," she said, her smile a mile wide. "I have something for you." She swung the gift bag off the tip of her index finger.

"For *moi*?" he asked, accepting the gift. "Should I open it now?"

"No, save it for later."

"Careful." He offered her an arm as they mounted the steps, looking pointedly at her feet. "I thought those had been retired."

"They will be after tonight. I'm wearing them for old times' sake. Call me sentimental."

That produced a deep belly laugh on his end. Jillian could really be charming when she set her mind to it. He was determined that he would not make this a sad farewell. It would be an evening he would remember for a very long time.

Anna peeked out the open front door and waved. Jillian managed a wave back before the housekeeper discreetly disappeared.

On the verandah, Ben linked his fingers through hers, but kept her at arm's length.

"Did I mention how nice you look tonight? I especially like the hair."

And she did look nice. She was wearing one of those very feminine dresses with a wide skirt that swayed as she walked. A wide belt cinched her waist, making it look tinier than ever. Jillian's hair had grown out and she kept it off her face with little clips that had butterflies on them. The severe woman he remembered was no more. To Ben, she was the most beautiful woman he had ever met, and the most feminine.

"Thank you," she said, her eyes holding a sparkle. "You're hardly chopped liver yourself. Just look at you."

Anna appeared, setting down a chilled pitcher of coconut water and the hors d'oeuvres she'd made from scratch.

"Nice to see you again, Ms. Gray."

"Jillian."

After she'd left, and they were seated on a wicker settee, Jillian said, "It was awfully nice of you to invite me to dinner. I thought you would be mad and want nothing to do with me."

"I am disappointed," Ben admitted. "I'm disappointed you didn't accept my job offer. And I won't pretend that I'm not feeling rejected, but I do realize you need to do this for you."

He wound an arm around her shoulders, bringing her closer to him. "I told you I loved you, Jillian. It's a blow to my ego you don't feel the same way. So I shall have to settle for friends."

Jillian turned to face him. She cupped his jaw with both hands. "We are friends and I do love you. "

Her sincere admission floored him. He needed to ask, needed an answer. "Then why aren't you staying and giving us a chance?"

There was a startled flicker in her eyes. He could tell his directness had taken her by surprise.

"Because Michael is offering me everything I have ever wanted and what I've worked for. If I stay I'll have regrets. I'll be thinking what if. I won't want my feelings to turn into resentment. I care about you too much."

There, he had it, though it didn't make her leaving any easier. How could two people who professed to love each other want such different things? What about the storybook endings he read about, where people declared their love and tiptoed off into the sunset together?

Still, he was touched that she'd opened up to him. Jillian came across as tough, but she was vulnerable. This was a case of bad timing on his part. But repeating that to himself didn't help much. Somewhere he'd read if you loved something enough you should set it free. If it came back to you then it was meant to be. He'd let Jillian go, but he still had tonight. He would live in the moment.

Ben picked up the platter, selected a plump scallop wrapped in bacon, and popped it into Jillian's mouth.

"Mmmm, delicious," she said.

"What are your plans when you get home?" he asked.

"First I'm going to air out my condo. Then I'm going to call my parents. I've only been in touch with them through e-mail."

"No boyfriends?" Ben asked, needing to know.

"No, no boyfriends. I have friends but no one I'm serious about."

"And this company you mention, Rowan's International. You think you will be happy with them?"

She nodded. "They're progressive, diverse and open to change. A far cry from Elite and less set in their ways."

"Then I wish you well," Ben said, kissing her on the cheek. "Shall we go in to dinner?" He offered her his arm.

Jillian took it and together they entered the cottage.

Anna served up a five-course meal but Ben barely registered what he ate. Jillian also seemed to have problems digesting. She shoved food around her plate and made appreciative murmurs.

When coffee was served they retired to the living room.

"Shall I open up my gift now?" Ben asked.

"Yes, go ahead."

Ben untied the bow on the bag and removed an oblong object. It was wrapped in purple tissue.

"Slightly bigger than a bread box," he quipped.

"Open it and you'll see."

Jillian's smile was that of the proverbial Cheshire cat. She watched with increasing anticipation as he tore the tissue apart and removed a framed photograph. Ben held it up to the light, squinting. "This is wonderful. Where did you get it?"

"Ah, wouldn't you like to know."

It was an aerial view of the Bula on a beautiful sunny day. The photographer had captured the buildings, gardens and ocean perfectly.

"I love it," Ben pronounced. "Thank you."

He couldn't help himself; he needed to touch Jillian, feel her, smell her. He wanted to carry the memory of Jillian in his heart forever.

"Come here, you," he said, enfolding her in his arms and kissing the top of her head.

A throat cleared behind them. "I'm leaving, Mr. Ben." Ben opened his eyes and over the top of Jillian's head, spotted Anna.

"Thank you for your help," Ben said graciously.

Jillian pushed out of his arms. He already felt a part of him was missing.

"Yes, Anna, thank you for a lovely meal. You will take good care of Mr. Ben for me."

"I don't understand," Anna said, sounding bewildered.

"I'm going back to the States," Jillian explained.

"You can't." The words were whispered. "You won't be happy there. You two belong together."

Ben's housekeeper echoed his feelings but he wisely kept quiet. "Good night, Anna," he said. "See you tomorrow."

When she was gone, he turned back to Jillian, rubbing her forearm. "I'd like to make love to you one last time. I need to hold you in my arms and show you how much you mean to me."

Jillian stood quietly looking at him. She seemed to be at war with herself. Then, turning her back to him, she raised her arms and said, "Will you unzip me?"

Ben eagerly complied.

It had all happened so fast. Ben asking to make love to her and her agreeing. Now she was lying on her back in nothing but the ridiculous Jimmy Choos that he insisted she keep on, claiming it was a turn-on.

Jillian closed her eyes, inhaling his unique smell and liking the weight of his body on hers. She wanted the moment to go on forever. She wanted to remember the texture of his skin against hers, to hear his rapid breathing in her head when she went to sleep at night. She wanted to savor these memories and remember it all.

The light from the candles flickered across the ceiling, bringing with it the scent of citrus and mango. The heat from Ben's body melded with hers. She twined her legs around his back, digging her heels into his buttocks and arched into him. Her nails scraped skin as she clung and he pumped into her. A feeling so sweet, so achingly wonderful took over. It needed release.

Release came in a spasm of convulsions and tangled limbs. Jillian now knew with certainty that Ben, wonderful caring man that he was, would always have a piece of her heart.

Chapter 24

Three months later, on a cold and blustery winter day, Jillian let herself into her apartment. She set her bags down in the vestibule, kicked off her boots and sank wearily onto her sectional leather sofa.

Jillian's limbs ached and her ears were clogged up. She was definitely coming down with a cold.

Times like this she wondered how different things would have been if she'd stayed on Taveuni. No point in regrets now. She'd made a choice—a choice that paid handsomely. She reasoned she was in a melancholy mood because negotiations in London had not gone well. Nah, if she were truthful, she hated the choice that she'd made.

Jillian had arrived in Chicago to find Rowan's International in turmoil. She'd taken over a position in what could easily be termed a start-up organization. And although the company was well-established in Europe, they didn't have a clue how business was conducted in the United States. The few European managers who'd been sent over clearly hated Americans and made derogatory comments about the U.S. and its people when they thought they could get away with it. Generally they were autocratic in their approach.

Jillian was being sent off more and more to put out fires the Europeans had started. She was wearing several hats and functioning in several capacities. The role of vice president of acquisitions came with little or no support staff and she was also saddled with the cumbersome paperwork.

Her mind wandered to thoughts of life on Taveuni and Ben, whom she'd kept in touch with by e-mail. His hastily written messages told her how busy he was getting the coconut manufacturing operation up and running, and he'd intimated the hotel was coming along. A staff member had been promoted to manager of operations. He'd said she wasn't innovative but managed to get the job done. Ben had also mentioned Ilya had flown in to help.

The mention of Ilya had set Jillian's teeth on edge. But there was nothing she could say or do about it. She'd made a choice. She'd chosen to return to the life she knew and was familiar with and in so many ways she regretted it.

Now the Christmas holidays were around the corner. In a few days she would be heading for Zurich to put out yet another fire. She barely had time to shop.

In stocking feet, Jillian entered the spacious kitchen where the answering machine sat on the counter. A blinking red light and a flickering dial indicated the machine wouldn't accept another message.

Wearily she depressed the button, listening with one ear to her mother go on. She wanted to know what Jillian's plans were for Christmas and if she would be joining them for the traditional holiday dinner.

There were messages from friends and a recent message from Michael. She wondered absent-mindedly why he hadn't called her cell. Duh. Because after getting off the plane, she'd forgotten to turn the thing on, that was why.

Michael's voice sounded frazzled and curt.

"Jillian, Jillian!" he yelled. "I need you to call me the moment you get in."

Jillian groaned. What could be this urgent? She'd been in London for two whole weeks and during that time she'd not had one day off. All she wanted now was a warm bath, food, and her familiar comfortable bed. Her grumbling stomach needed attention and soon.

She pushed the STOP button, delaying hearing the other messages. Opening up a kitchen cabinet, she found a mug, poured in water, and set the cup in the microwave. She badly needed to get rid of this chill. Sticking a slightly stale cracker in her mouth, she began nibbling on it, and then dumped the remainder of the box in the trashcan under the counter.

Better get it over with and call Michael.

Jillian punched in the programmed number. The phone never rang. Michael's words rushed out at her the moment the connection was made.

"Where the hell have you been?"

"What the hell do you mean, where have I been?" Jillian snapped back. "I've been on a plane heading home, that's where."

"Brace yourself," Michael said. "I need you again."

"For what?"

She knew she sounded churlish and irritated, but didn't care. The truth was she was tired.

"We've got problems. There's something going on in the Los Angeles office. One of the executives quit, taking with him a few key staff members. We were just days away from sealing that deal in Cabo. I'll need you on a plane first thing tomorrow. You might as well pack as if you're going to be there for a while. I don't know when you will be back."

Jillian's expletive was loud and colorful. She removed the steaming cup of water from the microwave and dunked in the tea bag.

"Michael, surely you can find someone else to go. You promised me these three days. I've earned them."

"That might be so, but things change. I need an executive's presence on the West Coast until things stabilize."

She took a huge gulp of tea, almost burning her tongue. "You don't know how long that will take. The holidays are coming up. I'd resigned myself to being in Zurich. Now you're telling me there's been a change of plan. I'm to go to L.A. Who's handling the problem in Zurich then?"

"We'll put Zurich on the back burner. Los Angeles takes priority now, then off to Zurich you go."

Well, she'd be damned. At times like these she wondered why even keep the condo. She was never there.

"Did you think to ask how I am?" Jillian said to Michael. "Well, I'm sick. I have a flu lurking. My ears are stopped up and still haven't popped."

"Take a couple of aspirins and go to bed now," his cold reply came. "You've got an E-ticket waiting at United's terminal. You'll have plenty of time to rest tomorrow in those comfortable business class seats."

"I'll see how I feel," Jillian said, hanging up. "I'm not promising that I'll make that flight."

But she already knew that as much as she bitched, she would be on that plane tomorrow. She couldn't help herself.

Tossing back a couple of aspirins, Jillian gulped the remaining liquid in the cup. No point in unpacking. She would take the same soiled clothing, toss in a few lightweight outfits, and have her laundry done at the hotel.

She'd just stripped off her clothing and climbed into comfortable flannel pajamas when she remembered that she hadn't listened to the rest of the messages. Exhausted and her temples throbbing, she trudged back to the kitchen, made herself another cup of tea, and sat down on a stool at the counter.

The droning went on: solicitors, her friend Angela telling her she had tickets for *Oprah*, a colleague inviting her to a wine-tasting—and then there was Ben.

Jillian set the warm tea mug down with a trembling hand. She turned up the volume on the machine with palms that were damp. Her cheeks were flushed from the fever, she decided. And when she heard his voice, an uncontrollable shiver skittered down her spine. The timbre of Ben's voice had her legs quivering and knees knocking. But she decided it must be the cold settling in.

"I'd hoped to catch you at home, Jill," he said in his deep baritone. "Looks like I'll be in the States for the holidays. I'm having difficulty getting some of the materials I need for the plant. The only way to assure that I do is to meet with the distributors before they disappear for the holiday. I'll be flying in to Los Angeles on December eighteenth. I was wondering if you'd consider taking a trip to Los Angeles, or maybe I can come to Chicago to you. And Jill—" The machine cut him off.

Jillian's heart practically stopped. Ben, who'd sworn not to set foot in the United States ever again, was flying into Los Angeles of all places. He'd be there when she was there. She needed to get in touch with him. But damn, she didn't even know where she was staying yet. He did have her cell phone number. Maybe he would call back.

She could try calling the Bula, she supposed. Where was her purse with her trusty pocket organizer and her cell phone when she needed it? She'd tossed it on the floor of the apartment when she entered.

Jillian hopped off the stool, knocking over the mug

of tea. Dark liquid sloshed on the floor. She grabbed for paper towels to sop the tea up, and despite a heavy head and a nose that was filling up, trotted into the vestibule to find her purse.

The cell phone was still in its case; she removed it and pushed the ON button. The icon on the face of the phone signified she had messages. Jillian dialed voice mail, punched in her password, and hearing Michael's voice again, impatiently skipped his message. There were several other rambling ones from business colleagues that she would return when she had the chance. Then at last she heard the voice she'd hoped for. This time Ben had left her the name and number of the hotel where he would be staying.

Hallelujah! Despite the congestion in her chest, and a lurking headache, Jillian's mood turned into a light and airy one.

She practically pranced back to the kitchen, wrote a check and quick note to her housekeeper, wishing her a happy holiday and explaining that she would be gone for an indefinite period. Then she reminded Bonita that she hoped she would care for the condo in her usual way.

Almost hugging herself with joy, and now kissing Michael for making this trip possible, Jillian went into the bathroom to run her bath.

Ben sat in the stuffy living room of his mother's apartment, wishing she would open a window or two. This was relatively new living quarters for her. He knew what a sacrifice it had been to sell the house in the Valley and move into an assisted living facility.

But this was better. She'd fallen and broken her hip and if it hadn't been for a neighbor checking on her, who knew how long she would have lain on that floor.

Ben's sister, Sasha, along with the doctor, had

insisted that Ava move into a place where meals would be delivered and there would be regular human contact. It had taken some argument, but Ava Fuller had finally agreed.

Ben had used this little trip as an excuse to see his mother, who in turn could be both selfish and loving. She had instilled in him a fierce independence and the desire to succeed.

Now they sat awkwardly facing each other.

"So how are you really, Mom?" Ben asked, breaking the uncomfortable silence.

"How do you expect me to be?"

Ben whooshed in a breath. So now she was going to play the martyr role. He wasn't in the mood to entertain her self-pity.

"The hip's fully recovered. The doctor said you're in excellent physical health," he said. "Is it your spirit that's damaged?"

Ava scowled at him. She was not a bad looking woman and wore her seventy-two years well. "There's nothing wrong with my spirit that being in my own home wouldn't fix."

"Your home's been sold, Mom," Ben answered, grounding her in reality.

"Don't remind me. So what really brings you here?" Ava sniffed, her eyes behind owl-like glasses giving him a speculative look. "You haven't been back to the United States in years. You've been hiding in that godforsaken place ever since Karen and my grandchildren went home to God. Something bad must be wrong."

Ava could be insensitive and cruel at times. He would not let her goad him.

"I built a home on an island that I love," Ben said evenly. "I bought a hotel and I'm building a manufacturing plant that I'll run. Mom, I've moved on."

"Hmmmph! And what about your drinking problem?" Ava charged on. "Who would ever have thought that I would have raised a drunk?"

Ben took several deep breaths. Best to take the high road on this. He'd done as much as he could do. His mother was in excellent physical health, or so it seemed. It was her own spirit and attitude that needed repair.

He rose, preparing to head back to his hotel.

"Look, I have to be going. I'm having dinner with a friend." He placed his business card on the table. "If you need me, Mom, you only have to call."

"What I need is my home," she said, her eyes watering.

Despite the fact that she'd said hurtful things to him, Ben wrapped her in a warm embrace.

"You can make this place home, Ma. At least here you have friends. The woman in the apartment next to you stopped me on my way in. She said she's tried talking to you but you don't seem particularly friendly."

"She just wants to get into my business," Ava sniffed.

"That might be so, but it's always nice to have friends."

Ben kissed her cheek and left her. Jillian had agreed to meet him for dinner and he had no intention of standing her up. He had a big surprise for her.

Chapter 25

"I'm meeting Ben Fuller," Jillian said to the formidable looking maitre d' who stood, arms crossed like a sentinel. "Has he arrived yet?"

Jillian had taken a taxi to the chichi restaurant in Beverly Hills that Ben had chosen. It was totally out of character for him, she thought.

The snooty looking man examined her as if she were something the cat dragged in and adjusted his half moon glasses. He continued staring at her as if she now spoke a foreign language.

What was the problem here? Jillian wondered. Did she have lipstick on her teeth, or maybe he just wasn't used to interacting with a successful looking African-American woman. But this was L.A. after all, not some backwards little town.

"I'll check my book," he said at last, stretching his lips into a thin smile. Straightening up he said, "Ah, yes, your Mr. Fuller's here. He is waiting for you at the bar."

Jillian frowned, at first not comprehending. Ben waiting in a bar was not a good sign.

She decided a side trip to the bathroom was in order, but not because she had to go. She needed a few minutes to check her appearance and gather what was left of her already shaky composure. How would she react to seeing Ben again? How would she handle it if he were drunk?

Inside Mirage's very feminine bathroom, Jillian managed to find a place at the mirror. She smiled politely at one woman flossing her teeth and nodded at another bent on recreating her face. Looking around, she took in the decor. The place was papered in pink and gold wallpaper and reminded her of Hollywood in the fifties. Muted lighting from the ceiling bathed the area in golden rays and lavender divans were angled in strategic corners. No one seemed to want to lounge. They were all intent on repairing worn make-up.

Jillian examined her profile in the oversized mirror. She tucked the hair that she'd let grow out behind her ears. After freshening her lipstick, she added a dab of blush and prepared to face the man she'd chosen a career over—a career she had come to hate.

One finger tucked under the strap of her pocketbook, she strutted into Mirage's glitzy bar, which was buzzing with people. She spotted Ben immediately. He had one foot propped on the brass railing and both hands wrapped around a highball glass. For a moment Jillian's heart stopped. She hoped he wasn't drinking again. And she hoped she wasn't the reason why.

As if sensing her presence, Ben turned toward her. Jillian was totally mesmerized by his gaze. Her steps slowed as Ben's eyes roamed the length of her. The months apart didn't seem to matter. Her stomach quivered and the tickle in her throat had nothing to do with developing a cold.

Ben raised his highball glass in greeting and took a slow sip.

Memories washed over her. Jillian remembered the selflessness that he'd exhibited, handing her over a hotel that he'd wanted badly. She remembered the passion and sensitivity with which he'd made love to her, and she remembered how graciously he'd let her go to pursue a dream that had quickly turned into a nightmare. God, she'd been so wrong to let him go. Could she possibly get him back, she wondered, and what would it take?

Smiling, Jillian made her way toward him. It had been years since she'd seen Ben in a suit and although he'd let his hair grow long enough to curl around his collar, the air of authority still remained. He was by far the most handsome man in the place, and certainly the most charismatic.

Ben set down his glass on the bar and met her halfway.

"You look wonderful," he said, sweeping her into his arms.

Although Jillian's breathing had quickened she still managed to say, "Not as good as you."

When he pushed her away from him, her hands remained on his lapels, stroking the fabric as if it was his flesh. Ben stood there examining her as if she were some precious gem. Finally he said, "You've lost weight, babe. Have you been on a diet? You could use a bit more meat on your flesh."

Was he saying he didn't like the way she looked?

"I've not been on a diet," Jillian answered. "I've been so consumed by work there are times I don't remember to eat."

"Not good. Not good at all."

She didn't smell alcohol on him and she heaved a sigh of relief.

"Why did you choose the bar of all places to wait for me?" she asked. "This has got to be tough on you."

His hand on the small of her back, he guided her back to where he'd been standing. "I needed to test myself and see if I could do it. And I have. For the first time in a long time I've not been tempted to have a drink."

"Good for you. So what's in that glass?" Jillian tapped the sides of the crystal with one finger.

"Club soda and lime."

"That's a relief. For a moment there, I wondered."

Ben gave her his infamous chip-toothed smile that had become his hallmark. Jillian wanted to die. That smile had kept her up at night. It had filled her dreams and left her tangled limbs aching. She gave into another urge, needing to touch him, and ran the tips of her fingers across his knuckles. "Okay, so now that you've passed your little test, can we eat? I'm starving."

Ben flashed her another devastating grin. "Of course, we can. Nothing's changed with you, ma'am. Still bossy as ever."

Jillian whacked him with her bag. Oblivious to the people around them, Ben pulled her up against the length of him and gave her a heart-stopping kiss. It seemed to go on forever. Behind them a couple of men cheered.

"We're making a spectacle of ourselves," Jillian hissed when at last he released her.

"Think so?"

Nothing had changed between them. The magic was still there. There was none of that awkwardness Jillian had anticipated. Taking her hand, Ben maneuvered them through the crowd, heading for an opening on their left, which was the entrance to the dining room.

There, a hostess greeted them as if they were old friends. They were shown to a reserved booth sheathed in champagne colored gauze and tied back with red and green ribbons. In a hidden recess, a quartet played traditional Christmas carols and a few brave souls gyrated on a very tiny dance floor.

Jillian inhaled the pine scent from the monstrous Christmas tree in the corner. For the first time she actually felt in the holiday spirit. Instead of sitting across from her, Ben slid into the booth beside her. His thigh rubbed against hers in a most intimate way. And the smell of his tangy cologne quickly replaced the pine.

"Tuscany?" Jillian teased, wrinkling her nose. "My favorite."

"Since when are you an expert on men's cologne, ma'am?"

Jillian winked at him. "Wouldn't you like to know? It's my all-time favorite scent, guaranteed to make me crumble."

"I'd like nothing better than to have you crumble," Ben said, sliding even closer. He was so close she could feel his body heat and her senses reacted to the delicious smell of him.

"What's the saying?" he said, eyeing her slyly. "When in Rome do as the Romans do. I've returned to the rat race, so no point in smelling like a rat."

His mood was light and made Jillian giggle. "Oh, you," she said. "How did your meetings go? Did you get everything settled?"

Ben had been tied up with appointments these last few days and she'd been so busy that it had taken some finagling to make tonight happen—she'd canceled her dinner appointment with a client, claiming to have a headache she just couldn't shake.

"I wouldn't say settled, but I did make progress. With the holiday coming up, most of the decision-makers were heading out of town. I offered to pay the express rate if I could get my supplies by mid-January. My mother's here as well, so I managed to kill two birds with one stone."

Jillian was surprised since Ben had never ever mentioned having a mother that was alive.

"Your mother lives here? How come you've never mentioned her?"

He shrugged. "We're not that close. My father passed away a few years ago. Six months before Karen and my kids died."

"Oh, Ben, I'm sorry. This has to be painful for you. All those losses in a relatively short space of time."

He nodded, "Yes, but I've come to terms with it. Time is a wonderful healer and I've learned to appreciate each day. Life is a precious gift to be savored and living is something one should do every day."

Ben then told her about his visit to his mother's assisted living home, and her reaction to his surprise visit.

"It's got to be a difficult adjustment for her," Jillian said, feeling for the woman. "I couldn't imagine giving up my independence and moving into a place that's not really my own. My parents are getting up in age but they're still active. If anything happens they have each other."

"I think we should order a drink?" Ben suggested when she was through. "How about one of those cranberry-colored drinks in the fancy glasses that that willowy blonde is holding?"

Two Cosmopolitans later, club soda for Ben, Jillian summoned up the courage to ask, "How's Ilya?"

Ben groaned. "Her usual overbearing self. Thankfully she went home for the holiday. With any luck I'm hoping that's where she'll stay."

That made Jillian feel somewhat better. Ben sounded as if he really didn't care where the woman was. She'd feared she had competition but Ben made it sound like there was none.

"So tell me about this job of yours?" he said, while

they were waiting for their entrees. "Is it turning out to be all that you'd hoped?"

"I hate it," Jillian admitted, a catch in her voice. "The position is what I thought I wanted, but now I don't know. I'm always exhausted and my life isn't my own. I'm beginning to think I made a huge mistake."

Their dishes were set before them. Both had ordered duck garnished in pineapple and asparagus tips in cream sauce.

Ben waited for Jillian to take her first bite before commenting. "It's not too late to chuck it all in, you know. A job at the Bula's still waiting for you if you want it."

Jillian looked at him in wonder. "You're kidding, right? I let you down once. Why would you trust me again?"

Ben claimed the fork she was holding and set it down on her plate.

"Because seeing you again has made me realize that you weren't some momentary distraction. I've missed you, Jill. Over time I've come to realize how much I miss having a family. You're the woman I want to have children with."

Jillian stared at him. How could he possibly be serious? But truthfully she'd been thinking along those same lines. Ben had simply articulated everything she felt.

Returning to Chicago had been a reality check. She'd immersed herself in work, hoping to forget, but work no longer had the effect it once did. There was an emptiness inside her. She'd felt an overwhelming need to connect with someone special and though she hated to admit it, she'd thought about the babies she might never have. Were she so blessed, she'd raise those children to do right and instill in them values that were important to her. What exactly was Ben suggesting?

"So what do you think about my proposal?" Ben pressed.

"What do I think about what?"

"Giving us a chance, quitting that job you hate and coming home to Taveuni with me. It would give us a chance to build something special."

It was all happening too fast, she needed time to process this. Ben hadn't come right out and said he loved her, but he'd said he was willing to give them a chance, and that said so much. It had taken her months and space to realize that she really truly cared for Ben Fuller.

During those months, Jillian had compared him to every man she encountered and all had come up short. No one, but no one, made her feel like Ben did.

Before she could change her mind, Jillian came to an immediate decision.

"I have several obligations I'll need to take care of," she said. "I'll need to give Michael a couple of months notice. I owe him that."

"Is that a yes, I hear?" Ben practically shouted, garnering the attention of the surrounding patrons and kissing her soundly on the lips.

Tears welled in her eyes and slid down her cheeks. She was making a huge fool of herself. The thing is, she didn't care. Let those surrounding them stare. She was just so happy.

"Waiter," Ben called, in the same loud voice. "Could you bring us the next course?"

"Right away, sir." Their waiter danced off into an area that Jillian assumed was the kitchen.

He returned minutes later, bearing a silver tray protected by a dome-shaped cover. A circle of holly garnished the rim, and the flames from tiny white candles sparkled against silver. He set the tray down and then discreetly disappeared.

Ben quickly plucked off the cover. In the center sat

a blue velvet pouch. Jillian looked at him puzzled. It was the kind of pouch that held expensive jewelry from a pricey well-known jeweler.

"What's this?" she asked, gazing at him in wonder.

"You'll see." Ben opened the pouch and the case inside.

A huge solitaire surrounded by emeralds twinkled in the candlelight. Jillian gaped at Ben, uncomprehending.

"Hold out your left hand."

Jillian stuck out her hand, wiggling her fingers.

"I'm asking you to marry me. I want you with me for the rest of my life."

She couldn't speak. Words stuck in her throat. What a fool she'd been. Here was a man willing to put himself out there and risk rejection. Ben was offering her himself and a whole new beginning. He was offering her a job and the babies she'd been thinking of. More than anything else, he was offering her his love.

Jillian spoke over the knot in her throat. "I've been stupid," she confessed. "And you've been very patient with me. It's taken me months to get my head straight and realize you are exactly what I've been looking for all of my life."

"Is that a yes?"

"It's a yes."

There was such love in Ben's eyes when he slipped the ring on. Accepting his proposal was not a mistake. Her priorities were now in order. A career and six-figure salary were a poor substitute for having this man in her life.

An outburst of applause from the people around them shattered the romantic mood. A few people ventured from their tables, coming over to extend their good wishes and wishing them all the happiness in the world.

"I say we go back to my hotel and order room service?" Ben suggested when the last person left. "Our meal is ruined and we would be much more comfortable." Ben pushed his coagulating entree away from him.

"The hotel sounds tempting but not for the reasons you suggest."

"Good to know we're on the same wavelength at last. Shall we get the hell out of here before we get arrested for indecent exposure?"

Jillian stood and watched as Ben tossed cash on the table. Then, tucking Jillian's left hand with the sparkling ring through the crook of his arm, he hurried her from the booth and out the door.

He would never have thought it felt this good to be home.

Three months later, Jillian was racing through the Bula with a clipboard in her hand.

"There's a spill on the lobby floor," she called to one of the maids in passing.

"Luggage needs to be delivered to the honeymoon suite on the double," she said to a bellman.

Stopping at the guests desk, Jillian told the surprised receptionist, "Please get the florist on the phone. The flowers in the restaurant are wilted. We'll need a fresh arrangement sent."

"I'll take care of it all, Mrs. Fuller," the woman answered, the receiver already in hand.

Jillian headed out. There were times when she hoped she was not coming off as a monster. But the bottom line was the Bula was beginning to fill up again. They'd already received a nice write-up in *Travel and Leisure* and that hopefully would bring them even more business.

Shortly after arriving back in Taveuni, Jillian and

Ben had been married by a justice of the peace. Ricky and Anna had served as witnesses. They'd decided to wait to have a more formal celebration after the hotel was up and running. They'd also delayed having a honeymoon.

"Mr. Fuller is looking for you, ma'am," one of the gardeners said when Jillian stopped to examine his work. "He said you should meet him in the usual place." The man smiled slyly and returned to his pruning.

"Thank you, Willy."

That meant Ben was expecting lunch. Jillian headed off to the kitchen where a packed picnic basket was usually waiting.

She and Ben had gotten into the habit of having a quick lunch together. It was the only time they were not surrounded by staff. They'd come to value this private time together.

Picnic basket in hand, Jillian made her way toward the renovated warehouse, now operating as a fully functioning plant. She was dying to tell Ben how much occupancy had picked up, thanks to the new advertising company she'd hired.

In the short space of time that she'd taken over, Jillian had made several changes. She'd wanted to make repeat guests feel valued and had suggested incentives to have them come back. Patrons, upon check-in, also received vouchers for a complimentary drink, plus the spa service of their choice.

Jillian had also insisted all employees learn to use the customer relationship management system she'd implemented. The software recorded each guest's preferences, even documenting the most finicky of wishes. And the word "no" was no longer a part of any employee's vocabulary. Employees were urged to take charge and make things happen.

"There you are," Ben said, spotting her and separating himself from the staff. He came over to plant a kiss on her lips.

Jillian kissed him back with passion, then pushed him away. "Lunch time, Lothario. Let's go to your office."

Inside Ben's attractive office, which Jillian had made even more comfortable by adding feminine touches, he said, "Have you heard the latest?"

She shook her head. "I'm afraid not. I've been too busy today to entertain gossip."

Jillian was quickly getting used to what was considered newsworthy on a very small island. Sometimes it paid to be aware of the slightest little grumble.

"Desmond's been arrested," Ben said, looking for a reaction.

"Our Desmond, from the scuba shop?"

"Yup, that's him. Dr. Charles' court case was scheduled for tomorrow and I guess he decided to come clean. He and his attorney worked out a plea bargain with the judge. The good doctor confessed he and Desmond were in it together. Desmond was the person who discovered the marijuana field and was the one responsible for the Bula's troubles.

"He didn't want the place sold because his capital would cease to exist. So he decided it made sense to scare off the prospects. It was he who hired an employee to set fire to the bure. And he persuaded a few of the kitchen staff, his employees, of course, to serve tainted fish. Desmond tampered with his own scuba equipment. While Dr. Charles was the money collector, Desmond remained the brains behind the operation. It worked perfectly until you and I stumbled onto that field. Who would suspect an aging hotel doctor and a lazy one at that?"

"Well I'll be . . ." Jillian said, clapping a hand to her cheek. "And that would explain why there were always hotel pens left at the site. I wonder what made Desmond do it?"

"To use his own words, money and greed. But at least it's done with now. The entire marijuana field was cleared before you got here. I made sure that it was taken care of by trusted employees. And to ensure no one gave in to temptation, the police were there to supervise."

Jillian shook her head in slow disbelief. "I hope they throw the book at that awful man."

"Actually he'll probably be sent back to the States where he'll be sentenced. Now can we talk about more positive things?"

Ben turned Jillian's hand over, examining her ring. "That's a beautiful wedding ring, Mrs. Fuller. I think we should start working on those babies we planned."

"Working? I never considered it work." Jillian winked at him. She slowly began unbuttoning her shirt, then made a production of glancing at her watch. "You've got forty-five minutes left to do the job."

Ben slid a hand into the opening of her blouse and slowly began caressing her flesh.

"I've got a lifetime, baby, and don't you forget it."

Dear Reader:

I was really pleased when asked to write this story set in the South Pacific. After all, who could ask for a more romantic setting for Ben and Jillian to embark on a relationship?

Call me Pollyanna, but most of us have been Ben and Jillian at some point in our lives. We've been sitting on top of the world; then *bam*, life throws us one of its curves.

The resilient ones brush themselves off, and charge on, emerging better equipped to handle the next challenge.

That said, I hope you found Ben and Jillian's story uplifting. If so, please write to me at one of the following addresses and tell me why:
Mkinggambl@aol.com or P.O. Box 25143, Fort Lauderdale, FL 33320

Thank you for reading my books.

Romantically yours,

Marcia King-Gamble
www.lovemarcia.com

More Sizzling Romance From
Marcia King-Gamble

__**A Reason To Love**   1-58314-133-2   **$5.99**US/**$7.99**CAN

__**Illusions Of Love**   1-58314-104-9   **$5.99**US/**$7.99**CAN

__**Under Your Spell**   1-58314-027-1   **$4.99**US/**$6.50**CAN

__**Eden's Dream**   0-7860-0572-6   **$4.99**US/**$6.50**CAN

__**Remembrance**   0-7860-0504-1   **$4.99**US/**$6.50**CAN

__**Change Of Heart**   1-58314-134-0   **$5.99**US/**$7.99**CAN

__**Come Fall**   1-58314-399-8   **$6.99**US/**$9.99**CAN

Available Wherever Books Are Sold!

Visit our website at **www.arabesque.com**.

COMING IN AUGUST 2005 FROM ARABESQUE ROMANCES

__ALL MY TOMORROWS $6.99US/$9.99CAN
by Rochelle Alers   1-58314-653-9

Chef Lydia Lord returns home to Baltimore with plans to launch a gourmet market. But when Lydia volunteers at a summer camp for disadvantaged kids, her life takes an unexpected turn—into the arms of former football star Kennedy Fletcher. Muscular, broad-shouldered Kennedy may look like a typical jock, but four years ago he proved otherwise when he opened Camp Six Nations. In its inaugural summer, the camp may deliver one more dream come true, as evening walks turn into passion-filled nights. But what happens when one of them believes their relationship is just a sizzling summer fling?

__LOVE RUNS DEEP $6.99US/$9.99CAN
by Geri Guillaume   1-58314-655-5

When Jessica Ramsey awakens one morning to discover her Mississippi home is threatened by flooding, her stubborn nature won't let her leave. Even after Police Chief Malcolm Loring drops by and encourages her to seek safety, Jessica still resists. Since they began dating in high school, Jessica and Malcolm have had a stormy history. But with danger from the rising waters around them, Jess will need Mal's level head to see her to safety, and both may finally find themselves ready to put their hearts on the line . . .

__FREE VERSE $5.99US/$7.99CAN
by Kim Shaw   1-58314-600-8

Self-described party girl Kimara Hamilton is a poet who likes her drinks strong, her music loud, and who has yet to find a man who could tame her. When she meets NYPD officer Jared Porter during a disturbance at a nightclub where she works, his sex appeal doesn't even register. But the second time around, when Jared comes to her friend's rescue, his confidence and easy smile melt her heart and make her want to forget her wild ways.

__DÉJÀ VU $5.99US/$7.99CAN
by Elaine Overton   1-58314-584-2

When dynamic prosecutor Victoria Proctor enters the courtroom, determined to kick some butt, the last person she expects to see representing the defense is Nicholas Wilcox—once the love of her life . . . and now her nemesis. Her heart was broken eight years ago when Nick left town, and her career almost ruined when he returned. She's determined not to be beguiled by his handsome face, since she learned it hid a selfish heart. And she isn't—but she *is* attracted to the honorable man he seems to have become . . .

Available Wherever Books Are Sold!

Visit our website at www.BET.com.

BOOK YOUR PLACE ON OUR WEBSITE AND MAKE THE ARABESQUE ROMANCE CONNECTION!

We've created a customized website just for our very special Arabesque readers, where you can get the inside scoop on everything that's going on with Arabesque romance novels.

When you come online, you'll have the exciting opportunity to:

- View covers of upcoming books

- Learn about our future publishing schedule (listed by publication month and author)

- Find out when your favorite authors will be visiting a city near you

- Search for and order backlist books

- Check out author bios and background information

- Send e-mail to your favorite authors

- Join us in weekly chats with authors, readers and other guests

- Get writing guidelines

- AND MUCH MORE!

Visit our website at
http://www.arabesquebooks.com